This is a work of Fiction. All charac
although based in historical settings. If
the story, it is a coincidence, or maybe I

Acknowledgements

Thanks to Dawn Spears the brilliant artist who created the cover artwork and my editor Debz Hobbs-Wyatt without whom the books wouldn't be as good as they are.

My wife who is so supportive and believes in me. Last my dogs Blaez and Zeeva and cats Vaskr and Rosa who watch me act out the fight scenes and must wonder what the hell has gotten into their boss. And a special thank you to Troy who was the grandfather of Blaez in real life. He was a magnificent beast just like his grandson!

THANK YOU FOR READING!

I hope you enjoy reading this book as much as I enjoyed writing it. Reviews are so helpful to authors. I really appreciate all reviews, both positive and negative. If you want to leave one, you can do so on Amazon, through my website, or on Twitter.

About the Author

Christopher C Tubbs is a dog-loving descendent of a long line of Dorset clay miners and has chased his family tree back to the 16th century in the Isle of Purbeck. He left school at sixteen to train as an Avionics Craftsman, has been a public speaker at conferences for most of his career and was one of the founders of a successful games company back in the 1990s. Now in his sixties, he finally writes the stories he had been dreaming about for years. Thanks to inspiration from great authors like Alexander Kent, Dewey Lambdin, Patrick O'Brian, Raymond E Feist, and Dudley Pope, he was finally able to put digit to keyboard. He lives in the Netherlands Antilles with his wife, two Dutch Shepherds, and two Norwegian Forest cats.

You can visit him on his website

www.thedorsetboy.com

The Dorset Boy, Facebook page.

Or tweet him @ChristopherCTu3

The Dorset Boy Series Timeline

1792 – 1795   Book 1: A Talent for Trouble
Marty joins the navy as an assistant steward and through a series of adventures ends up a midshipman.

1795 – 1798   Book 2: The Special Operations Flotilla
Marty is a founder member of the Special Operations Flotilla, learns to be a spy and passes as Lieutenant.

1799 – 1802   Book 3: Agent Provocateur
Marty teams up with Linette to infiltrate Paris, marries Caroline, becomes a father and fights pirates in Madagascar.

1802 – 1804   Book 4: In Dangerous Company
Marty and Caroline are in India helping out Arthur Wellesley, combatting French efforts to disrupt the East India Company and French-sponsored pirates on Reunion. James Stockley born.

1804 – 1805   Book 5: The Tempest
Piracy in the Caribbean, French interference, Spanish gold and the death of Nelson. Marty makes Captain.

1806 – 1807   Book 6: Vendetta
A favour carried out for a prince, a new ship, the S.O.F. move to Gibraltar, the battle of Maida, counter espionage in Malta and a Vendetta declared and closed.

1807 – 1809   Book 7: The Trojan Horse
Rescue of the Portuguese royal family, Battle of the Basque Roads with Thomas Cochrane, and back to the Indian Ocean and another conflict with the French Intelligence Service.

1809 – 1811   Book 8: La Licorne
Marty takes on the role of Viscount Wellington's Head of Intelligence. Battle of The Lines of Torres Vedras, siege of Cadiz, skulduggery, espionage and blowing stuff up to confound the French.

1812   Book 9: Raider
Marty is busy. From London to Paris to America and back to the Mediterranean for the battle of Salamanca. A mission to the Adriatic reveals a white-slavery racket that results in a private mission to the Caribbean to rescue his children.

1813 – 1814   Book 10: Silverthorn
Promoted to Commodore and given a viscountcy, Marty is sent to the Caribbean to be Governor of Aruba which provides the cover story he needs to fight American privateers and undermine the Spanish in South America. On his return he escorts Napoleon into Exile on Alba.

1815 – 1816   Book 11: Exile
After 100 days in exile Napoleon returns to France and Marty tries to hunt him down. After the battle of Waterloo Marty again escorts him into Exile on St Helena. His help is requested by the Governor of Ceylon against the rebels in Kandy.

1817 – 1818   Book 12: Dynasty
To Paris to stop an assassination, then the Mediterranean to further British interests in the region. Finally, to Calcutta as Military Attaché to take part in the war with the Maratha Empire. Beth comes into her own as a spy, but James prefers the navy life.

1818 -- 1819   Book 13: Empire
The end of the third Anglo-Maratha war and the establishment of the Raj. Intrigue in India, war with the Pindaris, the foundation of Singapore, shipwreck, sea wars and storms.

Contents

Chapter 1: River Patrol

Chapter 2: Battle on the River Tapti

Chapter 3: Opportunities

Chapter 4: Sindhudurg Fort

Chapter 5: Cutting Out and Delving Deep

Chapter 6: A Heroes Return

Chapter 7: The Plot Thickens

Chapter 8: Burma

Chapter 9: Pursuit.

Chapter 10: Festival

Chapter 11: Consequences

Chapter 12: The Narmada River

Chapter 13: Skirmish at The Third Ford

Chapter 14: A Celebration.

Chapter 15: Endings and Beginnings

Chapter 16: Murder Most Foul

Chapter 17: The Java Sea

Chapter 18: Confrontation

Chapter 19: Trial by Combat

Chapter 20: Foundation

Chapter 21: Epilogue

Historic Notes

Chapter 1: River Patrol

The Silverthorn glided into the mouth of the river Tapti. It was dawn on a late winter morning in 1818 and Midshipman James Stockley had the watch. It was hot and humid. The thermometer the captain hung from the mizzen mast showed it was already seventy degrees Fahrenheit and rising. Mosquitoes and flies were beginning to plague them, and they had lamps burning citronella positioned above and below decks to fend the little monsters off.

"James, rub some on your skin," Captain Trevor Howarth, who had come up from below, said and held out a bottle of citronella oil.

James took it gratefully and liberally applied it. His face was already showing signs of being attacked.

"Wind is from the northeast and light. We are making eight knots with the incoming tide, I have leadsmen in the bow sounding the bottom," he reported.

"How far up is the river tidal?"

James knew he was being tested, "For around sixteen miles, Sir."

"And what depth do you expect?"

"The river is navigable for much of its length being five fathoms here in the central channel of the estuary and rises to around ten feet after we pass the basin."

"Good, you have done your homework."

"I asked Mr Panda, he is very familiar with our patrol."

Mr Panda was the East India Company representative they had taken aboard in Calcutta. He was a quiet man but answered any questions asked of him as honestly as he could.

A leadsman called, "Four and half fathoms, mud on the bottom."

They were passing a mass of mangroves on their port side which formed an island in the middle of the estuary that split it in two. They were taking the southern channel that took them past the fishing village of Dumas. Fishermen were already out casting nets and watching the elegant but dangerous schooner glide by.

Egrets stalked the banks, supremely indifferent to their passing as they concentrated with deadly efficiency on catching small fish and reptiles. A cormorant dove into the water near the ship, emerging with a silver fish in its beak. It paddled along while it flipped the fish, so it was head down, then swallowed it whole.

James was aware they were entering enemy territory and called up to the lookouts, "Mastheads report!"

"Nothing but a few rowboats on the river, women on the beach washing clothes."

"I will be below. If anything happens, I am to be informed immediately," Howarth said.

"Aye, aye, Sir," James said and tugged his forelock.

"Keep her to the centre of the channel helmsman," James said as he noticed they were cutting a corner. "We will be joining the main river at the end of this island."

As they left the estuary and entered the river proper, the dome of a large temple came into view. It was the first indication they were approaching the town of Surat and, in accordance with the captain's standing orders, he called the ship to quarters.

Captain Howarth appeared, dressed in full uniform, and wearing his sword. "I have the deck, Mr Stockley," he said formally then grinned. "Go and get your sword or Dennis will fidget a hole in the deck."

Dennis was one of James's followers, not because James had chosen him but because of all the officers that Dennis had ever known James had been the only one to treat him kindly. That was because Dennis was not only a mountain of a man but touched. He had, what had recently been named, mongoloid features and the intelligence of an infant of around seven years old. He did, however, adore James and with him beside him along with Joseph and Eric, his other two followers, they formed a very effective fighting unit.

Dennis strapped his sword belt around his waist with a happy grin. "There, Mister James is ready now."

"Thank you, Dennis," James said.

The captain called, "Raise the colours."

James walked aft to oversee the raising of the huge white ensign that was a statement of power and a challenge to the Maratha Empire.

He looked along the shore. They were passing the town proper now and people were coming out to see what to them was a big threatening ship.

"Load for salute, run out the guns!" the captain shouted.

James walked to his station at the mainmast. His gun crews already obeying the command.

"Well done, number three," he said, praising them for being ready first. The crew grinned, enjoying the praise.

Both sides were run out, the Silverthorn bared her teeth. The thirty-six-pound carronades ugly against the sleek lines of the hull.

"Fire salute."

"Number one. Fire," James said. He had his watch in his hand and five seconds later said "Number two. Fire" as he progressed aft on the port side and forward up the starboard until all sixteen guns had discharged.

"Well done, Mr Stockley," the captain called.

The effect on the shoreline was amusing. Clouds of birds took to the sky. People started running as soon as the salute started fearing they were being attacked, but as soon as they realised nothing was landing on shore they started to come back. Some brave souls shook their fists at them. Children ran along the shoreline trying to keep up with them. Dogs all over the town were barking. There was an enraged trumpeting and a large grey shape appeared on the north shore.

"A bull elephant, and a big one at that!" the captain said.

The elephant raised its trunk and trumpeted again following it with a bass rumble that James could feel in his bones.

"Don't they travel in herds?" James said.

"The females and young males do, but the older males are solitary beasts. That one is fully mature."

"I don't think I have a gun capable of stopping a beast like that. A normal rifle would just annoy it," James said in awe.

"I read that they are most dangerous when they come into must in the breeding season. Then they will kill anything that gets in the way of them finding a mate."

"Then I will look out for randy elephants and stay well clear," James laughed.

The river turned sharply to the north-northwest at a point overlooked by an ancient fortress. Its forty-foot-high walls were imposing: bounded at each end by round towers

"Guns? Mr Stockley."

"Look like six pounders to me and old," James said after studying them with a glass. "I can only see one or two people on the walls and there isn't any sign of them being manned."

"Thank you, please be so kind as to ready the sweeps we will be turning into wind soon."

The river curved around to the northeast. The sail handlers were kept busy, and the sweeps were needed to get them around the corner to head southeast again. They were passing the edge of town now. The smoke from their salute had drifted away across the rooftops and peace had returned. The children had been left behind. A lone horseman paced them.

"Where did he come from?" James said.

"From the fort," Joseph said.

"Keep an eye on him."

The river swung northeast again putting them dead into the wind. The sails were furled, and sweeps deployed. Progress slowed to a crawl, then stopped as the tide slackened, then stopped at its peak before turning.

"Drop anchor, we are going nowhere until the tide turns again," the captain said. "James, put together a shore patrol. I saw some deer earlier and we could do with some fresh meat."

"Aye, aye, Sir."

James gathered his team. His followers and four marines all of which had backgrounds in poaching or scouting.

"Make sure you only take water or small beer. I will be checking your bottles. Dress in civilian clothes. Rifles and ammunition."

They boated to the shore and landed on a shallow beach. The marines fanned out and moved quietly into the undergrowth. James followed keeping Dennis behind him.

A twig snapped. James looked at Dennis who was frozen in place a look of chagrin on his face.

"Place the ball of the foot down first and gently lower your heel as your weight comes on it. That way you will feel any twigs before you snap them," James said and demonstrated.

Dennis moved forward; a look of intense concentration on his face as he exaggerated the movement.

"That's it, well done."

"Sir," Eric said softly, and pointed ahead where one of the marines was knelt on one knee his left arm cocked over his head.

James signalled for the others to stop and quietly moved up beside him.

"What is it, Tremaine?"

"Over there, Sir."

James looked ahead to a small pool of water formed where a stream had gotten dammed by a fallen tree. Three deer were drinking, and he was about to raise his rifle when a movement caught his eye. He stopped and looked. A tiger slunk from under a bush, its belly close to the ground. It moved silently, stopping, frozen in place for seconds at a time. Its lip curled revealing massive canines. It took another slow step, then another. The deer were oblivious. Its muscles under its glorious fur bunched and it drew its hind quarters up under itself. It sprang forward, its speed astonishing, and felled one of the deer with its huge front feet, claws cutting into flesh. The deer stood no chance once the tiger clamped its jaws around its throat, choking the life out of it.

"Phew! That was something to see!" James breathed.

They tracked the tiger for a while before duty overcame curiosity and they started looking for meat for the table. They found a family of wild boar. There was a male, three females and a swarm of piglets of various ages.

"That female must weigh three hundred pounds," Marine Cooper said. He was from Shropshire and had worked as a farmhand as well as a poacher.

"You take the female. I'll take the male."

They raised their rifles and took aim, the male sensed something was wrong and looked in their direction. James felt a breeze on his neck. The wind had shifted.

With an angry squeal the boar charged straight for him. He had never seen something move that fast. He hesitated and that was nearly his undoing. Strong hands grabbed his shoulders and literally threw him to one side. His rifle fired into thin air.

James rolled onto his back. Dennis was stood over him protectively. He picked himself up and dusted himself down.

"Are you hurt, Dennis?"

"Dennis is alright, Mister James. Are you?"

"I'm fine. Thank you, Dennis, you saved me a goring."

He looked around; the sow was lying on the ground. Cooper had shot true. Three of the larger piglets had also been taken.

"Well done, lads. Let's get them trussed and back to the ship."

The carcasses were well received, and the cook and his mates fell to dressing them out. Not a piece would be wasted.

"Well done, James. The crew will eat well tonight. A suckling pig for the officers."

"Sir, can I give something to Dennis? He saved me from a goring when the boar charged me."

"Did he indeed? Well, a reward would be appropriate if what you say is true. You can tell the story over dinner."

Captain Howarth decided that the men needed a day's rest and that allowed the cook to create fire pits on the shore and set up spits which the crew took turns to turn. The sow was spitted and turned slowly over one and the piglets over the other. The smell of roasting pork was incredible. Foragers went out and gathered edible plants and fruits under strict instructions only to gather things they recognised as edible. Luckily a few men had sailed the Indian Ocean before and had some experience they could share.

The results of their endeavours were spread out for inspection by Mr Panda who was the final arbiter of whether it was edible or not.

"This is Methi. The seeds and leaves are very good for the digestion. This is waterleaf, this jangli." He held up another plant, "That is not edible and will give you the shits if you eat it." He threw it over the side. He advised the cook whether to boil, fry or make a salad of the various plants and the result that evening was a feast for the crew.

The captain, James, Phillips (the master), Mr Panda and Simmonds (the surgeon), gathered for dinner on the quarterdeck where the captain's steward, Grimsthorpe, a dour Yorkshireman, had set up a table and chairs.

"I thought it would be nice to eat under the stars. The nights are beautiful here," Howarth said.

They were served glasses of madeira. James sipped his, all too aware of the effects of alcohol on his young body.

"Dinner's ready," Grimsthorpe declared, and then to James, "and mind the cloth, it's not for wiping your nose on."

James laughed at the thought that anybody would do that then remembered that Terrance, the previous mid, had lacked some of the social training he had.

They sat and were served a fried river fish and a salad of the greens that had been foraged.

"James, tell us of your hunt," Terrance Howarth said.

James told them the story, making them oooh and aaah when he described the encounter with the Tiger and laugh when he related the incident with the boor.

"Your man Dennis, reacted quickly," Howarth said.

"I have bruises where he gripped my shoulder and arm, but yes he saved my life."

"Did you reward him?"

"I gave him one of my fighting knives."

"I saw that," Phillips said, "he is as proud as punch of it. It is a prodigious blade."

"It's a Pesh-Kabz. I bought a couple in Calcutta where they call them Afghan knives. I prefer it to the fighting knife my father has. Here, I have its twin."

He passed over the knife. It had a well-formed hilt with a hooked end formed around a through tang. The blade was eight inches long and recurved with a fuller that ran a third of its length. It was razor sharp along one edge and ended in a wicked point that was thicker than normal. The letter J was ornately carved into the hilt.

"Definitely not a hunting knife," Howarth said, "why is the point so thick?"

"Because it was designed to penetrate chainmail and armour," Panda said.

"Really." Howarth handed it back to James who slid it back into its sheath.

The main course was served. A whole spit roast suckling pig was presented on a platter surrounded by pieces of fried liver and kidneys.

"Will you carve, James?" Howarth said.

James stood and took up the carving knife and fork. He tested the edge of the knife with his thumb.

"Blunt as a turd," he muttered and fished in his pocket. He produced a stone and set it to the edge. Half a dozen strokes set the blade right and he carefully wiped it before carving the meat.

A gravy flavoured with methi, roast yams and greens accompanied the tender pork.

"I say, this crackling is perfect." Phillips said.

"It is a thing of wonder. We do not roast our meat in India and this is a revelation!" Panda said.

The virtues of the traditional British roast were expounded upon and argued. Whether beef should be eaten rare, or well done was discussed and Panda went very quiet.

"Is something wrong, Mister Panda?" James asked.

"It is this talk of eating beef. I am a Hindu, and the cow is a sacred animal to us."

"Aah that is why you cook for yourself!"

"Yes, your men eat salt beef and that is forbidden to us."

"The beef isn't always beef," Phillips said. "Sometimes it is horse."

"Whichever, I prefer my own food." He looked embarrassed and added, "Not that this isn't the most excellent meal."

Howarth laughed, "I shall remember that when I dine you in again. More wine James?"

The main was replaced by desert.

"What fruit is this? It's wonderful!" the normally reticent Simmonds said.

"That is mango, and this is chalta or elephant apple. Both grow wild here."

The meal was finished with port and nuts, they had run out of cheese days ago.

The river forked around an island, and they took the wider southern channel. They were heading northeast and sailing as close to the wind as they could. James watched the sails carefully. The slightest shiver would indicate they were about to go into irons. They had ten miles more on unfavourable headings as the river wound through the lowlands before it settled a point or so south of east for fifty miles. Then they would be in the river basin.

"Sir," the lookout called.

"What is it?" James called back.

"That horseman is back with some friends."

James climbed atop a carronade and used a small glass to examine the riders. He heard the captain step up behind him.

"Four men on horseback, military uniforms like I saw when we rescued Father. One looks to be an officer. He has a plume in his turban that is bigger than the others," he said without looking around.

"Armed?"

"Swords and lances. Hold on, one has turned and is riding back towards the town we passed. He has a carbine in a saddle holster. The rest are pacing us."

The officer must have spotted him. He stopped, reared his mount and drew his sword.

"Been reading too much romantic literature," Howarth grunted.

"A clear challenge," James said.

"You can joust with him later, young knight, for now keep this ship on course."

"Aye, aye, Sir," James grinned and jumped to the deck.

"I will be below," Howarth said in farewell.

Once he had gone, Jim Martin, one of the marine sharpshooters, wandered aft and said, "You want me to knock him off his horse, Mr Stockley, Sir?"

"Not today, Jim, let him pose for a while."

Jim lent on the rail and spat tobacco juice over the side, then put his Baker rifle to his shoulder, "I could get him right through that smug face of his." Then he sighed and put the gun's butt back on the deck. James hid a grin by admonishing the helm to keep to the centre of the river.

Nothing happened for the rest of the day, they sailed on and the horsemen kept pace. At the end of the day when they made anchor another of the troops left and headed back towards the town.

"They are definitely up to something," Howarth said. "Double the watch tonight and have some illuminating rockets ready."

James slept until two in the morning when he took the watch. Liberally smeared in citronella oil he came up on deck and relieved the captain.

"All quiet so far. Keep the men on their toes."

"Aye, aye, Sir."

James walked around the deck quietly checking on each of the lookouts.

"All quiet, Barnaby?"

"Aye, Sir, just frogs singing."

He moved to the next at the bow

"All quiet, Thompson?"

"Heard some rustling and splashing over there. Probably animals."

James focussed on the area but could see nothing. As he turned to walk away, he registered a movement out of the corner of his eye. Aware like all sailors that his night vision was better at the periphery of his eye. He looked ahead and softened his focus.

There it was. The anchor cable was bobbing up and down.

Now why would it be doing that?

He walked over to the rack where the rockets were stored and selected one. Nearby was a coil of slow match burning over a tub of water. He took the match and blew on it. When it glowed nicely, he set it to the rocket's fuse. He held the rocket at arm's length, lightly between two fingers so when it ignited it flew into the air freely.

With a soft thump the rocket burst into bright white light. James was already looking down the length of the cable.

Frozen in shock at being discovered was an Indian man wearing nothing but a breach clout clinging upside down to the cable, his hand frozen in the act of trying to saw through it with a knife.

James had a pistol in his hand and raised it, pulling back the hammer with his thumb.

"Good evening, would you care to come aboard?"

He beckoned with his free hand. The man didn't move. He beckoned again, then the rocket's flare sputtered and died. There was a splash, James fired but was fairly sure he hadn't hit him.

"What's going on?" the captain asked from behind them.

James turned and saw he was in his nightshirt. He forced the grin off his face. "An Indian was trying to cut our anchor cable with a knife."

"Did he do much damage?"

"I don't know. I was about to go and have a look."

"Pull a boat around. No point in getting wet."

The gig was pulled alongside and with the help of two crew it was walked to the bow. James stood and ran his hands down the anchor cable to the waterline. The only damage he could find were some frayed threads. Nothing that would weaken the cable unduly.

The next morning at the end of his watch, which was just before dawn, Captain Howarth said, "What do you think their intention was, James?"

"Probably to cast us adrift so we would run aground somewhere their cavalry could storm us."

"Just what I thought. I want a man up the mast."

James chose a man and went up with him. The schooner had a topsail spar and they sat either side of it waiting for the sun to rise.

"Do you think them Indians are out there, Mr Stockley?" Eric Jones said. He was a twenty-year-old Welshman and one of their best topmen.

"Somewhere. Look, false dawn."

They both scanned the shoreline as the sky turned grey. A line of blue appeared on the eastern horizon and then the golden ball of the sun peaked up and it was officially dawn.

"Clear this side," Eric said, then when James didn't reply looked past him to the other bank. "Bugger."

"Looks like a squadron of cavalry about a mile off the south bank. They must think that because they are behind the trees that line the river, we won't have seen them," James said.

"They are just camping?" Captain Howarth said after James reported.

"My guess is they are waiting for something, but what? I don't know."

"Your father once told me about a raid they did in Holland where they nearly got trapped in a port when the French brought up horse artillery."

"We are somewhat like ducks on a pond here." James said thinking about what well-aimed field pieces could do to them.

"Yes, get us underway, lets speed things up we have been dawdling up to now."

The river had settled on a roughly Easterly course and with the wind further round they could set more of their gaff-rigged sails. The current was sluggish, and they could make eight knots of land speed.

"We should be in the main river basin by early afternoon."

The lookouts reported that the cavalry was still pacing them.

The river opened out into the river basin and James wondered why they had been ordered to go this far up the river.

"There's nothing here, it's too shallow to patrol and has marshes either side," Howarth said after the boats had done a short reconnaissance.

"Then why did we sail up here?" James asked.

"Ours is not to wonder why," Howarth said.

"Ours is but to do or die," James finished for him.

"Quite,"

"What now?" James said.

"We turn her around and go back."

"Can we start now? This place is teaming with mosquitoes."

"Yes, and they will only get worse after dark. Use the boats to swing her around and get us out of here."

James commanded the cutter and called orders to the gig as they pulled the schooner around to face down river. The mosquitoes swarmed around the sweating men getting their fill of good British blood. The task was over none too soon. Some men's faces swelled they had been bitten so badly.

With the current and a favourable wind, they moved back down the river at a trot. Only anchoring when it got too dark to see. They were moving again as soon as it was light the next morning.

"Any sign of that cavalry?" Howarth called up to the lookout.

"No Sir, not a sign of them."

"Damn, what are they up to?"

James didn't answer, he had his own fears.

Chapter 2: Battle on the River Tapti

The Silverthorn fairly raced back down the river, going faster than any cavalry could sustain. The lookouts were on constant watch and her officers on edge. The entire crew had the feeling that something was about to happen and quietly prepared the ship for a fight.

James prowled the deck. The armourer had set up his stone and the sound of cutlasses, boarding pikes, knives and tomahawks being sharpened grated on the ear. James slid his hanger from its sheath and looked along the edge. It was flawless and razor sharp. His dirk and knife were also perfectly sharp, his guns loaded and primed. He had even brought his rifle up onto deck and it was stored, conveniently, on the rack that normally held the telescopes along with a pouch of cartridges.

Captain Howarth had the quarterdeck.

"Deck there, there is an island approaching and there looks to be a boom across the river from it to the shore."

"Back foresails, loose the others," Howarth barked.

The Silverthorn came to a rapid halt as the sails spilled their wind and the foresail came hard against the mast. The backed sails held her against the current.

"Go to quarters!"

The crew cleared the ship for action in no time, the gun crews stepped to their guns from where they had been waiting on the centreline and looked expectantly to James. He walked, almost nonchalantly, to the quarterdeck.

"If they have boomed the river then we can expect they have brought up artillery as well. We may be in for a hot time."

"Deck there, horsemen on the south bank."

"We need to see what we are up against, join me in the tops."

The two of them dropped their sword belts and clambered up the mast. Howarth was fit and James worked hard to keep up with him. Once up and settled they could see the tableau laid out before them.

The main channel of the river was blocked by a log boom consisting of a half a dozen logs that had been chained together and secured on either side to sturdy log frames that had been dug into the banks. The island was fortified with gabions that protected four cannons. Infantry could be seen sitting around, waiting as well.

"They look like six-pound horse artillery pieces," James said.

"There are more on the south bank. Another eight guns."

"Two batteries then," James said absently.

"What?"

"Oh! Sorry, Sir. A battery is six guns so they must have brought up two batteries."

"Quite. Mr Panda says the north channel is too shallow for us to take. So we are stuck until we can clear that boom."

"The horseman is waving a white flag, Sir," the lookout said, having made way for the officers by moving higher up.

"Is he? He must want to parlay," Howarth said and started down.

James followed him to the deck after studying the island again.

"What do you want?" Howarth called to the horseman.

The horseman kicked his horse forward until it was knee deep in the river.

"I am Major Gayakwad of the Peshwa's Cavalry. I am here to offer you terms of surrender."

"You want to surrender to us?" Howarth said.

The major looked annoyed, "You are trapped, you cannot pass the boom and my artillery will destroy you if you try. You have until dawn tomorrow to surrender, or we will bring up our guns and blow you to pieces." He turned his horse and spurred it out of the river and along the bank, throwing the white flag to the ground once he thought he was out of range.

"Cheeky git," an anonymous voice said.

"What will you do?" Mr Panda said.

"We will not surrender, that's for certain," Howarth said.

"You plan to run the blockade?" Mr Panda's voice went up an octave at the end of the statement.

"Sir, can I make a suggestion?" James said.

After dark the Silverthorn's marines and an equal number of sailors gathered on deck. "All present and correct, Sir," Sergeant Anfield said to James who was dressed in dark clothes like the rest of the men and had his face and hands blackened with burnt cork.

"Thank you, Sergeant. Men, we are going to take the island." The men listened intently. "Now, the enemy have four guns, each of which is manned by a crew of nine."

"Strewth, that many for those popguns?" one of the sailors said.

"Only four man the gun, the rest are cavalrymen who ride the horses," James explained, then continued.

"There is also what looks like a platoon of infantry as well. That gives us a total of sixty men to deal with."

"Two each, Sah, we have them outnumbered," the sergeant said.

"Indeed. Now we will land on the beach at the corner of the island. That will allow us to circle behind the fortification for the guns and take them. I don't want any shooting until they do. Bayonets and blades only. Am I clear?"

"Aye, Sir," the men said in unison.

James carried a boarding pike, the extra reach it gave him cancelled out any advantage an infantry man had with his bayonet. He had drilled himself and the men with it.

"Good luck. Get in the boats."

Howarth met him at the entry port.

"Good luck, James and good hunting. I will see you in the morning." They shook hands.

The boats had rags tied around the rowlocks to silence them and the oarsmen were careful not to splash. It was a dark night, but the Indians had lit fires to cook with which the tillermen used to guide them. The boats were overcrowded with fifteen men in each which meant the oarsmen would be part of the landing force.

A man called out on the bank and was answered by another. They all tensed but nothing happened. They continued until they heard the sound of the river lapping against the small beach. The boats drifted up to it and ground with a soft crunch.

James was first over the side and helped pull the boat up, Dennis by his side adding his prodigious strength. Soon all the men were ashore, the boats pulled up and secured.

"Get the men deployed," James whispered to Sergeant Anfield.

James had chosen to arrange the men in a line as the island was low and flat with few trees. He was at the centre with Dennis, Eric and Joseph, the marines formed up either side of him with the sailors out on the flanks. A pair of scouts disappeared into the dark to eliminate sentries.

He stepped forward and the line moved with him, *not bad*, he thought for no practice. They could see Indian soldiers gathered around the fires ahead of them.

A grunt from in front and to the left, followed by a sigh as a sentry was disposed of. One down fifty-nine to go. They got to the edge of the light cast by the fires.

"AT 'EM, MEN!"

James threw himself forward and engaged the nearest man to him who looked around in shock at the cry.

"GRAAAAAAGH!" James screamed and thrust forward with his pike. He took the man in the side and ripped the blade out sideways. Dennis was beside him with a short spear that Sam, his father's cox, had given him. He stabbed the next man with it and almost took off his head with a follow-up slash.

It was pandemonium, the marines advanced in a disciplined line, bayonets to the fore. Stabbing, withdrawing, and stabbing again. The sailors, less disciplined but no less effective, using their boarding pikes to good effect.

The soldiers on the far side of the camp got organised and a volley of musket fire illuminated the night. A marine screamed as he was wounded, and a sailor fell dead, silently, not knowing he was gone it was so quick.

"Marines, halt. Present arms," Sergeant Anfield ordered, and the marines stopped "Fire!" fourteen Baker rifles fired in volley. Aimed low, the shot scythed across the camp. Dennis unlimbered a volley gun he had been carrying on a strap across his back and added that to the mix. More Indians fell.

"Bayonets! Forward march."

The marines moved forward driving the remaining Indian soldiers towards the river. Those that resisted, died. Those that ran, had to swim for their lives. Those that surrendered, if they were lucky, were disarmed and taken prisoner. The unlucky ones were killed anyway.

"Island is secure, Sir," Sergeant Anfield said. "One dead and three wounded on our side, twenty prisoners secured. What would you like us to do with the guns?"

"Thank you, Sergeant, please allocate gun crews. Have you located a magazine?" James said.

"They have brought over caissons; they are loaded with cartridge."

James followed the sergeant to the caissons, "Take a pair of cartridges from each." Men jumped to it then he led them to the anchor for the boom.

There was shouting from the far bank, and someone started firing across the river at them.

"They will get organised soon. Place the charges around here." James indicated which timber he wanted taking out. "Run a fuse out then pack dirt on top." The men obeyed with enthusiasm.

"Good, get clear." James lit the fuse and ran back to join the men.

The charges exploded shattering the timber. The structure critically weakened; started to shift.

"The pressure of the water should do the rest," James said.

It took a long moment then it gave way completely, the boom swept aside by the current.

"Proper job." James grinned, putting on his father's Dorset accent.

The men rested. There was a lot of shouting on the far bank causing a wag to shout over, "Can't you shut up? We're trying to sleep over here."

Dawn came. James was tired, not having slept at all. He had tried to help the wounded, cleaning and binding their wounds. Luckily only one was serious enough to need more than a bandage. All they could do was make him comfortable until they could get him to the surgeon.

"The ships making sail!" a sentry shouted.

They could just see a grey goose at a mile and the battery on the other side of the river was in clear view. James took charge of the guns.

"Let's keep them occupied he said and had the guns trained around to fire on their brothers."

"Ready?" the gun captains raised their arms.

"Fire." The linstocks were lowered to the touchholes. No flintlock igniters on these old pieces.

The guns barked and dirt spouted up around the far battery.

"Reload, let 'em have another."

The gunners adjusted their aim, getting used to the guns.

"Fire!"

This time the shot slammed into the gabions. They saw an officer waving his sword at his men who started turning half the guns towards them.

Marine Jim Martin was knelt to one side and wetted his foresight with his thumb. He raised his rifle, "You're mine this time," he said. He breathed in and slowly let it out, his finger caressed the trigger. The rifle kicked as it fired.

"Good shot, Jim!" Marty called as the officer was knocked off his feet. "Can you get any of their gunners?"

Jim called a couple of other men to him and the three of them knelt in a row. They started to fire, suppressing the gunners on the other side. More marines joined them and soon there was an almost constant crackle of fire.

"One more round then spike them!" James ordered.

The men fired and then drove nails into the touchholes, rendering the guns useless. Cartridges was placed on the carriages and fitted with slow fuse to further render the pieces useless.

The Silverthorn was entering the channel. Her carronades spoke and the huge thirty-six-pound smashers demolished the gabions and upturned the guns, sending bodies flying.

"To the boats!" James ordered, and the men ran back to the beach.

On the Silverthorn, Howarth acted on faith that James had completed his mission and as soon as it was dawn, set sail. They had been bothered by indiscriminate musket fire from the shore during the night, and he was ready to start handing out some retribution.

"Well done, James," he said as he saw the guns on the island targeting the shore battery. "Run out!" he ordered. The port carronades were loaded with solid shot. "Target those guns."

A six-pound shot flew across the deck, one of the few that were fired. Howarth looked down in amazement as his right leg disappeared below the knee.

"Fire!" he shouted as he toppled.

He lay on the ground and ripped his sword belt off, discarding the sword and wrapped it around his thigh. "Get me a marline spike!" he shouted to the nearest sailor who stood looking at him in shock. The man moved and handed him a spike which he used to tighten the belt over his femoral artery.

He was faint but had stopped the blood flow.

"Get me a damned chair!" he barked.

The sailor ran below and came back with one of the folding canvas chairs from his cabin and placed it on the deck. He just stood and gawped at his captain.

"Don't just stand there, you idiot, help me sit in it!" Howarth snapped. Two men picked him up and got him comfortable. The surgeon arrived.

"It will wait!" he snapped as the man started fussing over the gory mess.

"Keep hitting those guns!"

Marty and his men got their boats into the water and piled aboard. They rowed around the back side of the island to rendezvous with the Silverthorn further downstream. James was pleased, they had only lost one man with another seriously wounded. The other men that had been hurt only had minor injuries.

The Silverthorn sailed past the end of the island and hove to. Her port carronades barked again, discouraging anyone from getting too close. They brought the boats up to the starboard side and the men scrambled aboard. James was the last up, against protocol, to ensure his wounded were taken safely aboard.

"The captain wishes to see you right away," a worried-looking seaman said as soon as he was aboard.

He turned to the quarterdeck and saw Howarth sitting in a chair. He thought it odd and walked towards him with a smile and then he saw the stump, ragged and still dripping blood, the surgeon hovering in the background, the paleness of the captain's face.

"I have command," he shouted and saw Terrance nod. Then his head slumped forward.

"Get him below at once!" he barked. The surgeon's loblolly boys moved in to be shouldered aside by Dennis who picked him up and cradled him in his arms like a baby as he carried him below.

"Don't just stand there, man! Get down there and treat him!" James barked at the surgeon who was stood to the side.

He took a deep breath; this was not what he expected but the training he had received at the college kicked in and he looked around his ship.

"Make sail, I want us out to sea as fast as possible."

Sailors ran to do his bidding. He was young and still covered in blood from the fight, but they trusted their Jim and reacted immediately.

Joseph came to him. "Can I check your legs?" he said.

"What? Why?" James said.

"Leeches. Several of the boys had them."

James pulled up his trouser legs and there on both his legs were the disgustingly, bloated blood suckers.

"Ugh," he said.

"Best take off your trousers." Joseph said and James didn't hesitate.

Joseph used salt to make the leeches release their grip. James had them on his calves and one had climbed up as far as his thigh. James shuddered when Joseph tossed them over the side.

"All done," Joseph said, cheerfully.

"Get me a clean pair of trousers. I do not want to put those back on," James said.

What the women thought as they sailed past them as they washed clothes on the riverbank, he neither cared nor wondered.

As they approached the town, he ran out the guns. The fort was manned this time and smoke blossomed from the parapets.

"Let's show 'em what real guns can do. Round shot and fire when ready."

The gun crews gleefully went about their business. The carronades, at full elevation, belched smoke and flame. A whole section of the ancient parapet crumbled under the onslaught. A second broadside and they were past. James let them keep firing as they passed the town, only stopping as they entered the estuary. The Silverthorn entered her natural element and spread her wings.

"Sail ho!" the lookout called.

"Where away?" James called back.

"Windward, about a mile off, just turned towards us. It's a felucca or sommit like it. Lot of men on board."

James was feeling belligerent still. He ordered a reduction in sail.

"Load the guns with cannister over small ball, but don't run out. Rear carronades shift to stern positions."

From bitter experience, the Silverthorn had mounts for carronades at her stern and the two rearmost guns could quickly be repositioned there. The bow could be protected by the forward guns being trained around. The foremost gun ports were elongated to allow it.

There was a bellow of pain from below.

"I'm reckonin' that the surgeon just cauterized the skipper's leg," Harry the helmsman said. A faint whiff of burning flesh confirmed it.

The felucca-like craft approached. It was flying the Maratha flag. It made to cross their stern.

"Ready?" James asked.

"Aye, Sir," the gun captains answered.

"Fire as they bear."

Guns sprouted along the felucca's side.

Don't they have anything bigger than a six pounder? James thought. The starboard carronade fired as the bow came into line. The front eight feet of the boat disappeared. Water rushed in. One cannon fired.

"Hardly worth getting up for," James grinned. "Heave to. Boats away, pick up survivors."

Chapter 3: Opportunities

Commodore Martin, Viscount, Stockley had discovered that being Defence Attaché involved a lot of paperwork. Reports on this or that, requests, demands and invitations all came in and reports, letters and responses went out. On top of that was the endless cycle of functions he had to attend, mostly in full uniform which he hated, and the balls and parties that he and Caroline were expected to attend.

At least Beth was on her way back to England now to enter the Intelligence Service Academy and he didn't have to worry about her anymore. It had taken a superhuman act of will to allow her to follow her ambition of being an agent. She was a superb study of all the techniques needed to be undercover, an expert shot and more than capable with a blade. But she was still his little girl and he loved her dearly.

All he had to worry about now was James. He wondered what they would be doing. The Silverthorn's mission would send them deep into enemy territory and into danger. Terrance Howarth was a very capable captain and knew his ship and crew intimately. He told himself that James would be as safe as he could be.

A knock on his door and Adam stuck his head inside.

"Frances Ridgley to see you."

"Show him in and bring some tea."

Frances was the head of British Intelligence in Calcutta and ran the Northern India office.

"Morning, Martin," he chirped.

"Morning, Frances, you are perky this morning. Have you killed someone?"

Francis was notorious for not being a morning person and he was definitely out of character this morning.

"Ha ha, not today. I've just had a talk with Chopra junior."

"That explains your out-of-character behaviour. Did you leave any of him for the crows?"

"Didn't need to use violence, just the threat of telling his father and disgracing his family was enough."

"Blackmail! Your second favourite pastime." Marty smiled.

Frances grinned. "He caved in like a house of cards. His excuse was that the consul knew about him having an affair and was blackmailing him."

"Highly unlikely, his wife couldn't do much even if he was, under Hindu law."

"Exactly, and it's all thanks to your daughter."

Marty acknowledged that with a nod.

"How do you want to use him?" he said.

"I'm gifting him to you. You can send whatever messages you want through his network."

Marty thought on that.

"We will have to be careful to keep sending some real information or they will smell a rat."

"There is also the open issue of the French consul's son," Frances said. Beth had discovered he had a gambling problem and had cultivated him until he discovered her real purpose.

"You can join me this afternoon if you like. There is a Kabaddi tournament at the park. I'm fairly sure he will be there."

Frances looked, if anything, even happier. Then he started as he remembered something.

"Have you heard of the Maratha Navy?"

"They have one?" Marty said, amazed.

He pulled a paper from his inside pocket.

"It's what you sailors call a green water navy. I would call it a bunch of pirates."

Marty laughed. "An inshore force made up of smaller boats. It was made popular by the barbary pirates?"

"That sort of thing. Well, they took a Company Marine sloop last week and the Company want it back. You can expect a summons from his lordship the governor any time now."

Adam knocked, then stuck his head inside the door, "Sorry to disturb you. The governor is outside. Wants to see you immediately."

Marty raised an eyebrow and Frances grinned. "Show him in please."

Governor-General Sir Francis Edward Rawdon-Hastings KG, PC, entered and dumped himself in Marty's second comfortable chair. He looked around, "Where's m' niece?"

"Justine is running an errand for me; she will be back in an hour or so," Marty said.

"Harrumph, can I get some tea?"

"Adam, would you be so kind as to bring another cup and a fresh pot please," Marty said.

Adam bowed and did one of his best exits.

"Damn marine has gone and had one of its sloops stolen by pirates."

"By pirates you mean the Maratha Navy?" Marty smiled.

"You knew already," the governor said looking accusingly at Frances who did his best to look innocent. "Well, we want it back. The last thing we need is them having that sort of firepower."

"Don't they have sloops of their own?"

"Yes. They are armed with old nine-pound guns," Frances said. "They are the biggest ships they have."

"And the ship that was captured?" Marty said.

"The Aurora is armed with sixteen twenty-four-pound carronades and a variety of small, long guns."

"Where are they holding her?" Marty asked, knowing full well if the marine wanted him to get her back it would be somewhere very well protected.

"Sindhudurg Fort." Hastings stood and walked over to the large map of India pinned to Marty's wall. He peered at the west coast. "Here on the Goa border."

Marty peered at the map and couldn't see it so he retrieved a magnifying glass from his desk.

"There," Hasting said, and Marty focussed the glass on the end of his finger.

"It's an island." He stepped back and looked at India as a whole. "Why have you let them keep a fort down there?"

"It's too well defended. The fort is the whole island and it's been there since sixteen hundred and something."

"And that is where the Aurora is being held. What about her crew?" Marty said then held up his hand, "Don't tell me they are inside the fort."

"Yes, you will need your best skulduggery skills to get them back."

Frances had a coughing fit and Marty had to exert iron control.

"Very well, Sir, I will get the ship and her crew back for you."

"Good." He stood just as Adam came in with the tea.

"I'm looking forward to your successful report." He nodded to Adam and left. As soon as the door closed Frances collapsed in laughter, "Skulduggery skills!"

Marty lost his control and burst into laughter. Soon tears were running down their faces, they hiccupped to a halt then Adam said, "Skulduggery skills?" and set them both off again.

Justine came in and Adam looked at her with a shrug as if to say, "What did I say?"

"Are they drunk?"

"No, it's something to do with skulduggery."

That set them off again.

Adam shook his head and left.

Marty and Frances attended the Kabaddi tournament in the park. They didn't have to wait long before Ghislain Blanchette, the son of the French consul, turned up. He went straight to one of the many betting booths and stood in line. Marty and Frances moved in behind him. Garai, Matai and Sam stood nearby.

"Hello Ghi, we thought we would find you here," Marty said. Ghi spun around like he had been stung. He looked at Marty and Frances then bolted.

"It's funny how they always run," Frances said.

Ghi bolted for the nearest gate and skidded to a stop when Antton stepped into it. He turned and ran for the next one, Adam was blocking it. He turned to run again and slammed straight into Sam, who wrapped him in a bearhug. He kicked and struggled but Sam just held him.

"That's enough of that," Marty said in French. "I only want to talk to you. Put him down, Sam."

As soon as Sam let him go, he tried to run again but Sam was ready and grabbed his collar.

"The sooner you stop being silly, the sooner we can get this done."

Ghi looked frantically around for help, but all the Indians were studiously ignoring what was happening.

"Where is Beth?" Ghi asked.

"She has gone back to England to finish her education," Marty said.

"Is she really your daughter?"

"Yes, and I am very proud of her. You know, you are very lucky she didn't kill you that night in the consulate."

"What?"

"Yes, it was her, but you knew that, didn't you."

"Did she tell you everything?" Ghi said, a sense of dread settling into the pit of his stomach.

"Absolutely everything, she was working for me you know. Now if you want to keep your gambling secret from your father and the fact that you are stealing from him to fund it, you will listen to my friend Frances here and do exactly what he says."

"I only stole one," Ghi said.

"Really?" Marty said, dipped into his pocket and pulled out a handful of gold coins. "We got these from the money changers you used, and if you look carefully, you can see the secret mark your father puts on them."

Ghi deflated, he thought he had been so clever using different money changers to exchange the gold louis for Indian currency.

"What do you want?"

Frances put a fatherly arm around the boy's shoulders and led him away. Talking quietly and giving him instructions.

Marty watched them go then looked at the two teams getting ready for the next contest. He flipped a louis and said to no one in particular, "I might have a little bet myself."

They had a progress meeting with Hastings and two of the East India Company officers.

"In summary we control the feed of information to the Maruthans, and have an informer in the French Consulate," Marty said, rounding up a half-hour briefing.

"Why not just put this fellow Chopra on trial for treason and hang him," William Scott, the commissioner said.

"He wouldn't be of any use to us dead and it would tell the Maratha Pasha that we are on to his game with the French consul."

"And we couldn't send them false information at the moment it would do them most harm," Frances added.

"I think we should let the professionals do their job, William," Richard Rocke, the president of the board, said.

"Hmmph, I suppose you know what you are doing," Scott said.

"We will keep sending verifiable information so the Maruthans believe he is a genuine source and then, when our army is ready to strike, we will send them a piece of information that will cause them to make a fatal mistake," Marty explained again.

"To gain his cooperation we offered him a free pardon." Frances got another Harrumph from Scott.

"You are taking personal charge of the retrieval of the Aurora?" Rocke said.

"I am. The flotilla leaves on the next tide," Marty said.

"You really think you can retrieve her and her crew?" Rocke said with an air of scepticism.

"Failure is not something I contemplate this early in a mission, Sir," Marty said, suddenly fed up with the civilians.

Rocke looked taken aback by Marty's quite firm answer.

Frances nudged Marty's knee with his, "What the commodore meant was that until he knows what he is up against its impossible to say what the chances of success are. Although, I might say that the naval tradition does not allow or easily forgive failure. I believe your commission says, "Fail at your peril," or something like that."

"Any failure results in a court martial," Marty said.

Rocke nodded, "I see. My question was indelicate and ill timed."

Francis Hastings suddenly knocked his fist on the table, "Gentlemen the time for talking is done and the commodore needs to prepare for his departure."

"One last question if I may?" Rocke said.

"Sir?" Marty said.

"Have you any news of the expedition up the rivers?"

"Not directly, but we have intercepted a telegraph message that talked about a battle near Surat, which is on the Tapi river."

"You think your ship was involved?"

"If I know Captain Howarth, he was in the thick of it. We will have to wait and see what transpired when he reports."

Hastings looked at Marty, "Your son is aboard that ship, isn't he?"

"He is, and James would rather be nowhere else than in the middle of whatever action took place."

He bowed and took his leave, and just before the door was closed behind him, he heard Scott say, "You would have thought he would have kept his heir out of harm's way," and Hastings reply, "You don't know our Martin, that is the last thing he would do."

Marty boarded the Unicorn to the sound of the bosun's pipes and the crash of musket butts on the deck. The men were happy to see him, many admired him, all respected him and more, his return meant that they would be going to sea very soon.

"The squadron is in all respects ready for sea," Wolfgang said after they had finished the usual round of greetings.

"Take us out as soon as the tide is right."

"Aye, Aye, Sir!" Wolfgang said.

Marty had every piece of information he could gather about Sindhudurg Fort, and it was scant. He wrote a summary.

Sindhudurg Fort

    Island, curtain wall completely surrounds

    Complement – unknown

    Guns – unknown

    Layout – unknown

    Built 1664

    Considered impregnable

Just because it was built in 1664 didn't mean it was decrepit. They built forts to last then, and it would take a serious pounding to breach the walls. No, it would take what Hastings described as skulduggery to make this work.

"Adam!"

"Sir?" Adam said from the scullery door.

"Ask Zeb to attend me please."

"Certainly, Sir."

Marty grinned. No matter how hard he tried he would never make a sailor out of Adam.

The marine on his door announced Zeb.

"I have a task for you." Marty took a large chart from the rack. He opened it and laid it on the desk. "This is the largest scale map of the coast of India where our destination lies. Here is the island fort Sindhudurg. It's quite detailed but very small."

"You want me to draw it larger then?"

"If you would."

Zeb went to get his writing and drawing instruments and returned with a large sheet of fine paper.

"Would this be big enough? I can fill in details once we get there."

Marty had been studying the map with a glass. "There is a second fort on the very end of the point there. Pad-mag-ad," He pronounced it one syllable at a time.

"I can include that if you want."

"Yes, please do." Marty thought about the set up. The second fort was tiny compared to Sindhudurg. What was the point of it? He was still trying to figure that out when Zeb finished.

"It looks more like a fortified island than a fortress on an island," Zeb said.

"It does, doesn't it." Marty said.

Chapter 4: Sindhudurg Fort

It was a good two weeks of sailing to get close to the fort and Marty sent Zeb ahead on the Endellion to fill in the details on their map. The Endellion had a new crew, Philip Trenchard was still Master and Commander, having recovered from his ordeal at the hands of the pirates. Marty and Wolfgang wanted to see how he would hold up on a solo mission. They had given him Jon Williams as his mid leaving the Nymph with a vacancy. Zeb had a watching brief and was to report back on Trenchard's performance.

Philip had taken time to physically recover from the abuse meted out by his captors. He had trained hard to recover the lost muscle and fitness and was now as fit as he had ever been. Mentally he was not quite so recovered. His mind was full of doubts and guilt over losing his ship even though the court of inquiry hadn't deemed it necessary to hold a court martial. He had not struck. He and his crew had fought until they were beaten to the ground by sheer weight of numbers. He had a flashback, seeing young William Reynolds fall. Pierced through with four blades, he still swung his sword one last time before crumbling to the deck.

"Sir. We are coming up on the island," Midshipman Williams said, wrenching him back to the present.

"Very good, we will stand off a mile and heave to, to give our artistic friend a chance to take a good look." The island was about eight hundred yards long and five hundred at its widest.

Zeb had taken his pens and a sheet of paper pinned to a board up the mainmast to the topmast yard and was comfortably ensconced and scanning the island with a telescope. He sketched the wall noting the height and frequency of towers. He counted the guns he could see between two towers. *Brass nine-pounder field pieces from the glint of the sun,* he noted. Then he looked inland. Houses and what looked like a temple came into view. A couple of long low buildings appeared to be barracks as there were men streaming out of them and running to the walls.

Philip was watching the walls from the quarterdeck and saw the men appear to man the guns. He checked his watch. It had taken a good twenty minutes for them to react to their presence.

"Zeb! Can we move on?" he called up.

"Aye, Sir, if you would."

"We will circle the island at a mile. Make sail for five knots."

His heart was pounding, and his chest was tight. Not fear as such but anxiety. He took a deep breath and let it out slowly and looked aft to where the white ensign flew proudly. He thought about the crew of the Aurora being held on the island somewhere and his shoulders squared.

A puff of smoke from a gun on the wall. The bang followed and he watched as the black dot of the ball landed half a cable past them and a cable ahead.

"A warning shot," he said to his mid.

"Nine-pounder from the sound of it," Williams said.

Philip raised his telescope and the sleeve of his uniform coat fell back exposing his wrist. Jon noticed the still pink scars where he had been shackled. He knew the captain carried more on his back where he had been whipped.

"Maintain this speed and distance," Philip said.

"Deck there, just caught a glimpse of some masts on the far side of the island," the lookout shouted down.

They progressed up the west side of the island and were about to turn around the north end when the call came down,

"Gunboats coming out from behind the island. Feluccas and dows. Seven that I can count."

"Zeb, are you finished?" he called up.

"Give me two more minutes please."

"Bring us to quarters, Mister Williams, guns to be loaded with chain over small ball. Shift the aft quarterdeck guns to the stern mounts."

Like the Silverthorn, the Endellion had been modified in the light of experience with pirates. The forward carronades could now be pivoted to face forwards to protect the bow and he had added an extra twenty-four-pound-carronade on the foredeck that could be swept seventy degrees either side of the bow. The foremast rigging had been modified to give as clear an arc of fire as possible. The aft pair of the four twenty-four-pound carronades on the quarterdeck had a second set of mounts at the stern and the rail had detachable sections made for them to be deployed rather than gun ports.

Philip had done a lot of thinking about the loads for combatting ships full of men and, based on what he had seen, decided that chain over small ball would be most effective. Chain was very effective against rigging and even more so against people. Whereas small ball smashed light hulls and people indiscriminately but was no good against rigging. At a cable's range a hit with a single load of chain and ball would be devastating.

Zeb waved to say he had finished and saw the activity below. Trenchard wasn't changing course; he was going to go into the boats coming out from between the island and the mainland. He heard cheering and looked at the wall of the fort. It was lined with soldiers who were jumping up and down with excitement. He was about to get down when Trenchard called up, "Zeb, as soon as you can identify the ship in the harbour, report and we will get the hell out of here!"

There's a fine thing. He ain't lacking in bottom that's for sure, he thought and got his telescope out again.

"Ship is cleared and ready for action, Sir," Jon said.

The enemy ships were fast and divided into two groups with a felucca leading each one. The larger group of four was swinging around to get behind them. The other three would go for the bow. When the three got to a cable and a half away, he ordered, "Run out, fire as you bear."

The ports went up and the battery ran out. Marines manned swivels. There was a pause then one of the attackers fired a bow gun. The ball whistled along the deck and parted a halyard. A crewman rushed to repair it. The gun captains knew their stuff and waited until the boats came within effective range, ignoring the incoming shot.

A cloud of smoke from the bow and the foredeck twenty-four-pound carronade fired followed by the two foremost thirty-sixes. Then the port battery opened fire in sequence.

"That surprised them," Jon shouted above the noise. "John, Company ships don't have carronades."

Philip didn't answer he was totally focussed on the unfolding battle. Three of the four ships had gotten past the battery and were swinging around to his stern. One turned to point a big bow chaser at his stern windows.

The port carronade fired, sending its load directly at the boat's bow. The thin timbers shattered, sending splinters flying. The ball hardly slowed, and the chain howled through the gap. A head flew up in the air as the bow chaser was tossed aside. Blood sprayed, rigging came down and the boat drifted to a halt. The following boats swerved aside. Frantically trying to open the gap. The starboard stern chaser fired; its load shimmered across the water, the chain howling.

Zeb appeared on deck having slid down a stay. "The Aurora is in the harbour. I was shouting but you couldn't hear me."

Philip grinned, an almost manic expression, and pointed, "No matter, Zeb, look at them run!"

He was right, the Maratha Navy had lost three ships in a number of minutes and had decided that discretion was better than valour. That, however, cleared the way for the gunners on the walls. The top of the wall opposite them was suddenly covered in smoke.

"Wear ship!" Philip shouted and the Endellion spun on her heel as balls started to rain down around them.

"Philip, welcome. A glass?" Marty said and had Adam pour Philip a glass of port. "You had some warm work."

Adam looked at Marty and cocked his head at Zeb, who had followed Philip in. Marty nodded and Adam served the grinning Shadow a glass as well.

"What have you to report?"

"Three enemy boats destroyed, minor damage to the upperworks which will be repaired by dark. No casualties. We ran up the west side of the island and charted what we could see. It is eight hundred yards in length and five hundred at its widest. The walls are forty feet high with towers every eighty to ninety yards. The wall follows the edge of the cliff. There are nine-pound field cannon mounted at intervals. The top of the wall is flat, and the guns protected by gabions."

"Hmm, that means the walls are very thick," Marty said.

Zeb stepped forward and laid his sketches out, "This here is what the wall is like with the towers, and this is what's inside them from what I could see."

"Barracks?" Marty said, pointing to the two long buildings.

"Yes, and it took them a good twenty minutes to respond to us arriving," Zeb said.

"You think the harbour is here?"

"That's certain, the Aurora is tied up to a dock, I could see it through a big gate in the wall. A boat was coming in and the gate were open. A lot of civilians were milling around waiting for it."

A light went on in Marty's mind, "I will bet you a glass of rum that it was a supply boat. Were there any fields or animals on the island?"

"A few goats is all I saw, the ground is mainly rock," Zeb said.

"Did you get a look at the other fort?"

"Not much, it's not very big and just looks to be protecting a jetty."

"Gentlemen, welcome. We will carry out an action to recover the Aurora tomorrow at dawn," Marty said to the assembled officers in his cabin. It got their attention. Grins and nudges were exchanged.

"It will be in two parts," he said, and pulled the cover off an easel that was set up beside his desk. On it was Zeb's detailed map of the island and the adjacent fort.

"This is objective one," he pointed to the harbour. "A boarding party will take the Aurora and get her under sail by the time the sun rises. It will be led by Mr McGivern and consist of boats from the Unicorn, Eagle and Endellion. Ten men will be taken from each ship to make up the boarding party, The boats will assist if the Aurora needs to be towed out."

McGivern was congratulated by the men as he would be in command of the ship once it was at sea. Marty let them settle, "The second part is the taking and holding of Padmagad Fort. It is located here, and is only an island at high tide. At low water it connects to the mainland by a sand bar."

"Just like Mont San Michel," James Campbell said.

"Indeed," Marty said, then continued. "We do not know the strength of the defending force. Zeb saw some cannon on it but was too far away to identify their size. So given that, I and the Shadows will infiltrate the fort at midnight and eliminate any sentries. A force led by Captain O'Driscol will follow an hour later. We should have the doors open by then and their job will be to hold the fort and prevent any supplies being sent across to Sindhudurg Fort. The squadron will blockade the fort from the seaward side."

"Starve them out," Wolfgang grinned.

"Offer them a parley," Marty said. "We will give them back the fort in return for the Aurora's crew."

"What if they start killing the crew to force us out?" James asked.

"Then the combined firepower of our frigates will be brought to bear, and we will pound the walls to dust. We will demonstrate our firepower in advance. The Unicorn will come to a mile offshore an hour after dawn and fire a single broadside of her eighteen pounders. You will aim for this hammerhead-shaped section of wall which is the furthest west point. All the buildings are further north so we should only upset a few soldiers."

Marty got down to details. "The boats will be towed in by the Eagle and Endellion to a half mile of the gap. Once they have cast off the ships will return to the squadron. All lights will be shown on the other ships to divert any sentries' eyes away from the unlit boarding party. Any questions or suggestions?"

"The Unicorn and Leonidas could fire signal rockets," James Campbell said.

"Good idea, in fact the Nymph can join in that as well. We want them to know there is a strong force offshore," Marty said.

Sleep was short that night, Marty dressed in his black coveralls and had his uniform packed in a small chest the marines would bring ashore. Adam dressed the same and was making sure Marty's weapons were all in their correct places on his fighting harness. He held it up and Marty shrugged into it, looping the shoulder straps onto his belt and positioning the Manton double-barrelled, percussion cap pistols comfortably under his arms. His fighting knife with its nine-inch Damascus steel blade was on his belt at the back positioned for a left-hand draw. His hanger on his left hip, a pouch containing darts on his right along with cartridges to reload the Mantons.

The two went up on deck to find the rest of the Shadows and Sam waiting for them.

"Ready?" They were. "Let's go."

The Unicorn slipped within a mile offshore and hove to. All her lights were out. The cutter was alongside with a mast stepped and sail ready to raise. The first men dropped silently into it and took the equipment handed down from the deck, stowing it under the thwarts.

Once they were all aboard Sam took the tiller and they pushed off. As soon as they had sea room, a black sail was raised and they moved away into the night. Wolfgang turned the Unicorn and headed out to sea to join the squadron guided by the Leonidas firing a rocket.

Sam steered the cutter, guided by the stars and a beacon that the Indians burned all night on the fort.

"Very nice of them to show us the way," Adam said.

"It's to guide the fishermen home. A dozen boats went out at dusk," Marty said.

They approached the island, dropping the sail at the last minute and ran the cutter up onto the sand. Someone jumped over the side and ran a mooring line up to a large rock making it fast.

Antton and Garai took point and they moved out as a unit towards the castle walls. They all carried backpacks with equipment and were armed with a variety of silent ranged weapons.

They reached the wall and spread out. The moon rose over the horizon casting a faint light.

They waited and then the sound of a man's voice drifted down to them. He was humming softly, singing the words intermittently as if he hadn't quite learnt them yet.

Marty drew his knife and scraped the blade gently on the wall. The humming stopped and a head appeared over the parapet silhouetted against the stars. It grew a crossbow bolt in the forehead and fell back. Sam stepped away from the wall and twirled a grapnel on the end of a strong line. He let it fly and gently pulled it in until the tines bit and held. Chin, being the nimblest, was up the wall in a flash slipping over the edge.

There was a tug on the rope and Garai went up next followed by Matai, Antton, Billy, Zeb, Sam and Marty last of all. The sentry's body had been pushed into the shadows. He had hardly bled as the bolt had killed him instantly and blocked the hole at the same time.

They split into two teams. Antton's went clockwise around the wall and Marty's anticlockwise. Any sentries were taken down quietly with bollos, bolts, knives, or garrottes.

They met up again at the gate, a simple wooden affair set into an arch in the wall. They lifted the crossbar and tried the gate. It threatened to squeak. Zeb took a bottle of light oil from his pack and liberally treated the hinges. They gave it time to penetrate then tried again. The gates opened with the faintest of groans.

Sam placed a shuttered lamp in the middle as a guide and set off down to the landing dock to guide in the marines. He used a second shuttered lantern to flash a signal. He got two short, a long, and two short flashes in reply and the first of the marine's boats came alongside.

Marty and the rest of the Shadows started a reconnaissance of the fort. They soon discovered the barracks and chained the door shut. Chin came and found Marty. "The officer's quarters are over there," he said, indicating a building far enough away from the men to be officer territory.

Marty walked over and listened at the door. He made out two different snores. One decidedly male the other, probably, female. He grinned showing white teeth through his blackened face, pulled a pistol and gently opened the door. It was very dark in the room, so he opened the shutters on a small lamp he had in his left hand. It gave out the faintest of beams but was sufficient to reveal a beautiful, naked Indian girl lying next to an Indian man with an impressive moustache.

He put the lamp on a shelf and paused for a moment admiring her form. With a sigh he gently tapped her on the leg with his pistol. Her eyes opened and so did her mouth. His left hand clamped over it. She bit him. He wrapped her forehead with his pistol then pointed it at her eye. Her teeth relaxed, her eyes round in fright.

"Shhh," he said and indicated she should get out of the bed. She did and he was surprised that she was only about five feet tall. *She looked taller lying down*. He pushed her to the door, gathering a robe of some sort from a chair and threw it to her. The door was still open, and Sam took charge of her as soon as she exited.

"Careful she bites," Marty warned him and went back in. He sat in the chair and waited.

The marines arrived and soon there was shouting and banging as they entered the barracks in force. The officer woke with a start and sat upright. It took him a second or two to realise his companion was missing and there was a man with a gun sat in his chair.

Outside, the marines were not having it all their own way. One came backwards through the door to the barracks without touching the ground skidding across the cobbles to an untidy halt. He didn't get up. He was followed by an enormous, bare-chested, and turbaned Sikh. The marines levelled their guns at him, and he eyed them disdainfully.

Billy stepped forward and said, "This one's mine!" while taking off his shirt and bearing his chest. He looked quite impressive apart from the fact his chest was lily white and his head and arms a golden brown. The Sikh was impressed enough to flex his muscles and assume a fighting stance. The Shadows sat in a row on a low wall and cheered him on.

Marty pushed the officer out of his room in front of him and took in the tableaux in a glance.

"This could be quite interesting, no one has ever beaten Babbar in a fight," The officer said in English. "Why do you not stop your man?"

"He's been waiting months to test himself. He would never forgive me if I stopped him now."

The girl was still stood next to Sam, she had been crying and Sam looked awkward beside her.

"Tell her she can go and dress," Marty said.

The officer spoke to her, and she entered his rooms. Marty signed to Sam to stand guard at the door.

The combatants were circling each other. Suddenly they came together, grappling for supremacy. Muscles bulged, sweat glistened and they parted. They were equally matched. Babbar swung a haymaker at Billy's head which he ducked and responded with a right hook to the ribs which landed. Babbar grunted and backed away. Billy followed, his left jabbing out at his face. He had him off balance and was keeping him there while he waited for the right moment. The right cross took Babbar on the chin. The big man staggered back, blood trickling from his lip. He shook his head then bellowed as he charged. Billy met him face to face with a boot to his gut and as he double over brought his knee up into his face.

It was all over, Babbar was out cold. Billy rolled him on his side and rubbed the back of his neck.

"Bring me a cold wet cloth," he said but Matai was already there.

"You broke his nose and I think you might have cracked his jaw."

Billy's right hand was swelling up and turning blue.

"Think I might have busted my hand on it."

"Shelby is going to be mad at you. He might just have Anabelle fix you.

"That ain't no 'ardship." Billy said thinking of Shelby's beautiful wife.

The fort was secure, but the officer didn't seem bothered and that bothered Marty. He had the marine's man, the guns and when it was light walked around to see what was there. He discovered what had to be a drydock, it was a channel cut into the rocks big enough to take a large boat or small ship. A boat could be floated in at high tide and left to settle as the tide went out. There was also evidence of shipbuilding. He found a point where he could see into the harbour on the bigger island. He had heard shooting just before dawn and wondered if McGivern had been successful.

Chapter 5: Cutting Out and Delving Deep

First Lieutenant Gordon McGivern would be the first man aboard the Aurora if they found it on this damnably dark night. They had been towed, as planned, to within half a mile of the channel between Sindhudurg Island and the smaller fort that Commodore Stockley and his team of rogues should have taken by now. The beacon was still lit, and he steered well to the right of it. His other two boats were close in behind, following his lead.

His cutting-out team consisted of thirty men taken from the three biggest ships in the squadron. Top men, gunners, landsmen everything he needed to run a sloop and even fight one side if he had to. All he had to do was find the damn thing.

A break in the cloud allowed the moon to shine through and he could see he was a little close to the rocks around the big island. He eased his rudder a little to port. They passed the point and Padmagad Fort was a beam of them. He knew there was a low sea wall that protected the harbour jutting out from the fort, so kept to the middle of the channel while they headed Southwest.

He identified the wall by the fact it was an unmoving shadow in the moonlight and eased his tiller to come around behind it. The waves suddenly reduced, and it became quite calm.

"Steady, lads," he said, and the men reduced the stroke.

He caught sight of masts above the wall. *There she is,* he thought, mightily relieved. He canted the rudder to starboard a touch, aiming for the fore mast.

"In oars," he whispered, as he swung the tiller to port to bring them up beside the Aurora. There was a gentle bump and a boat hook snagged in her chains pulling them close.

"Follow me, lads," he whispered and grabbed the batten that ran around the hull. He pulled himself up and reached up for the rail. His hand found it and he hauled himself over onto the deck. Men joined him either side. The lithe topmen making light work of it.

His team were going in over the bow, the second boat was to go in over the beam and the third over the stern. It was classic boarding technique. The men paired off to their individual tasks. Landsmen to secure the dock and let go the mooring ropes. Topmen to get up the mast and make sail. The rest sweep the ship and get rid of any enemy that were aboard.

A hatchway burst open, and men started to boil up out of it, Soldiers!

"It's a trap, lads! At them!"

The first soldiers up, formed a line and fired their muskets. A sailor screamed as he was hit, another dropped to the deck, dead.

Gordon was a descendent of the highlanders that had fought the English at Culloden. He carried a basket-hilted Scottish sword ground down from its original thirty-six inches to a more manageable twenty-eight for deck fighting. It was still a prodigious weapon, and he knew how to use it to good effect.

He charged the embryonic line screaming a Gaelic war cry, his family, originally from County Cork in Ireland had moved to Scotland in the seventeenth century and aligned themselves with the Cameron clan. "Chlanna nan con thigibh a' so 's gheibh sibh feòil!" (Sons of the Hounds Come Here and Get Flesh!). He swung his sword at the hastily-presented bayonets, knocked them aside and crashed into the soldiers.

Now he had the advantage, the soldiers were unused to, and untrained for: deck fighting. He pulled a second blade and fought like a demon. Slashing and stabbing, not giving the Indians time to reform or room to use their long spear like bayonets. His men pilled in behind him and it became a melee.

He didn't hear the shots from forward. His sword became a living thing. He didn't think. He was possessed. Suddenly there was no one left to kill. He paused and looked around. His men were standing back, away from him. Looks of awe or fear on their faces.

"Get this ship underway," no one moved. "NOW!" he barked.

Men moved, running to get the sails set.

He walked down the deck checking on his men stopping only to put his sword through any wounded Indians he came across on his way. There was a shout from the dock.

"More Indian troops coming from the gate!"

"Get the swivels loaded," he said.

"Cast off!"

The men on the dock let go the lines, then ran to leap aboard. The gap widened as the offshore breeze filled the topsails pushing the Aurora away.

A platoon of infantry lined up on the dock in two ranks. The front knelt, and presented their muskets, seeming to point straight at him.

"Fire," McGovern said, and the swivels barked.

His order was a fraction faster than the officer in charge of the troops. Canister ripped through the ranks. Even though there were only three the effect was devastating. On the other hand, the balls from the muskets were not well aimed. Most went high, those that didn't hissed across the deck and landed somewhere out to sea.

"Trained by the French," he scoffed, "couldn't hit a barn door with a short axe."

The main sails caught the wind and they pulled rapidly out into the fading dark. It was dawn and he suddenly felt very tired. He shrugged and realised he was still holding his sword and dirk. They were covered in blood, so he wiped them on the nearest corpse and sheathed them.

"Get this offal off my deck," he said to a pair of landsmen.

He walked to the quarterdeck as the first of the splashes was heard.

Marty and his marines had the fort secured and the Indian prisoners safely stowed in a couple of storage sheds. However, the officer's behaviour still bothered him. He was far too – blasé, yes that was the word, blasé about being captured for Marty's liking.

"Zeb, come with me."

Zeb put down the piece of scrimshaw he was working on and followed Marty.

"How can I help?" he said.

"You have an eye for line and form tell me if you see anything out of the ordinary."

"Anything in particular?"

"I don't know what we are looking for, but that officer is too damn smug for a man who has lost his command."

"A trap or something then."

"I don't know, but I do know that we have the defence set to withstand an attack from both land and sea. So, if he thinks one is coming it's coming from inside."

They walked around the small castle, inside the buildings and around the inside of the wall.

"I ain't seen nothing," Zeb said.

"Me neither," Marty said grimly.

They returned to the place the men were gathered for their midday meal.

"Who has guard duty on the Indian officer tonight?" Marty asked O'Driscol.

"Corporal Edwards, who has the watch on the officer tonight?" O'Driscol asked.

"Marine Standish. Sah." Evans barked, snapping to attention.

"Bring him to me," Marty said.

"Sah! Standish, front and centre!" Evans bellowed.

"Quietly man," Marty said, wincing at the volume.

"Sah!"

Standish appeared and Marty took him by the arm, talking to him quietly as he walked away from the others. Standish nodded and grinned before saluting and returning to his meal.

Captain Satish Kumar was under house arrest in his rooms. That evening he ate his meal with an air of anticipation. He had secreted a rock in his jacket earlier that day and had fashioned a kind of cosh from a stocking. He waited patiently for it to get dark and for the guard to be changed. It was creeping up to midnight and the fort was quiet. Most of the sea soldiers that the hateful British officer commanded would be asleep and the sentries were on the walls.

He stood slowly so his bed wouldn't creak. Hefted his rock in the stocking a couple of times to get the feel of it and tiptoed to the door. There was a noise and he paused.

It was snoring!

He cracked the door open an inch and peered through the crack. The guard was fast asleep, a bottle beside him on the low wall he was slumped on. He caught the smell of rum.

He grinned, carefully opened the door, and looked around. Nobody was about, only the guards on the walls moved, silhouetted against the stars, and they were looking outwards.

He crept past the guard and headed towards the magazine. Ducking dramatically behind cover on the way, scuttling from a wall to a building to another wall. He paused at the top of the ramp that led down to the magazine. It was unguarded something he would never allow.

He looked around again. It was silent so he slipped down the ramp and opened the door. Inside it was as black as pitch and he felt his way around the wall to an alcove. He felt inside and found the slightly protruding brick he was looking for. He pushed it firmly and there was a load click followed by a creak.

A cold, very sharp blade touched the side of his neck, right over the main artery.

"Don't move," a soft voice said.

As soon as Marty spoke, Antton and Garai opened the shutters on the closed lamps they were carrying. The three of them had shadowed the captain as he had left his room. He had been laughably easy to follow despite dramatic dashes from cover to cover. Now Marty could see the open entrance to a passage that, by his reckoning, headed straight to the other fort.

"Good evening," he said in a light tone. "Now where would you be going on this lovely clear night."

He took the captain's arm and moved him away from the door, still holding the blade of his fighting knife at his neck.

"No sudden moves now, I'd hate to kill you by accident," Marty said. "Antton, see where it goes."

He led the captain out of the magazine where the rest of the Shadows waited with a grinning Marine Standish. Marty pushed the captain towards him.

"Thank you, Standish, take him back to his room. Billy, go with them."

They waited for Antton to return, and a pair of marines resumed guard duty. Marty checked his watch; a half hour at least had gone by since he left. Ten minutes later he stepped out of the magazine. He looked damp.

"It goes down under the sea and comes up at the other fort. The end is closed with a door, and I found the release mechanism. I didn't open it in case it came out in the barracks or something. It drips water and at its lowest has a foot of water in it."

Marty thought about it. There were close to three hundred men in the fort so a surprise attack through the tunnel wasn't an option. He needed to know where it came out. They closed the door to the passage after making sure they knew how to open it. It was time to get some sleep.

In the morning Marty had Captain Kumar brought to him. The first thing he noticed was he was no longer smug and had an air of defeat about him.

"Sit down, captain," Marty said. He was sat in a chair with his feet up on a stool. Beside a second chair there were two barrels stood on end with a plank laid across them and a row of water buckets all full to the brim.

"Do you know what that is?" Marty asked, indicating the barrels and buckets.

Kumar shook his head.

"That is a device for extracting information from reluctant subjects. It leaves no marks, it doesn't harm the outside of the body at all, but it never fails to work."

He leaned forward conspiratorially, "I've used it on fully-trained agents of the French secret service, they were blabbing all their secrets in an hour."

It was then that Kumar realised that the man opposite him wasn't in uniform, and his eyes had a coldness to them that was frightening.

"What we do is strap you down on the plank face up. Then Billy there, he is the big one, holds that cloth," Billy snapped the cloth between his hands, "over your mouth and nose so you can't turn your head. Then Antton," Antton waved with a smile, "pours water from one of the buckets over your face continuously. It goes up your nose and you can't breathe so you open your mouth. It goes in there too and soon you are drowning."

He paused, reached out, turned Kumar's head towards him and looked at him with those cold eyes.

"So you see, you will tell me what I want to know. It's up to you whether we do it the easy way or the hard way."

Kumar looked around for a uniform, a military man who he could appeal to. There were only the grim-faced men in black.

"I protest, I am an officer and I demand to be treated as such."

"Protest noted and ignored," Marty said. "Now, where does the tunnel come out in the other fort?"

Kumar tried very hard to be brave but then the men started making the board ready. Straps normally used by a surgeon to tie his patient down before an amputation were unrolled. The one called Billy moved to the end of the plank in readiness; the cloth stretched between his huge hands. Antton picked up a bucket.

His will to resist dissolved, "It comes out in the tower to the right of the gate."

"What is in the room that it comes out into?"

"It is a guardroom, and the mechanism for the gate is in there. There are ten men in there at all times."

"How do I know you are telling the truth? You could be lying to trap me."

"On my honour, I am telling the truth, may Shiva forgive me."

Marty believed him.

"Bring one of the other prisoners."

A sergeant was brought forward. "Tell this man he has to carry a message to the commander of the fort."

Kumar translated.

"The message is, we will release the prisoners we are holding here and return the fort to you in exchange for the crew of the Aurora. If they do not agree or harm the prisoners in any way by sundown this evening my ships will start to bombard the fort."

Marty signalled to Sam, who was stood atop the wall. He fired a rocket that rose, red, into the sky.

"What follows now is a demonstration of our firepower."

It sounded like thunder as the eighteen-pound main armaments of the Unicorn and Leonidas fired their broadsides.

"The next time I fire a red rocket, the bombardment will not stop until we have reduced a whole section of wall to rubble."

This was a bit of a bluff as he didn't think they had enough shot to do that.

"I will also detonate the magazine here and destroy this fort."

When Kumar finished, he added, "I expect you told him we know about the tunnel." The look on his face was all the answer he needed. "If they try to use the tunnel to attack us, we will collapse it. Charges are already in place. Tell him I want the reply brought by an officer of the Aurora who can testify to the wellbeing of his men."

Kumar talked to the sergeant for a while seemingly repeating the message so he wouldn't forget any of it. Once he was happy he had it, he turned to Marty.

"He has the message memorized now and can be giving it."

One of the boats was used to ferry him across under a flag of truce. The sergeant stood in the bow franticly waving the white shirt back and forth.

The boat dropped him off then backed away to a safe distance. The sergeant was met by an officer who kicked his ass through the gate. Marty watched through his telescope and chuckled at the pantomime.

An hour later the gate opened and a man in Company uniform stepped out. He waved to the boat, and they picked him up.

"Lieutenant Conner, East India Company Marine." He introduced himself as he debarked. He was thin and dirty Marty could see vermin crawling around his neck

"Commodore Stockley, Royal Navy," Marty replied. He didn't offer his hand.

"The commander of the fort is in a right funk. Your ships made a mess of one of his walls. He does, however, agree to release the crew as per your demands."

"How many and what condition are they in?" Marty said.

"I am the first, the captain was killed in the action. We have forty-two survivors. All our wounded died weeks ago. The Indians refused to have a doctor treat them. Some of my men have dysentery."

"When will they be released?"

"At dawn tomorrow."

"Do you trust the commander of the fort?"

"Not as far as I could spit him."

That was what Marty thought.

"Fire a blue rocket," he said to Sam then turned to the lieutenant. "Get a bath. There's one in the officer's quarters. We will give you some clean clothes. This marine will show you the way."

The officer turned away to follow then stopped and said, "Thank you. What does the blue rocket mean?"

"That the squadron should stand by, if I fire a red one, they will start sending shot over the walls into the compound."

The lieutenant grinned; he was beginning to like Commodore Stockley.

That night more boats arrived and by dawn they were lined up in the harbour waiting for the prisoners. Lieutenant Conner stood in the prow of the centre boat holding the white flag of parlay. The gate opened and his men staggered out. They were a sorry bunch, malnourished, crawling with vermin, some so sick that their mates had to carry them.

The boats went alongside and took ten each. The commander of the fort glared down at them from the wall. The boats moved away, rowed out around the seawall and out to sea where the Endellion and Eagle were waiting for them.

Once they had been recovered Marty and the shore party embarked in their boats and made to follow. The commander shook his fist at them. Marty saluted smartly.

A gun fired from the wall. The ball screamed overhead and sent up a plume of sand on the beach. Before Marty could order the red rocket fired, there was a rumble of thunder.

"Shall I fire it anyway?" Sam asked.

"No need, Wolfgang has our backs," Marty said as more guns fired. "Get the sails up and get us out of here."

On the Unicorn Wolfgang directed fire. "I want the balls to pass low over the wall so that they hit the far wall or land in the compound."

The gunners went at it with a will. Trajectories were calculated and elevations set. The first broadside fired. About half the balls cleared the wall; some by such a scant margin that they cleared anything on top away. Others hit the top of the wall and ricocheted away knocking large chunks out of the ancient rock.

On the Leonidas, James Campbell was treating the affair as a competition. "Come on, lads," he exhorted, "we can outshoot the Unicorn. Put your backs into it."

The Nymphe sailed in under the cover of the frigates' guns. Her job was to pick up Marty and the shore party. That didn't prevent her from joining in the bombardment. Her nine pounders and carronades didn't pack the punch of the eighteens, but they could disrupt the guns on the wall.

Chapter 6: A Heroes Return

Marty took a deck pump bath luxuriating in scrubbing himself down. The crew were used to that, and the pump team worked with vigour. As soon as he was done each of the shore party followed in groups. They had all picked up fleas and the odd lice while in the fort and their clothes were being boiled to remove any stowaways.

Extra rum rations were given to the men and a certain amount of horseplay ensued. Marty, now wrapped in a dressing gown watched indulgently. Adam, who was, somehow, bathed, shaved, and dressed in livery brought him a welcome cup of coffee and a brandy.

"Mr Shelby, how are the survivors?" Marty said as Shelby walked up beside him. He had ordered the surviving men to be brought to the Unicorn once they had been cleaned.

"Most have malnutrition and scurvy; some have ulcers in their skin and some dysentery. All of which can be treated. Annabelle and Matai are nursing them along with my boys."

"Excellent. We will be back in Calcutta in three weeks so there's time to feed them up."

Adam served Shelby a coffee. "Bless you, my boy," Shelby said and sipped the bitter brew. "Just how I like it."

Marty looked along the deck. Lieutenant Conner was standing by the rail watching the two of them. Marty beckoned him over.

"Mr Conner, I hope you are well?" Marty said.

Conner looked a little abashed at being addressed by a navy commodore and lord in a dressing gown.

"I am well, thank you, Sir." He didn't know whether to salute or not and his arm sort of hovered halfway to his forehead.

"You don't need to salute, I'm not in uniform." Marty grinned looking almost boyish.

"I have been admiring your ship," Conner said.

"Not mine anymore, she's Wolfgang's. I gave up the privilege when they gave me my broad pennant." He glanced up at the pennant that flew from the mainmast. "Though it's more fun being a captain."

"The armament is somewhat unusual," Conner said looking at the huge carronades on the foredeck.

"You noticed Bertha and Brenda." Marty chuckled. "The men came up with the names."

"Are you interested in gunnery?" Shelby asked.

"Oh yes, it's the reason I joined the marine."

"Have you met Wolverton the gunner?"

"I can't say that I have."

"Mr Stirling," Marty said to a passing midshipman. "Please give Mr Wolverton my compliments and ask him to join us."

The mid squeaked an 'aye, aye' and disappeared below.

A couple of minutes later, the misshapen gunner came on deck. Conner started at the sight of him and was openly astonished when he reported in a refined, educated voice."

"Close your mouth, Mr Conner. This is Wolverton our gunner and he is the best in the navy. He will give you a tour of our armaments."

Wolverton looked him up and down, "He's a weedy one."

"He was imprisoned on the island," Marty said, hiding a grin.

"I'll go slowly then."

The two went forward and Marty could hear Wolverton going into detail about the carronade mounts and their benefits.

Marty had Allan Conner, Shelby, Anabelle and Wolfgang to dinner. They met for a pre-dinner drink. Marty was pleased that the Company sailors were all recovering well and even contributing to the watches.

"We will be in Calcutta in a week if the weather holds," Wolfgang said.

"I told Caroline you two should get together when we get back," Marty said to Anabelle. They hadn't had a chance to meet up before now, though Caroline knew about her. "The crew will be due some shore leave when we get in."

Connor was not used to having women onboard especially one as beautiful as Anabelle.

"How did you meet, Mr Shelby?" he said.

"Just Shelby," Shelby said.

"In Malta," Anabelle said.

Marty came to her rescue as he knew she didn't like talking about it. "We were there working with the Maltese government on a situation they had, when the two of them met. It was love at first operation, one might say."

Anabelle blushed while shooting him a grateful look and Shelby laughed.

"She is a dab hand with a needle, stitches them up better than I can, and I am a fair hand if I might say so."

"Your ministrations have been well received by my men," Conner said. He looked thoughtful and said, "I gather from the wardroom that you are not quite a regular navy squadron. The men haven't said anything directly but some of the operations they talk about are, shall I say, unusual?"

"We are a special unit and take on the navy's less public missions." Wolfgang said.

"Like when you were here last time?"

"With Wellington? Yes, like that."

Connor was struggling with something, and by the time desert came he had worked his way up to saying, "I found the tour with Wolverton fascinating. His description of your armaments and the way you use them was very interesting. I was wondering," he cleared his throat. Marty waited patiently. "I was wondering if you had room for another officer in your squadron."

"You would give up your rank in the marine?" Marty said.

"Yes, I would go back to a midshipman if that is all you could offer."

Marty looked at Wolfgang; eyebrows raised in question.

"We only have vacancies for mids right now, but I suppose the Nymphe could do with an extra officer. Andrew and Stanley are stretched with no mids aboard."

"That would be a second lieutenancy," Marty said.

"That would be perfect." Conner smiled.

Calcutta still stank when they came up the river to moor outside of Fort William, but the telegraph had been busy, and the shoreline was full of people cheering and waving. There was a band playing and Marty could see Caroline and the twins amongst a group of dignitaries. He saw Hastings and Ridgley stood together. Frances Ridgley looking like the cat who ate the canary.

Conner looked at the crowd, "Do you often get that kind of reception?"

"You think that it's only for us?"

"Why would they be cheering the marine? We lost."

"But you have been returned to the fold, and for that they are happy. They will cheer you and buy you drinks to hear the story of how bravely you fought."

"You understand people better than I." Conner sighed.

"Just experience, now smile and wave." Marty laughed.

The Unicorn eased up to the dock and the mooring ropes were secured. The gangplank pulled across. Hasting and Ridgley were the first aboard.

"Well done, Martin. I see the Aurora, did you recover the crew as well?"

"What was left of them, they didn't go down without a fight and then the Indians treated them roughly." Marty turned to Conner, "Governor Sir Francis Hastings, may I present Lieutenant Conner. The sole surviving officer from the Aurora."

Hastings shook his hand, "You can tell me about what happened over dinner tomorrow night. You too, Martin."

Marty plastered a smile on his face which turned genuine when Caroline stepped aboard with the twins. He swept all three into a hug, and bussed Caroline with a smacker on the lips.

"Martin, control yourself!" she whispered but returned it soundly.

Marty grinned and stepped back over to Hastings who had now been joined by Rocke.

"Well done, Milord," Rocke said.

"Thank you, I will be putting the Aurora up in front of the prize court, or do you want to settle the salvage bounty privately?"

Hastings choked, Ridgley walked away, his shoulders shaking, and Conner looked astounded.

"What?" Rocke spluttered.

"Any ship lost to the enemy and/or abandoned by her crew that is recovered by a Royal Navy vessel is deemed to be either a prize or salvage. Either way a bounty will be paid that is divided amongst the ships in sight of the action. In fact, the admiral or senior officer present can also decide to buy said ship in for use by the navy. But in this case, as that would be me, unless an admiral has arrived while we were away, I would say I have no need for another ship of her size."

Rocke listened in amazement. "How much will this cost the Company?"

"One officer and one thousand, one hundred pounds. That is one pound for each of the sailors in the squadron to have a drink while they are ashore and one hundred pounds to kit the officer out with a full set of lieutenants' uniforms and equipment."

Rocke looked at Marty then at Hastings, who was trying hard not to smile, and realised he had been had.

"I assume the officer is Mr Conner?"

"Why yes, now you mention it, it is."

"And what reward do you require?"

"His service in my squadron will be enough."

"I will see he is transferred."

Rocke shook Conners hand and said, "You may think this is a good idea now but flying your flag next to this pirate will bring you to a bad end."

"I think I will risk it, Sir." Conner grinned.

Rocke turned back to Marty, "Thank you for your help." He smiled genuinely.

After that they made their way ashore.

Dinner at the governor's residence was low key but lavish with many courses and a lot of wine. Marty and Caroline, Allan Conner, Wolfgang, James Campbell and McGivern were invited. The story of the rescue had to be told from all points of view.

"Did you do much damage to the fort?" Hastings said.

"We knocked some large chunks out of the wall but it's still standing. We assume we did some significant damage to the interior as we targeted the barracks and the keep-like building behind the gate. We also cleared the wall of artillery pieces along that section."

"I assume you can replace the expended powder and shot?"

"Yes, there is a store here we can access."

"Any news of that other ship of yours?"

"The Silverthorn? She isn't due back for another month."

A week later Adam entered his office with a message from the telegraph.

"This was just delivered. The Silverthorn entered the river an hour ago."

"What? They are early."

"Yes, and they signalled that they are in need of medical assistance."

"Get a message to Shelby to get here as fast as he can, and one to Wolfgang. I want the Silverthorn moored here in front of the fort."

Marty was waiting when the Silverthorn slid around the bend in the river with the Unicorn's cutter leading her. The midshipman in charge of it signalled they should moor at the dock. He saw the surgeon's flag was hoisted on the mainmast and a clatter of hooves announced that Shelby had arrived, just in time, in a dog cart. He had Anabelle with him.

Marty pulled a small glass from his pocket and focussed on the quarterdeck.

"Thank God, James is alright," he said, then looked again. "Where is Terrance?"

James saw him and waved, then got back to bringing the ship alongside.

As soon as the gangway was in place Marty, Shelby and Anabelle raced up ignoring the side party.

"What's happened?" Marty said.

James held up his hand and said, "Mr Shelby, Captain Howarth is in his cabin, he has lost his leg below the knee, and I fear gangrene has taken hold."

Shelby and Anabelle hurried below.

"Sorry, Sir, but he is in a bad way," James said to his father by way of apology for side stepping him.

"No matter. Report, Mr Stockley."

James gave his report, factually without embellishment.

"Let me summarise," Marty said, "Terrance lost his leg when you fought your way out of the river Tapi, you took command at that point and, in consultation with him, decided to continue the mission into the Narmada River."

"Yes, Sir."

"How far up did you get?"

"About one hundred and fifty miles."

"Then Terrance's wound turned bad."

"Yes, Sir, he got feverish and started rambling."

"So, he was no longer capable of command even in an advisory role."

"No, Sir."

Anabelle came up on deck. "Shelby is going to take his leg off above the rot. It is the only chance to save him. We will do it here on deck."

"What do you need?" James said.

"A table that is scrubbed clean, our instrument boxes from the cart, and a brazier of hot coals."

James shouted orders and the men sprang to obey without hesitation. A pair of trestles were brought up and one of the mess tables was repurposed. Two men with soap and water scrubbed the table with stiff brushes. The surgeons' boxes were brought onboard. Finally, a brazier was placed on a metal plate and a charcoal fire started.

Terrance was brought up on deck and Marty immediately caught the stink of corruption. Anabelle had already prepared the saw and knives by washing them in spirit and burning it off in the flames. She also placed several cauterizing irons in the coals.

Burley men placed their captain gently on the table and held him still. Shelby tied a torniquet around his thigh and tightened it. He took a knife, a wickedly sharp one with a curved blade and reached under Terrance's thigh. In a single movement he cut the flesh to the bone all the way around the leg. Blood spurted from an artery. Anabelle moved in quickly with a clamp and sealed it.

"Thank you, my love," Shelby said, and flayed the skin back far enough to form a flap, then removed another inch or so of flesh. He folded the skin back out of the way and took a saw to the bone. The discarded lump of blackened flesh was thrown in a bucket. He carefully cauterized the veins and arteries to stem any bleeding before sprinkling the raw flesh with sulphur powder and wrapping the end in the skin that had been folded back. Anabelle stitched it into place.

Throughout the entire operation the crew of the Silverthorn watched and when they finished and washed their hands and arms in a bucket of water, gave them three cheers and a tiger.

"There is at least a slim chance he will pull through. He was unconscious throughout so the shock will be minimal. The flesh I cut back to was clean. We can only hope," Shelby said to Marty.

Marty took the time to look around the ship. Her repairs had been done well, she was tidy and as clean as a ship could be after being at sea and freshwater. He was at the bow when he saw Wolfgang doing the same.

"Very tidy, not a rope out of place," Wolfgang said.

"Brass could do with a polish," Marty said, straight faced.

"I'm sure he will get around to that now they are in port." Wolfgang said, then realised Marty was teasing him.

"Can't be seen being soft on the boy," Wolfgang said.

"Have you talked to any of the crew?" Marty said.

"Yes, the purser and the bosun, they corroborated his report."

"I will step away and support any recommendation you make." Marty said. "I expect a full report on my desk by tomorrow."

It was another day before James was able to visit the family at their house. He walked through the door unannounced except for the coded whistles of the marines on guard at the gate. Caroline met him at the door and swept him up in her arms.

"I swear you have grown," she said as she held him at arm's length, looking him up and down. "Your arms are outgrowing your uniform."

"I will get it adjusted, there's a very good tailor near the navy dock."

Marty came out of his study, he stood and looked at his son, then slowly stood to attention and saluted.

"You have performed in an exceptional way, Wolfgang has mentioned you in dispatches, and you will, no doubt, be gazetted. I am very proud of you. Now come here and give me a hug."

Father and son hugged for the first time in what seemed like an eternity and when they parted the twins descended on James like a tornado.

"The only thing missing is Troy," James said.

"He is too old for all this nonsense now; he is much better off at home with Ryan and Louise," Marty said suffering a pang at the thought of the big Dutch Shepherd dog that had shared so many of his adventures.

James looked like he wanted to ask Marty something.

"Come with me," he said and led him to his study.

They sat by the open window and Marty looked at his son, "What is on your mind?"

"Will Philip have to give up his career?"

"Not necessarily, it depends on if there are any other side effects from the gangrene and whether he can adapt. The Tool Shed are adept in constructing artificial legs."

"Oh yes! I forgot Louise. She is so good with hers you wouldn't know she had one," James said, referring to the former French spy who had worked for British intelligence and was now wife to Ryan Thompson, who was the factor and manager of the Stockley estates. She was also his mother's business partner.

"Who will take the Silverthorn now?"

"Gordon McGivern is senior, but I believe he has expressed the wish to stay with Wolfgang. Angus Fraser is next in line."

"Can I stay on the Silverthorn?"

"I don't see why not. The men obviously respect you."

James realised he had probably pushed his luck as far as he could and looked around. He noticed a new sword lying on his father's desk.

He stood, stepped over and picked it up. It was a hanger, twenty-four-inch blade, shagreen wrapped hilt, brass knuckle guard, cross guard, and pommel, with a finger loop for added control inside the cross guard. The sheath was plain but fashioned of high-quality leather and tipped in metal.

"Draw it," Marty said.

He clicked the blade free from the scabbard with his thumb and drew the blade slowly, it was drawn from extremely high-quality steel.

"Toledo?"

"Yes, the finest."

He drew it all the way and held it up to the light.

"It has the family crest etched on the ricasso."

"Yes, it's to remind you to use it with honour."

"Remind me? This is mine?"

"It was meant for your birthday but now is also a good time for you to receive it."

"Thank you, I will try to live up to your expectation."

"I'm sure you will." Marty stood. "It's time we re-joined the others, with Beth gone your mother needs some time to exercise her motherly instincts."

James winced, but then decided he wasn't too big to enjoy a bit of mothering.

Chapter 7: The Plot Thickens

Frances Ridgley loved his job, especially when he was playing puppet master. Right now, he had the French consul's son dancing to his tune and feeding him all sorts of useful information. The fly in the ointment was the small stack of papers by his elbow. They hinted that there was another player in the game other than the French and he had no idea who it was.

He picked up the top paper. It was a message he had intercepted when a known courier had an unfortunate accident. His people had gotten to the body first and found the message. It was in code; one so complex it had taken him a week to crack it.

It said simply, "The peacock has landed, rendezvous at Mandi's"

What the hell did that mean and who or what was Mandi? They didn't know who wrote it or who the intended recipient was. The message on its own was meaningless. It could be someone writing to their lover that they were in town. But who would use a double shifted Caesar code that was date stamped to send a message like that?

Then one of his agents had spotted a man using a dead drop. He had copied the message and passed it to Frances. They had intercepted two more messages since then. All were encoded the same way.

"Sometimes strokes of luck just spoil the party," he muttered to himself.

He spread the messages out in date order.

The Peacock has landed, rendezvous at Mandi's.

The time is set, be prepared when Durga rises.

The tiger has arrived.

After Vijayadashmi, gather the loyal.

What the hell did it all mean? He slumped back in his seat and stared at the ceiling. He was lost in thought when the door opened, and Marty stuck his head inside.

"Got a moment?"

Frances sighed, "Come in, maybe you can make something of this."

He showed Marty the slips of paper.

"Double shifted Caesar's?" Marty said.

"With a date stamp."

"Somebody is going to a lot of trouble to keep these a secret."

"Yes, but who and why?"

"Have you tried following the man who leaves them?"

"Of course, but he is as slippery as an eel." Frances sighed.

"Is he an Indian?" Marty said.

"Who?"

"The man who drops these off."

"Yes, he's an Indian."

"And what about the person who picks them up?"

"That's the thing. We haven't seen anyone pick them up. They just disappear."

Marty shook his head, there was no way they were magicked away, someone had to be picking them up.

Marty went to the door and called over a messenger, he spoke to him then went to the ever-steaming samovar and made a pot of tea, He laid out three cups. Frances noticed but decided to wait and see what his ever so clever colleague was up to.

There was a knock on the door,

"Come in," Marty said.

"I will do that in your office next time I'm there," Frances said.

Marty ignored him as Mr Panda came in.

"What can I be doing for you, Lord Martin?" Panda said.

"Please take a look at these messages and tell me if they mean anything to you."

Mr Panda studied the papers then looked up and said with a typical Indian head wobble, "The peacock could refer to Bhimabai Holkar, he is known by that name by some of his followers. The next one refers to Durga rising, that is probably the festival of Durga Puja which is in September and October. I am afraid I have no idea what the tiger has arrived means. Vijayadashmi is the last day of the festival. The city will be crowded with worshipers and followers.

"The perfect time for a move against the British with added religious significance as well," Frances mused.

"Thank you, Mr Panda, you have been most helpful," Marty said. "I will put the Shadows onto trying to solve the mystery of the dead drop," Marty said after Panda had left.

"That would be appreciated, the local agents are alright but lack experience."

"I'm sure you will improve them."

Francis looked happier, then remembered that Marty had come to see him, "What was it you wanted to see me about?"

"Oh, I was just wondering, how you were getting on with that French boy."

"Ghi? He is terrified we will expose his larceny and is passing copies of all his father's papers to us. We are rewarding him by funding his gambling."

Marty laughed, "Carrot and stick, works every time."

"Yes, and we have been able to discover how and when he is bringing in the arms. It would have been easier with Beth here, but we are managing."

Marty wondered how Beth was getting on, she was probably halfway home by now.

Beth was in fact having a lovely trip. She was unaccompanied except for one of the Indian servants that she had established a relationship with. The girl, Sarika, had jumped at the chance to go to England and be Beth's maid of all works. The Company ship had luxurious cabins, served excellent food and as the only single female passenger she got plenty of attention.

That attention had threatened to get out of hand in the first month of the voyage when a young officer had become somewhat over attentive. Beth had explained, by putting him on his arse when he tried for an unwanted embrace, that she wasn't interested. He got the full message when she produced a pistol seemingly out of nowhere, stopping his protest in its tracks.

She started practising her swordsmanship on deck early in the morning which was soon noticed by the other passengers.

"Can I spar with you?" The enquirer was a captain of the Lifeguards who had been on detachment in India with his wife and two children. Beth rather liked his wife, Nikola, who was from a good Bedfordshire family and had married for love.

"Certainly, it's always better to practise with an opponent," she said.

He soon discovered she was an accomplished swordswoman and had to work hard to match her. Her athleticism and natural grace made her difficult to make a hit on and he found himself thrusting or slashing at air as she slipped away. She didn't use any of the total fighting techniques that her father had taught her. That would be giving away too much.

His ten-year-old daughter absolutely hero-worshiped Beth and, much to her mother's dismay, asked if Beth could show her how to fence. Her father agreed despite his wife's reservations, as long as they used practice swords. Beth didn't bring hers, so used her charms on the ship's carpenter and had a couple of short wooden practice swords made.

"Hold it loosely, that way no one can knock it out of your hand," she instructed and demonstrated the correct grip. Emma was a bright girl and a quick study, and the clacking of wooden blades could be heard most mornings.

Matai and Garai dressed as Afghans for their shift watching the dead drop. It was at a crossroads under a teardrop-shaped stone. There were a significant number of the rugged northern tribesman trading in the city and their naturally dark complexions allowed them to be inconspicuous.

The crossroads was used twice a week as a vegetable market. They had been watching for two days now. It was market day, so they had the rest of the boys watching around the periphery. At dawn a vegetable seller laid out a blanket on which he displayed cauliflowers and aubergines to one side of the stone and on the other, another selling coriander, parsley and other herbs and spices.

Women came and shopped early, children picked up orders and delivered them to the houses of wealthier citizens. Then Matai saw a Buddhist monk enter the market. He moved from vendor to vendor holding out his bowl. Matai got an itch that something didn't ring true and moved in closer to him. Some gave him vegetables or rice. He got to the cauliflower seller, he held out his bowl and the seller waved his hand at his goods indicating they were all too large.

The monk said something. The vendor dug into his pocket and dropped a few coins into the bowl. Matai caught a flash of white. The monk moved off and Matai followed. Garai joined him for a moment and then took over following the priest while Matai went back to watching the vendor. He spotted Antton across the way and signed to him that they had a hit.

Chin and Zeb linked with Garai setting up a perimeter tail. The three basically surrounded the target at a distance, the idea being one of them would keep him in sight at all times. The monk made his way unhurriedly through the city to a nearby temple. They couldn't follow him in but there were only two exits, so they covered those.

That evening Matai and Garai reported to Marty.

"The pass was made in broad daylight from the cauliflower seller to the monk. The seller looked surprised when the monk identified himself. He made a good job of the pass, but I spotted the paper." Matai said.

"We followed him to the Monsha Bari temple. He left in normal Indian clothes a half hour later, right out the front door," Garai said. "He walked to a farm in Dewan Bagan Lane near Nonapukur Pond. Only the farm hasn't been operational for a year or so. Chin is watching it now and we will hand the watch over to a local this evening."

"We followed the vendor to an address in Gorachand Road. He isn't a farmer. The house is owned by a merchant according to the man Frances sent along with us, they are looking for him now," Matai said.

"Good work, I can see why the locals were having trouble. The priest disguise is genius as they are almost invisible to the locals. I wonder if they suspected we knew about the dead drop and changed the way the message was passed because of it."

Marty took the Shadows to Frances's office to brief him and after a thorough round of questions Frances said, "Can I keep Matai and Garai for a while? We need to discover the rest of the network, who any co-conspirators are and their expertise will be invaluable in tracking them down."

Marty was grim and said, "You can use any of the Shadows except Adam and Sam. This is important and I have the feeling we are potentially looking at the Maruthans staging some kind of grand gesture at the end of the festival. We don't want that as it would be interpreted as the Company being vulnerable. Find out who and where they are so we can kill this before it happens."

He looked over another note from Francis Hastings, "In the meantime we need to investigate why the Burmese pirates have suddenly shifted their attention from the Straits of Malacca to the Bay of Bengal."

Chapter 8: Burma

Angus Frasier read himself in as Captain of the Silverthorn. He did so in a strong clear voice without a hint of the nervousness that he felt. Nervousness mixed with a healthy dollop of pride, the Silverthorn was a fine ship with a crack crew. He finished the reading in and looked around the crew who looked back at him expectantly. *They want a speech!*

"Terrance Howarth is a good captain who has, unfortunately, been laid low by his injury. He is in the best possible hands with Mr Shelby and his wife. We were trained by the same man, our commodore, and our expectations are the same. To have a taught, happy ship that is a prime example of the navy's tradition. You men are the best and I will expect nothing less than the best from all of you. In return I will bring all my experience and skill to making this the best ship in the squadron."

He paused judging his audience.

"We will take the ship out so that I can assess its readiness. We will perform sail and gun drills. Show me what you can do. Dismissed."

The men dispersed to their stations.

"Take us out, Mr Stockley."

James shouted the orders that would warp them out from the dock. He hoisted the pilot flag as soon as they were three feet off. A pilot who he had seen before came alongside and up the battens.

"I am wishing you a very good morning. I am Gupta, your pilot."

"Good morning, Mr Gupta," James said, "please take us down river."

"If you would set sail, please."

"Set foresails, spanker and topsails!" James cried.

The ship made way as the wind filled the sails and they were trimmed. James left the sail handlers to trim them. He would only intervene if it was necessary.

"Steerage way," the helm called.

They moved downstream amongst the other traffic. The river was busy with boats crossing from one side to the other which was a major hazard. Boats travelling along the river stayed to starboard, so it was a case of matching their speed to avoid problems.

As the river opened up and they had more room, they increased speed. The pilot's boat, a small sailboat, kept pace with them.

Suddenly there was a shout from the main mast. "Man overboard!"

James ran to the side and looked down. A barrel with a face chalked on it floated past. "What the hell?"

"Man overboard, Mr Stockley. What are you going to do?" Frasier asked.

It was a test!

"Haul your wind! Back the foresail. Bring the gig to the side!" he yelled in quick succession. The ship glided to a stop and the boat was manned. James delegated the command of it to Ivor Steenson, one of the mates.

"Get that barrel and bring it back here. Treat it like a person."

Balancing the ship in the current using the sails was tricky but he managed it. The barrel was recovered and brought aboard.

"Make way!" he said as soon as the boat crew was on deck.

It was a sign of things to come. As soon as the grinning pilot left, Captain Frasier let them settle, then ordered an evolution followed by others. Top masts down, replace a sail while under way, rapid changes of direction. Then there were gun drills. They fired a broadside, and he walked the length of the deck tapping men on the shoulder saying, "You're dead." The men would go to the centreline and James had to reorganise his gun crews to maintain full fire.

By dinner time the crew and James were exhausted, but that wasn't the end of it. Frasier had him and the warrants to dinner and went over each of the exercises in detail.

"Gentlemen, you did well today. Consider the improvements I have suggested when we do them again tomorrow."

James collapsed into his cot and fell asleep fully clothed.

The next day they started out with more evolutions. This time the captain took a more active role. He made small changes to the way things were done. Never anything large but just enough to stamp his way of doing things on the men.

During a lull he said to James, "I had heard about your large friend but now I've seen him he is prodigious!"

"Dennis is indeed a force of nature, if he is directed correctly," James replied.

"You have how many followers?"

"Three, Sir."

Frasier left it at that. He had brought his cox, steward and cook with him. He wasn't a great believer in having a lot of followers. As in many things his Lutheran upbringing in Glasgow kept him modest in his ways. He invited James for dinner again that evening.

"You did very well today, James," he said.

"Thank you, Sir."

"I was told you have an affinity for the marines."

James was surprised, he liked working with the marines but had not realised that anyone had noticed.

"I enjoy shore actions," he said truthfully. "They are often quite technically challenging."

"I liken our troops to amphibians," Frasier said, "at home on land and water."

"That is very apt." James laughed.

"What are your thoughts on amphibious operations?"

"My father developed a good method for getting men ashore quickly, which is very important when you are doing a landing."

"Yes, I was commander of the Hornfleur, she was the flotilla's troop ship. We spent a lot of time training our marines to get into and out of the boats quickly."

"I didn't know that. I would love to hear of your experiences."

The rest of the meal rotated around the use of marines as a spearhead for amphibious landings. It was the start of a real friendship.

On their return to the squadron, they found the other ships busy preparing for sea. Angus was called to an all-captains meeting and on his return said, "There has been a sudden resurgence in piracy out of Burma. It's strange because they normally restrict themselves to the Strait of Malacca. Your father and Mr Ridgley seem to think it's linked to the Maratha problem. Whatever the cause, they want us to go and sort it out."

James was kept busy restocking the ship as they rushed to get ready in time. He was still organising the hold when they warped off the dock. He came topside to find the Silverthorn bringing up the rear of the squadron sailing in line astern down the river.

"All done, James?" Angus said as James came up in deck,

"Aye, all stowed and secured, Sir," James said beating his coat to remove dust.

Dennis stood nearby and looked thoughtful.

"Something bothering you, Dennis?" James asked.

"Where is Burma?"

"It's the other side of the Bay of Bengal from Calcutta. Why?"

"I heard the captain say we are going to Burma. Dennis not know where that is."

James took him to the chart table and said to the master, "Mr Phillips, would you show Dennis where Burma is?"

"Certainly. Look here my large friend, this is where we are right now," he pointed to the mouth of the river Hooghly, "and all the way across the Bay of Bengal is Burma."

Dennis looked at the map, "How long?"

"How long? It will take us two days to sail across."

Dennis grinned.

"You look pleased about that," James said.

"Dennis happy."

Dennis walked away and James looked at Philips, "Who knows what he his thinking?" Philips said.

"It's probably because we will fight pirates, but as long as he is happy I'm content. An unhappy Dennis is not a good thing," James said.

The crossing of the Bay of Bengal was far from easy. An anticyclone came in and sat right in the middle of the bay causing the winds to rotate anticlockwise.

"The frigates won't be able to make headway against this," Angus said as the wind veered to a point north of east and increased to gale-force.

The Unicorn turned and, under storm sails, paralleled the coast heading southwest. The rest followed like ducks in a row. They soon picked up the western edge of the cyclone and were able to make minimal sail, scooting along with a following wind. The sail handlers took a much-needed rest. James and Angus had been on watch constantly for twenty-four hours so Angus handed over the watch to the master so they could both get some sleep.

"Where are we?" James said as he took over the watch from Mr Philips.

"Coming up on Coringa as far as I can tell. Wind is starting to swing around to the west so I reckon we will be turning east soon."

James looked up at the pennant. Philips was right, the wind was slowly veering as it followed the heart of the cyclone around.

He had a thought,

"Do cyclones often sit in the middle of the bay for this long?"

"They can do," Philips said, "this one is starting to move northwest, at last, as far as I can tell."

"Thank you, I have the watch."

It was easy navigation as all he had to do was follow the Eagle that was ahead. He was relaxed and enjoying the sailing as they turned east.

"Signal, our number!" the lookout called.

James took a glass from the rack and focussed on the Eagle. The signal was a repeat from the Unicorn.

"We are to take position out in front of the squadron." He read without having to refer to the code book.

"Set mains. Helm we will move up the windward side of the squadron at two cables' separation. Mark, please inform the captain we have been ordered to take up the point position." Mark was the ship's boy that was on duty on the quarterdeck as a messenger. The point was the tip of an arrowhead formation the squadron adopted when it was approaching an area of interest. The Eagle and Endellion would take up position either side of the lead ship with the Silverthorn ahead. All three ships would move out to be just hull up on the horizon to increase the search area.

Angus sent back a message for James to carry on as ordered and that he would take over the watch on time.

"Signal from the Unicorn, our number."

Proceed to A, then north, James read.

"Where are we Mr Philips?" James asked.

"About forty miles from the Andaman Islands."

"Looks like we have to head to the Andaman Islands then turn north."

"That makes sense as our destination is the Ramree Islands," Philips said.

James ordered a change of lookouts. He would change them every hour from now on.

"I have the deck," Angus said, as he stepped onto the quarterdeck for his watch.

"We are sixty miles north of the Anderman Islands, logging ten knots, course a point east of north. Weather is set fair; the cyclone has moved off to the north."

"Very good, James, send the hands to dinner."

"Aye, aye, Sir."

James joined the warrants for his own meal and enjoyed a pint of India Pale Ale. He had invested in several crates and had one chilling in the bilges. The strong, hoppy, bitter ale was brewed to be able to travel and he had developed a taste for it. After dinner and a chat with the men he went to his bunk stripped off and went to sleep.

He was woken by a commotion. Men were shouting and feet stamping on the deck above. The ship turned sharply almost tipping him out of bed.

"What the hell?" He looked at his watch. It was three in the morning. He pulled on his trousers and shoes and went up on deck.

"What's going on?" he said to Angus.

"We nearly hit a whale asleep on the surface. A blue. The lookout spotted it in the moonlight, and we just about avoided it."

The Silverthorn had re-joined the squadron at dusk and now rockets were shooting up from all the ships to illuminate the ocean around them.

"Good grief, it's a whole herd of them," James said as the sea lit up the glistening bodies.

"Reduce sail," Angus said. "The collective noun for whales is a school by the way."

"Take in the mains, reef topsails!" James shouted and men ran to do his bidding. "School, I didn't know that," he said to Angus.

"Get into the bow and steer us through them," Angus ordered.

"Whale dead ahead, two points to starboard!" James shouted almost immediately he was in position.

The whale slid down their port side.

"Resume course!"

The ship came back onto its original course.

"Keep the flares burning!" James shouted, then, "A point to port."

"Steady as you go!"

A big female with a calf rolled an eye at him as they passed, he would swear that she was being reproachful when he told the tale later.

He didn't see any more for five minutes.

"Looks like we are clear!"

He heaved a sigh of relief, not because the whales hadn't been hurt but because the Silverthorn hadn't been damaged. A collision with one of those behemoths could stove in the hull and sink them in minutes.

Morning dawned and James was back on watch. The Silverthorn had all sail set to resume her point position.

"Deck there! Land ho! Dead ahead!" came the cry when the sun was an inch or two above the horizon.

"That will be the Ramree Islands if my navigation is anything to go by," Philips said.

"A second man to the lookout," Angus said as he came on deck.

They cruised up the Burma coast towards the islands, reducing sail and slowing to ten knots. Fishing boats moved out of their way, the sailors looking curiously at them. The boats had high prows, twelve to fifteen feet long and four feet across the beam. They were propelled by a single oarsman stood in the back pushing a pair of oars.

One passed closely and James got a good look at his face. Lined from exposure to the sun and wind, his skin was light brown as if tanned, his eyes were almond shaped, strong chin and a straight nose. His head was covered in a loosely-wrapped turban. The man grinned showing uneven yellowed teeth. James doffed his hat and bowed. The man laughed and waved.

"Seem friendly enough," Joseph said.

"Fishermen, not pirates," James said.

"Funny how there are pirates along almost every bit of coast."

"Easy way to make money."

"Unless the navy comes after you."

They both laughed at that. Then James had a thought. "Do you think they have ever seen an American schooner before?"

"I don't know, but at a guess probably not."

James walked over to Angus.

"I don't think they have ever seen an American schooner before," he said.

"You have something you want to suggest?" Angus said. He was beginning to understand how his young mid thought.

"Fly a civilian flag, keep most of the men hidden."

"Look like a trader, yes I can see where you are going with that," Angus said. He thought about it, "Have the men go to quarters but all gunners to stay below the thwarts. Only the minimum number of men on deck to handle the sails. Let's throw some bait into the water and see if we get a bite."

"Deck there Silverthorn has raised a Red Ensign," the lookout bellowed down to the quarterdeck.

"Have they now," Wolfgang said. "I bet there is hardly anyone on deck as well."

"Sir?" McGivern said.

"Our young guns in the Silverthorn have decided to be the bait. I want the ship ready to go to full sail and quarters. We will stay under the horizon. Signal the Eagle and Endellion to close up. Signal the Leonidas and Nymphe to standby."

"Was that in their orders, Sir?"

"No, but we expect initiative and in this case they are in a better position than us are to make that particular call."

"Sir," McGivern said.

Wolfgang had noticed that since the fight to retake the Aurora McGivern was troubled by something.

"Gordon, walk with me," he said, and stepped to the windward side walking the deck to the rail before turning and walking back. "Do you want to talk about it?" he asked.

"About what, Sir?" Gordon replied, surprised at the use of his first name.

"Ever since you took the Aurora something has been on your mind. You are not your old self, my friend."

Gordon sighed and gazed at the Leonidas following behind a cable distant.

"I went berserk."

Wolfgang stopped and turned to him, eyebrows raised.

"I charged the line of Indian soldiers, my Claymore and dirk in hand. I cannot remember anything after killing the first one until I found myself stood in a circle of dead men. I was covered in blood and the deck was running in it. The dead men had been slashed and stabbed with such force their wounds were terrible to see."

"Has this ever happened before?"

"I have led boardings and other actions, I am no stranger to combat, but this…this is terrifying."

"Terrifying for the enemy perhaps, disturbing to find out about oneself, definitely. What frightens you most about this?" Wolfgang continued the walk.

"The loss of control and finding out I am capable of such violence."

Wolfgang stopped again and looked into Gordon's eyes. "Did you really lose control or did your body, honed for years to fight, just react to the situation and do what was necessary to survive and win?"

"I…" Gordon hesitated so Wolfgang started walking again. After two more lengths of the quarterdeck, Gordon said, "I think what is bothering me, is the fact I cannot remember what I did."

"I see, let me tell you something that happened to me when I first joined Lord Martin as a lieutenant. In those days I fought with my zwiehänder sword. I thought it terrifying to the enemy and the ultimate weapon. We were engaged in a hot deck to deck action and I was trying to keep up with Martin and the men around him. He was so elegant in the way he fought, the sword and knife combination always in balance and then there was that brute of a dog of his. Pulling down foes and either ripping their throats out or holding them for Lord Martin to dispatch. Afterwards I mentioned it to him, and he told me that he often didn't remember much of a battle as he trained so much his muscles knew what to do before he thought about it."

Gordon listened, it was true he trained hard with sword and dirk. Often against more than one opponent at a time. He nodded and Wolfgang continued.

"The wounds you mentioned. You use a Claymore and a broad-bladed dirk. Both are slashing and chopping weapons. The wounds they inflict are often quite terrible. Were these worse than any before? Or was it the number that affected you?"

Gordon nodded again he was deep in thought as they walked, and Wolfgang just let him think it through.

"I believe you may be right," he said at last. "Thank you."

"You can talk to me at any time. Think on this and we can talk some more or you can talk to Mr Shelby. He often has deep insights."

They parted; Gordon slightly lighter of spirit, knowing it was but a step.

On the Silverthorn, uniforms had been replaced with civilian clothes and sail handling reduced to the level of a civilian ship. Dennis didn't understand and watched with a confused look on his face.

"Dennis not understand, why we doing this?"

"It's a game of pretend," James said. "We don't want to frighten the pirates away, so we pretend we are not navy but a civilian trader. Then they will attack us, and we will surprise them."

Dennis's brow furrowed as he thought that over, "When they come, do we still pretend?"

"No, when they come, we go back to being navy."

"Hu hu hu, Dennis like that," he laughed

James patted his arm and walked away.

"You are very patient with him," Angus said as James re-joined him.

"He is a good man. I would rather have him at my back than many others," James said.

"Prodigiously strong and loyal," Angus said.

"Yes, just don't ask him to solve any problems that need more than sheer muscle."

"I will leave him entirely to you."

They were approaching the first island and as per orders steered to stay to the seaward side of it

"Deck, there is a large galley-style ship pulling out from behind the island. It's got a dozen oars and a lateen sail," one of the lookouts shouted.

"Deck," the second lookout called, "there's a smaller one coming around the outside of the island, ten oars, no sails but crammed full of men."

"Interesting," Angus said. "Want to wager which one comes and takes a look first?"

James grinned. "A guinea that the smaller one comes in fast. Then the bigger one will join if they think we are what we appear to be."

"You're on."

The oarsmen on the smaller and, probably the nimbler of the two, put their backs into it and the craft fairly flew across the slight chop.

"It's got a bow gun," Angus said, as he examined the oncoming craft through his telescope.

"Marines, to the tops!" James called, and the men moved up. Not many because of the schooner's sail arrangement but enough to pick off obvious officers. Like the rest of the crew the marines were not in uniform. "Gunners, make ready but stay down. Load will be canister over ball."

"Sail handlers, be ready to set more sail," Angus said. "Helm, keep her steady as she goes. They will try for the bow and stern."

"Good job we already shifted the aft guns then." James said, he was watching the galley trying to judge whether they would go for bow or stern.

"Go to your guns, James, and good luck," Angus said.

James saluted by touching his forelock and walked casually down the deck to the middle of the gun batteries. The forward carronade was covered by a tarpaulin but judging from the way it was undulating the men were underneath loading it already.

Dennis followed James, carrying his weapons, he already had a meat cleaver of a sword hanging from his waist and had a big two-handed mallet normally used for driving plugs in propped up against the mainmast. Joseph and Eric were at their stations, but James knew if it came to a hand-to-hand fight, they would be either side of him.

James took his sword belt from Dennis and once he had clipped it around his waist, took his pistols. He checked the priming and, satisfied, used the belt hooks to secure them to his belt.

"All ready?" he said.

"Aye, Sir!" his gun captains responded.

The smaller galley was half a mile away and a puff of smoke from her bow warned him that shot was incoming. He dropped to the deck and shouted for everyone to get down. The ball snarled overhead, and James looked surprised at the distinctive sound.

"Stone balls!"

"Ship to quarters!" Angus bellowed when they were a cable away.

The men sprang to their feet and the deck vibrated as they ran out the guns. James moved to the fore carronade.

The crew pulled the tarp away and swung the gun into line with the oncoming galley. The two forward guns were trained as far forward as their extended ports would allow. This meant they had an almost continuous arc ninety degrees either side of the bow covered. The only blind spot was directly in line with the bowsprit.

The galley was heading as if to pass down their starboard side but suddenly started to swing back in line with their bow. They were half a cable off.

"Fire!" James shouted, and the fore deck gun barked, closely followed by the starboard gun.

Angus was watching the galleys closely and saw the smaller one accelerate. *Damn he was right.* James would have to deal with the one approaching from ahead, so he concentrated on the larger currently circling to get behind them. A shot snarled overhead. He looked up in surprise at the sound. Only one thing made a sound like that. Stone shot, the irregularities in their surface made the snarling sound.

The larger galley fired its bow gun. The deep boom evidenced it was a twenty-four-pounder. The ball was well aimed, and he threw himself to the deck as it smashed through the rail sending splinters flying. He took a breath. Nothing hurt so he leapt to his feet.

"Fire as you bear!" he cried.

"Make all sail!" Wolfgang ordered as the ships on the horizon started firing on each other. The Unicorn would bear down directly on the Silverthorn, the Leonidas and Endellion would swing towards the coast to get between the pirates and prevent any to escape in that direction. The Nymphe and Eagle being the fastest pairing would endeavour to get beyond the conflict to cut off any retreat in that direction. It would take at least an hour to come to the Silverthorn's aid, he hoped they could hold out that long.

The foredeck gun missed, and the starboard gun only got a partial hit. The galley was wounded but not disabled. The gun crews raced to reload.

The galley came on and the lookout shouted, "There's another come around the island."

"Idlers and wasters to the centreline. Prepare to repel boarders!" James shouted. Men came up from below and lined up down the centreline. Armed to the teeth some swung their swords to loosen their shoulders. Some prayed and others looked scared.

The marines in the tops started firing. The foredeck gun fired again. James pulled both his pistols, double-barrelled Mantons just like his father's, and cocked a barrel on each. The small galley had again avoided any serious damage from the foredeck gun. It was now too close to be engaged and James braced himself.

Dennis moved up to be just off his left shoulder and behind him. A hook flew up from the bow and dug into the rail. It was followed by a half dozen others.

A face appeared above the rail, James fired his right pistol and it disappeared to be replaced with a half dozen more. "Repel boarders!" he shouted. The Burmese were agile, and the men had to move fast to stop them establishing a bridgehead. Pistols fired and swords were swung. Dennis roared and swung his mallet. A pirate's head was stove in like a melon. He swung again but the man ducked under it and made to stab him with a spear.

James fired his left-hand pistol, cocked the second barrel on his right and fired that. The spear tip just cut through Dennis's shirt when the sixty-calibre balls took his assailant in the chest.

James swapped the righthand gun for his sword and threw himself forward. He fired his remaining shot into a boarder's face, reversed the gun and used the butt as a club. The fighting was intense, and he had no time to think about much else. The galley must have had forty men on it.

The second galley got aft of them by staying far enough away to be safe from the carronades. They turned bow on and powered forward to get alongside what they thought was the Silverthorn's unprotected stern. Angus kept the stern chasers hidden until they were a cable away and then, "Guns out and fire as you bear!"

The hinged sections of the stern rail dropped down and the guns rolled forward. The advantage of carronades was they traversed and elevated quickly. The gunners had loaded with a mix of everything, small ball, canister and chain. A veritable hailstorm of iron shimmered across the water to take the galley on the prow. The ship was full of men. The prow turned into a shower of splinters from a foot above the waterline. Anybody stood above the thwarts was shredded, Angus saw a red mist of blood with body parts form above the ship. Battle cries turned to screams.

Astonishingly, the aft section of the ship remained intact and relatively unharmed. They could see the skipper exhorting his remaining men to pick up the pace and attack. Another two ships were powering in.

James was tiring, the bow guns had succeeded in stopping the second ship but another two were approaching. He heard the captain order more sails to be set. He stood in a brief respite and caught his breath. Dennis was beside him.

"Damn this is hot work," James said.

"Dennis have fun!"

"You, my friend, are a machine," James sighed as a clunk announced the arrival of another shipload. He had an idea.

"Dennis, get that ball and drop it on their ship," he said pointing to a thirty-two-pound smasher.

Dennis picked the ball up and trotted to the bow, glanced over, then tossed the ball over the side. There was a scream and a crunch. He ran back, picked up another and tossed it over the side as well. Before he could get away from the rail a face appeared. Dennis reacted. He punched the man in the face. His nose was flattened, and he fell back. There was a splash. He was about to get another ball when James said, "Time for sword work, Dennis."

Angus was busy. The pirates had made the deck by sheer weight of numbers. "Fall back!" he cried, and the men fell back behind the rearmost guns. Swivels were mounted on the rail and turned to rake the quarterdeck. "Fire!" Canister blasted across the deck from four swivel guns. "AT THEM SILVERS!"

Wolfgang was squeezing every last knot of speed out of the Unicorn he could, he could see that the Silverthorn was sorely pressed with ships at bow and stern. The wreckage of at least two ships could be seen drifting nearby.

The Eagle and Endellion were racing ahead. Faster and nimbler than the frigates they were rushing to their sister ship's aid. Guns run out, battle ensigns flying. Wolfgang smiled; his young guns were eager for a fight.

James parried a slash from a sword but couldn't avoid the thrust from a spear that came in from the side. It stung his side as the head skidded across his ribs. Dennis bellowed as he saw his friend cut and he swung the huge meat cleaver of a falchion he carried overhand severing the spearman's arm. He followed that by grabbing the wretch by the neck and throwing him against the rail. His foot stamped down as the man landed on the deck crushing his ribs. Blood spurted out of his mouth as he died.

James was dealing with the swordsman. He parried the next slash with his dagger and thrust his sword into his opponent's gut, twisted and withdrew. He looked for another opponent but saw that the pirates were running for their ships. Confused, he looked around and saw the Eagle and Endellion bearing down under full sail, smoke drifting away as their guns fired. He became aware of the sounds around him. The cries of the wounded, the cheering of his men as help arrived. He looked down, his foe was clutching his stomach. He noticed that his intestines were sticking out between his fingers.

Joseph stepped up beside him, "He's done for." He slashed down with his cutlas almost severing the man's head. *It's a kindness,* James thought, *a quick death rather a slow and lingering one.*

Chapter 9: Pursuit.

The pirates ran, they were absolutely not interested in fighting a full British squadron. Wolfgang had planned for that, and the Endellion was pre-tasked with following them while the rest of the ships dealt with any that were either incapable of, or, too slow to escape. It was a short messy fight with few prisoners as the pirates preferred to fight to the death rather than surrender.

"Bring my boat around, I wish to visit the Silverthorn and ask Mr and Mrs Shelby to join me with their equipment."

The Silverthorn was hove to and the sea around her was a mass of sharks. The water had a pink tinge and carcases floated slowly away on the current. The boat negotiated both the sharks and carcasses to reach the side. Wolfgang went up first followed by Shelby then his wife who had worn trousers for the occasion.

The deck was mainly clear of dead except a few unfortunates from the crew that had perished in the encounter.

"Looks like you had a warm hour's work, Angus," Wolfgang said after he had shaken hands with the somewhat dishevelled captain.

"A little, Sir. The Endellion and Eagle arrived in the nick of time."

"That bad?"

"They had numbers and were bringing in fresh men all the time. They were wearing us down. They knew how to attack us. They sacrificed the first ships in order to get the second under our bow and stern."

"Interesting."

Wolfgang looked at the row of dead.

"Are they all you lost?"

"Yes, so far that is, six dead, three badly wounded and a lot of minor wounds."

"Mr Stockley?"

"Wounded a couple of times but he should be all right. Fought like a tiger, just like his father."

James was supervising the clearance of the foredeck and had the pumps washing away the gore and filth when Anabelle Shelby came to him. She was carrying a tray of instruments and unguents.

"James, let me look at your wounds."

"They are just scratches, please look after the others first."

"Shelby has them in hand, now take off your shirt."

The men around him grinned as they heard the exchange and stopped work to watch. James decided to let them if it took their minds off the fight. He pulled the shirt over his head, it was one of his silk ones as, like many officers, he preferred to wear silk in a fight as it didn't contaminate the wounds like cotton or linen.

Anabelle tutted as she looked at the four-inch gash along his ribs and another three-inch cut on his upper left arm. She sat on an upturned bucket normally used for slow match.

"Come here, raise your arms over your head."

James placed his hands on his head interlocking his fingers while Anabelle examined the gash.

"What did this?"

"A spear. Dennis dispatched the wielder."

She took a cloth from the tray, wet it from a bottle, "This is going to sting." She proceeded to clean the wound and James tensed as the raw alcohol on the cloth bit. He did not flinch, nor did he cry out.

"You have a high tolerance for pain," she said.

"Father always said pain is inconsequential."

"Did he." She was busy threading a medium-sized needle. James kept his gaze on the horizon, so he didn't see that Angus and Wolfgang had stopped talking to watch.

The first stitch went in.

"I think ten should do it," she said.

Ribs stitched and bound she turned her attention to his arm which only needed six stitches.

Wolfgang took the guinea Angus held out.

The squadron patrolled the islands for the rest of the day, moving out to sea for the night. The Endellion returned in the morning and Philip Trenchard reported aboard the Unicorn.

"What did you find?" Wolfgang asked.

"Well, the island isn't really an island. It's actually more of a peninsula. The charts are incorrect." He unrolled a chart he had brought with him and laid it on the table. "See here, the island is actually in a river delta and behind it are a maze of inlets where the pirates disappeared into. Their galleys are ideally suited for this area and can go places we cannot."

"What is on the north side of the island?" Wolfgang said looking at an almost blank part of the chart. "We weren't able to get around there in the Endellion, the rivers get too shallow. I was going to suggest we take her around the seaward side and finish the charting as it's my guess there is a village or town there that the pirates call home."

Wolfgang nodded thoughtfully, "Do that, the Nymph will act as escort. I don't want you getting stuck somewhere we will have trouble extracting you from, so stay in deep water."

"Aye, aye, Sir."

Wolfgang sat in thought, if he was to eradicate the threat, he would have to destroy it at source, but he also wanted to know why they had moved up here from the straits.

"Call Captain O'Driscol please," he said to the marine sentry, and the call echoed down the ship as he sat back at his desk.

Philip had lookouts in the tops and stationed around the deck. He was travelling upriver ahead of the Nymphe. He knew that Andrew Stamp would have men up on his higher masts as well. The master was busy taking sightings as they passed notable landmarks and was sketching the river and its banks as they passed. Midshipman Williams was busy noting the depth as two men in the chains called it.

They spotted several temples and were approaching a point where the river swung south when a lookout called, "Boat approaching, port side. One man in a yellow robe."

Philip walked down the deck and looked at the flatbottomed boat being skulled towards them. More interesting was the boatman. Dressed in a saffron yellow robe with a red sash, the short, rather fat man had a ponytail that was rooted in a topknot that was all the hair on his otherwise cleanly-shaved head. He was determinedly heading towards them and when he saw Philip smiled and waved.

He came alongside and threw a rope to a waiting crewman then scampered up the side. Beaming a broad smile, he bowed to everyone who came even close to looking at him. Philip stepped up and after the man had bowed three times in rapid succession said, "I am the captain; do you speak English?"

"Oh yes, and Hindi, Tamil, Burmese and Chinese as well."

Philip hid his surprise and said, "What can we do for you?"

"You are His Majesty's Navy?"

"Yes, we are."

"My name is Indazita, but you can call me Izzy, my monastery is on that island over there. Six months ago, several ships arrived full of pirates. More arrived every week and started attacking ships in the bay. They also started demanding we pay them a tax. Telling us if we didn't, they would burn our monasteries."

"Well, we are here to do something about that. Where are they based?"

"This is why I rowed out to you. They are in a village just around the corner of the river on a small island. There are at least twenty ships there."

And they know we are coming, Philip thought.

"Would you be prepared to come and meet my commanding officer?" Philip said.

"Oh, I would be most happy, I have a very big interest in ships." Izzy grinned like a kid in a candy shop.

"Bosun, get Mr Izzy's boat aboard. Mr Williams, signal the Nymphe, we will be re-joining the squadron."

Philip took Izzy with him when he reported to Wolfgang.

"Mr Izzy," Philip started to say.

"Please, only Izzy."

"Izzy came out to us and warned us that some twenty ships were waiting to ambush us. Their base is on an island around a bend in the river." Philip placed an updated chart on the desk.

Wolfgang traced their route checking the depths. Then asked, "Izzy, how many exits are there from this point?"

Izzy picked up a pencil, examined the point curiously and touched it to the paper. He smiled delightedly when it made a mark. Sticking his tongue out he started filling in the gap that was left by the incomplete survey. Fifteen minutes later he stood back and said, "As you can see, it is an island as it is surrounded by rivers that cut it off from the mainland. This gives them at least two routes apart from the main one which they can take."

"One comes out onto the channel that you surveyed when you followed them," Wolfgang said. He took a deep breath and let it out slowly. "I think we can put our rats into a trap of our own."

Wolfgang called an all-captains meeting that evening. He had a large copy of the chart of the island pinned to a board sat on an easel.

"Gentlemen, we have the opportunity to excise the pirates, but it will need us to set a careful trap." He used a rattan cane to point to the chart. "According to a Buddhist monk who approached the Endellion, the pirates have a base here on this smaller island, behind Ramree. The channel up to this island is more than deep enough for even the Unicorn to sail up." He paused and was not disappointed when James Campbell said, "If we go charging in from that direction, they will just scatter into all those inlets."

"Indeed, that is exactly what I will expect them to do if they see us coming," Wolfgang said. "If you look carefully at the chart, you can see there are two possible escape routes. This one that goes around to the north and then west would allow them to get around behind us. The other takes them around the island and out at the southern end."

"What we need to do is block one of those and force them down the other," Andrew Stamp said.

"We could, but I think we have enough ships to do something more. The Unicorn and Silverthorn will make a direct assault on the base. We know they shy away from direct confrontation with anything big even if they have twenty ships. So, we can expect them to bolt and there are only two routes they can take. The Leonidas and Endellion will sail into the Northern inlet and make their way up to a point where they can effectively shut off that escape route. The Nymphe and Eagle will similarly blockade the southern channel."

"Snap, the trap shuts," Trevor Archer laughed.

"Indeed, but there is a final twist," Wolfgang said. "You will each send half of your marines to the Unicorn or Silverthorn. They will make up a landing party in force that will drive any that stay behind on the island into the sea. They will be led by Captain O'Driscol with Captain Frasier and Mr Stockley in charge of, what they call, amphibious operations. I want senior members of the pirate's taken prisoner so we can find out the background to all this."

"We will need your boats as well," Angus chipped in.

The ships started manoeuvring into position by the light of the three-quarter moon. They progressed slowly, feeling their way down the channels with boats ahead sounding the depth. The Silverthorn and Unicorn had long lines of boats strung out behind and their decks were awash with marines in full uniform. James had transferred to the Unicorn to run the landing party there, leaving Angus to manage the Silverthorn's marines.

"The boats will come along both sides and their allocated men will board as fast as they can using the cargo nets, without falling into the water. Men who have not done this before, talk to the old hands who have, and do what they say," James told the fifty marines he had charge of. He was putting ten marines to a boat. The boats were commanded by experienced coxes and James would board the last boat, which he wanted in the middle of the line.

The Unicorn hove to just before the bend in the river and James went to work. The first boats came alongside, and the marines descended the cargo nets. As soon as they were all in, the boat moved away and the next moved up. It took ten minutes to load a boat so in under an hour all five were done. James stood in the prow of his and waved a flag. At the signal the boats moved away from the Unicorn and were joined by the five boats from the Silverthorn. They waited for the Unicorn to slip ahead and tucked in behind her.

The animals came in two by two, James thought as he looked back along the two columns. He and Angus had lectured the coxes about maintaining position, which was all they could do given they had no time to practise.

The Unicorn slid around the bend, gliding like a ghost, the moon dipped to the horizon and the darkness deepened. A light or two shining from the houses on the island served to guide them in. The stern anchor was dropped, the splash loud in the darkness. They ran forward for a cable then the bow anchor dropped. The clink, clink of the capstan travelled across the water to the village and a dog barked. Springs were set. They were ready.

The Silverthorn turned and anchored across the channel so she could fire along the shoreline to catch ships that ran. Angus had his hands full as he was missing his midshipman. The stern anchor was dropped late, and the ship drifted further than he wanted. Resisting the temptation to bellow at the crew he used two ships boys to pass orders. He eventually got her anchored and pointing in the general direction she should be.

It was just in time as the single dog that had started barking had set off every dog on the island and the cacophony had woken the locals. It wasn't long until dawn and as the light crept across the land from the east someone noticed that the frigate was parked on their doorstep. A shout went up and a gong started to sound the alarm.

Wolfgang waited until his gunners could see the ships moored in the harbour then ordered, "FIRE." A rolling broadside shattered the peace and thousands of birds rose up from surrounding wetlands in shocked surprise. The effect was devastating as her eighteen-pound main battery plus the fore and quarterdeck carronades opened up. Galleys were reduced to jetsam. Unfortunately, only half the galleys were in that part of the harbour.

As soon as the Unicorn opened fire, James signalled for the boats to form line abreast. He held his arms out to either side holding flags to give the bowmen of the other boats a reference. Someone down the line caught a crab as their oar clashed with one from the ship to their side, but apart from that it went relatively well, and all the boats hit the beach at roughly the same time.

The marines debarked as soon as the bow men had the boats steady and lined up along the sand. Now Declan O'Driscol took command.

"Form two ranks!" The men shuffled into two ranks.

"To the right, wheel!" The lines pivoted around the left most men to face the village.

"Advance!"

The line advanced, bayonets glinting in the sun. James walked beside O'Driscol at the front, a pistol in one hand and sword in the other. They could see men running for their ships.

"Keep it steady!" O'Driscol said.

A large group of men were crowded behind where the Unicorn was turning their ships into matchwood. They spotted the advancing marines and one of their number screamed an order.

"Mark him James, he is yours to capture," O'Driscol said.

James kept his eye on the man as the mob charged them.

"Marines halt! Front rank present arms!"

James stepped back through the line to get out of the way.

"Fire!"

The marines had been recently re-trained to fire as the light rifles regiments did. Not together and unaimed but targeted. This meant they fired when the targets presented themselves, so the volley appeared to be ragged. It was, however, highly effective, and as soon as the smoke cleared, "Second rank, fire."

A dozen pirates were down but still thirty or more were coming on. There was no time for the marines to reload.

"Present bayonets!"

James made his way to the end of the line. He waited until they were a mere thirty feet away and fired first one then the other barrel of his Manton before calmly putting it back on his belt and pulling his knife. Now armed for two-handed fighting he braced himself to meet his first opponent.

The pirates crashed into the line which held firm, this was fighting the marines excelled at. Thrust, twist, withdraw. Classic bayonet fighting. James worked his way around the edge of the fight to where the pirate office was screaming at his men and even hitting them with the flat of his sword. He had not seen James and he made the most of it, getting behind him.

James swapped his knife for a blackjack, the leather pouch of shot felt comfortable in his hand. He slunk up behind his target and rapped him firmly, but not too hard, under the ear. He dropped like a rock. A scream from behind him warned him of trouble and he spun sword ready. But he need not have worried, his attacker seemed to be being assaulted by a bear. There was a crack, and he went limp. The bear dropped him.

"Dennis? What the hell are you doing here?"

"Dennis come, James need help, not go without Dennis."

James looked at him; he was soaking wet. A suspicion dawned,

"How did you get here?"

"Dennis swim."

He didn't have time for any more questions as they had been noticed and were soon fighting side by side.

The marines pushed the pirates back beyond the pair and their prisoner who James stood over protectively.

"Got him then," O'Driscol said, then looked at Dennis in surprise,

"How?"

"Never mind," James said. "We will take this one back to the Unicorn. Then I will catch you up with some reinforcements."

"Can you take the wounded with you?"

"Certainly."

O'Driscol waved and went back to the fight which was turning into a rout.

"Hold the line!" he bellowed.

"Pick him up, Dennis," he said, and the big man picked up the gaudily-dressed pirate as if he was a doll.

They returned to the boat and James ordered it and two others back to the Unicorn once the crews had helped three wounded marines on board. Marty kept an eye on his prisoner and Dennis surprised him by tenderly caring for one of the marines who had taken a sword thrust in the groin. Luckily it had missed his 'wedding tackle' as he referred to it.

They reached the Unicorn, and the crew lowered a chair to bring up the wounded. Their prisoner had regained consciousness and James sent him up the side at the point of a sword.

"I will take charge of him from here," McGivern said.

"Thank you, Sir, I did search him, he is dirty but unarmed. We need reinforcements on shore, may I talk to the captain?"

"No need, he anticipated that. There are twenty-five men waiting at the side to be ferried over."

James got the men loaded after checking they were all armed with cutlases and pistols. They were on the beach in good order, and he hurried them along to catch up with the marines. He followed the sound of fighting and a trail of dead and wounded pirates. He came across a wounded marine,

"Hello there, where are you hurt?"

"It's my foot, Sir, one of them heathens stabbed me through it after I put him down."

"We will get you to the boats. How far ahead is the main body?"

"They are clearing the town, Sir."

"You two get this man to the boats and then re-join us," James said to the two nearest sailors.

"Come on the rest of you, we have work to do."

They found the marines hotly engaged near a large warehouse-style building. The pirates were defending it determinedly from behind a barricade. He found O'Driscol.

"I have twenty-five men, cutlases and pistols," James said.

"Did any bring grenades or swivels?" O'Driscol said.

"No, but I can go and get some."

"We need to dislodge them from this building, a field piece would be better."

"Let me see what I can do." James turned to his followers, "Come with me, lads."

He ran back to the boats, two had been fitted with six-pound boat guns. The problem was how to transport them as they had fixed mounts.

"Get those guns and their ammunition out of the boats."

The guns were almost nine-hundred pounds in weight and five feet long and, without wheels, hard to move. He thought about it. He had men and he had oars. The boats were also stocked with cordage. It took a lot of men to dismount the guns. They made A frames from oars and lifted them out. Eric, his more mechanically-minded follower, scratched his head as he looked at them.

"What we need are rollers or skids," he said.

"We passed some round timbers on the beach that the locals use to pull their boats up on," Joseph said.

"They will do."

"Come on, Dennis, let's go and get them."

James detailed four sailors to accompany them. While they were gone, ropes were attached to the guns. The men returned, arms full of timbers. They laid them out ahead of the first gun and two teams of men took up the ropes.

"Together, men, heave!" James cried.

The guns moved but tended to follow the slope, so James detailed more men with levers to keep it straight. It took them over an hour to get to the edge of town and another thirty minutes to reach the warehouse.

"Excellent," O'Driscol said, "set it up here and get shooting."

Setting up was easy, they just ran it off the rollers some eighty yards from the warehouse. However, training it was more difficult. The sailors sweated with hand spikes to turn it, then the gunners loaded.

"Fire when ready," James said.

They were targeting the barricade of crates and barrels the pirates had set up in front of the warehouse from which a steady musket fire was coming. The gun fired. The ball slammed into the barricade smashing a barrel into splinters. The damage was very localised, time for a change in tactics

"Reload, grape."

The marines kept up a steady suppressing fire while the gun crew went to work.

"Ready!" the gun captain called.

"Fire!" James said.

The grape shot was much more effective blasting out a section and killing a couple of the defenders.

"And again," James said.

He noted with interest that the gun crew could reload and fire much faster than on ship. The wheelless carriage didn't need to be hauled forward so it only took as long as it took for the crew to swab, load and ram. About thirty seconds in fact.

The next shot smashed through the section to the right of the first shot opening up a significant breach.

"At them marines!" O'Driscol shouted.

"Unicorns forward!" James cried, waving his sword over his head.

The pirates ran. O'Driscol made to pursue them but James was curious why they were so keen to protect the warehouse. He handed command of the Unicorns to O'Driscol and led his followers and the gun crew to the warehouse doors.

They knelt in front of them guns at the ready, "Dennis open the doors," James said.

Dennis lifted the locking bar and pulled. The doors opened. Light flooded into the interior and James lowered his pistol in astonishment. Inside were people. James walked to the door, cowering in the bright light were men in chains and several women.

"Hello, I'm James Stockley, midshipman His Majesty's Ship Silverthorn."

A woman fainted. Another stepped forward, she was no older than James, a girl rather than a woman.

"Have the pirates gone?" she said.

"Yes, you are safe now." James said.

She almost fainted in relief. James supported her by holding her arm.

The men turned out to me a mix of Indian, European and Asians. They had been spared because they could be ransomed. The women would have been sold at a slave auction somewhere or another. However, that didn't explain why the pirates were so determined to defend the place.

"What's your name, Miss?" James said.

"Melissa Crownbridge,"

"Do you know what else is in here?"

"All the goods they plundered from the ships they took." She walked towards the back of the warehouse and, as his eyes adjusted to the light, he saw piles of crates, barrels, rolls of fabric, sacks of rice, and other goods. Melissa pointed to a corner, "They kept the bullion over there."

"Bullion?" James said and walked forward. A large brass bound chest stood in the corner. "That's huge!"

The chest was five feet wide, at least three deep and three and a half high. It had an enormous padlock holding a single hasp shut. James knelt and examined the lock. "Primitive," he said.

He dug in his pouch and took out a lock pick. He pulled on the lock to put tension on the hasp and dug around inside the keyhole.

"What are you doing?" Melissa said.

"Opening it, there you go." The lock opened and James removed it from the hasp. Before he opened the lid, he carefully ran his hands around it, then stood behind it.

"Stand to the side, it may be trapped."

He lifted the lid and Melissa gasped.

Chapter 10: Festival

Marty sat with Frances Ridgley and reviewed what they had found.

"Our monk is not a local. According to his neighbours he turned up a couple of months ago. He keeps himself to himself. The farm isn't registered to anybody. The previous owner died of typhus two years ago. His wife kept it going for a year and then she went back to her home village."

"A squatter then."

"Probably. Then there is the vendor, he in himself is a man of little consequence. His master, the merchant, is however a different proposition all together."

"Intriguing, don't stop there."

"He is Ranjit Vaishnava. Originally from Bhubaneswar, which is still a Maratha stronghold, he has been noted for promulgating anti-British sentiment."

"A prime suspect then."

"Yes. We have been following him, well your men have, and they have found he visits a brothel in the docks district regularly. It is known as Mandi's."

"Not in itself very interesting if it weren't for the message that mentioned it," Marty said.

"Ahh, as well as that, the brothel only deals in girls and our man is decidedly only interested in men."

"Then who is he meeting?"

"Zeb drew the short straw and got the task of infiltrating the brothel. He did so by posing as an artist and persuaded the madam to let him paint some entertaining frescos."

Marty's eyebrows raised at the thought of Zeb painting erotic art.

"Another man visited the brothel. He drew attention to himself because he dressed as an Afghan but was obviously more Indian in colour and features. He would arrive and ensconce himself in a room at the back, one or more girls would attend him. When Zeb asked, they told him that the man only wanted them to wait on him."

"No sex?"

"Nope. When our merchant friend arrived, the girls were dismissed and the two men were left alone."

"A liaison?"

"No, a discussion." Frances handed over a sheaf of papers. "Transcripts of their conversations."

"How did you get these?"

"I visited the brothel and had a quiet chat with the madam. She saw sense and allowed us to have the adjoining room where I had a clerk transcribe the entire conversation."

"No trouble listening in?"

"No, the walls were paper thin, and I had one of those hearing devices doctors use for listening to the heart."

Marty settled down and read.

"It appears our mystery man is probably Holkar. He is giving instructions via Ranjit Vaishnava to Mr Squatter Monk who is coordinating the action on the ground."

"I gather from that you haven't identified him yet?" Marty said

"Other than he is Tiger, no."

"This hints that they are planning an ambush on Hastings and his party when they visit the temple. We need to bring Tiger in and question him."

"There's a problem with that," Frances said with a look like he was sucking a lemon.

"Oh?"

"He has disappeared."

"You lost him?"

"I took the Shadows off the watch and put my people on it. I thought they could handle it."

Marty closed his eyes and offered up a silent prayer.

Marty had no choice. If he was to stop an attack at the temple, he would have to do it immediately before it happened. He hated the idea but could not in all honesty do anything else. There were, in his opinion, several risks. The first was they had no idea who the attackers were, the second, they didn't know when it would occur and the third, they didn't know what form it would take.

"In other words, we haven't a clue precisely when, who or how. But we do know where and in broad terms when and against who," Marty told the team.

"Sounds like a walk in the park boss," Billy said, setting off a ripple of laughter.

Marty let them laugh, he was going to ask them to do the impossible.

"We will be at the temple in force. You will lead individual teams of marines and trusted Indians who will mingle with the crowd. You will remove any person that you think may present a threat quietly and without fuss."

"You want them alive or dead, boss, dead's easier," Matai said.

"Don't kill them unless you have to, as some may be innocent."

"Won't a lot of English men mingling with the crowd frighten them off?"

Marty grinned; he had been saving this for last. "That is why you will be dressed as Indians."

There was a moment of silence, then Billy said, "Ain't we a bit white?"

"Walnut oil," Marty said. The men looked at him blankly, "You rub it into your skin, and it darkens it. Of course, Antton, Matai and Garai don't need it as they can pass for Brahmins, but Billy is white enough to be a beacon and the ginger tint in his hair is a dead giveaway."

A turban solved the problem of the hair and the walnut oil tinted white skin to a suitable brown.

"Don't forget your hands and wrists, go up far enough so you won't accidently flash some white," Matai instructed. Billy did as he was told and with a selection of Indian clothes ended up looking like a passable Sikh. Zeb had a similar problem which was solved in the same way. He looked at a grinning Adam and said, "Why ain't he getting all dressed up?"

"Because, dear Zeb, I am on top cover. There is a convenient roof two hundred yard or so from the temple that overlooks the courtyard. If anybody gets past you, I will stop them," Adam said.

"You better hope it doesn't come to that," Marty said. "A shot into the temple courtyard is likely to cause a stampede, and that's the last thing we want."

Marty joined Hastings to attend the ceremony. He was loaded with silent weapons but no pistols. Over his dress uniform he wore a sash bearing his honours. Under the sash he had a bandoleer that carried throwing knives and drug-tipped darts. On his belt, out of sight, were his knife and a pair of punch daggers. Stilettoes were strapped to his forearms. A blackjack lay comfortably in his coat pocket.

He wore a sword but dare not draw it in the temple grounds. He and his men were at a huge disadvantage, and he knew it. Outside the odds were more even as they had Hastings military escort and a platoon or two of troops. But even if he called on them, he knew it would be too late.

The dignitaries gathered at Government House. Hastings, Marty, Rocke and Scott represented the British government. As the temple ceremony was a men-only affair, their wives would accompany them to the gate but stay outside until the men re-joined them once it was over.

Caroline, like Marty, decided to be prepared. She carried a small pistol in her purse and wore her special garters with forty-calibre muff pistols strapped to her thighs. Borrowing an idea from her daughter, she concealed a pair of darts in her hair. She carried a parasol and looked a picture, in a soft yellow dress with pale green ribbons topped with a matching bonnet.

The ladies had their own landau carriage and Caroline was joined by Flora Hastings, Jane Rocke and Emma Scott. The men in the carriage ahead of them. A squad of lancers led, and another brought up the rear. The clatter of hooves was loud as they started off.

The temple was not far from Fort William, but the streets were crowded with celebrants and worshipers. The lancers had to clear the way for the carriages without using the sharp end of their weapons. Well-trained horses and a great deal of shouting worked well enough for them to make slow progress and they arrived at the temple gates on time. Caroline looked to the rooftop to her left and caught a glimpse of a broad-brimmed hat. Adam was in position.

The men debarked and were escorted into the temple by an Indian worthy and his entourage. Marty stayed close to Francis and was trying hard to look relaxed while at the same time being on high alert. He looked around for his men and picked out Billy and Matai.

They moved across the courtyard to the temple door, nothing seemed to be happening. His men, he picked out Antton and Garia, were mingling with the crowd. Suddenly Antton moved. He pushed his way to a man in a dark coat and got behind him. Following his lead Billy moved to stand in front of the man.

The party moved into the cool, scented, dim interior. The sounds from outside dimmed as they moved towards the statue of the goddess.

Outside the temple grounds things happened very quickly. The half dozen lancers behind the carriages were suddenly engulfed by a horde of Indians who pulled them from their horses and beat them to the ground. A second mob charged the lancers in front and a mass of people milled around to stop any troops coming to their aid. The ladies' driver was hauled unceremoniously from his seat and his place taken by a shaven headed man.

Caroline was about to pull her pistol from her purse when an evil-looking individual stood on the step below the carriage door and pointed a gun at her. His head exploded as a large-calibre ball entered just above his right eye and exited from below his left ear. He dropped away but was almost immediately replaced by another. The carriage moved and a path miraculously opened for it through the crowd which closed as soon as they passed.

Marty heard a shot. Zeb appeared in the doorway.

"They are taking the women!" he cried.

"What in God's name?" Hastings said.

"By the time we got outside the temple the women and their carriage were gone. All that was left was a crowd of chanting and cheering Indians that were dispersed by the army," Marty said to Frances.

"They fooled us, they were never going after Hastings or the others. The women must have been the target all along!" Frances exclaimed.

The Shadows immediately spread out through the city to find them. Marty had the man that Billy intercepted brought to him. He was oddly confident and stood straight. As soon as Marty approached him, he produced a paper and handed it to him. It said, "Do not follow if you value your women. A messenger will deliver our demands in two days. Let this man go if you understand."

Caroline had her work cut out keeping the other women calm. Flora was the calmest being angrier and more outraged than panicked. Emma was crying and terrified and Jane in shock. The carriage was driven at speed through the city. Outriders joined and led, clearing the way. They moved out into the country and dropped back to a walk to rest the horses. Caroline took the chance to speak to their captor.

"Who are you?" she said.

The bald man turned on the seat so he could look at her, "You must be Lady Caroline," he said in accented English.

"I asked first."

He laughed, "I am known as Tiger."

"I have no doubt that is very fitting, why have you kidnapped us?"

"I would have thought that obvious, you are the wives of the four most powerful men in command of the British invaders."

"You intend to trade us for some kind of concession?"

"Not just a concession but the end of the war," he said.

"I assume by that you mean for the British to walk away!" Flora snapped.

"Why yes. That is it exactly."

They came to a crossroads, and they turned to the south. Caroline let her arm drop over the side of the carriage.

"Where are you taking us?" Caroline asked.

"Into our territory," Tiger replied. He turned back to guiding the horses, closing the conversation.

They had stayed on the same trail for over an hour when they stopped.

"Ladies, if you would care to get out and stretch your legs. There are bushes over there where you can relieve yourselves. Food and tea will be prepared by my men."

The bushes offered some concealment but guards surrounded them so there was no escape. She lifted her skirts and squatted to pee. Once finished she dug in her purse for a visiting card and a small silver propelling pencil. She wrote quickly and precisely, encoding it with the family cypher as she wrote. She placed it under a rock and arranged other rocks around it in a S shape.

She left the bushes and walked to the area where the food was being prepared, a guard followed her. Lentils were cooking and breads baked on the fire. The man doing the cooking handed her a glass of tea.

She sipped it and looked around the camp, it was disciplined like the men were regular soldiers. Two men were cooking, another three were caring for the horses. Guards were set and alert. A headcount revealed there were fourteen men including Tiger. She had three pistols. She would be patient.

Adam had seen the kidnapping taking place and gotten off one shot before the carriage had been moved. As soon as it did, he started to move across the rooftops keeping pace with it. He came to a gap he couldn't jump and used a convenient tree to swing down to ground level. His heart was pounding with the effort to keep up and he was thankful that the crowd slowed the carriage down.

He kept up for several miles before he had to stop, but by then knew by which road they left the city. He recovered his wind and trotted back to the temple. He found Marty and the other men organising search parties.

"My lord," he said.

Marty looked at him and saw the fatigue, "Adam, you have news?"

"It was the one who played the monk, Tiger. They had a lot of men in the crowd outside the temple and easily overpowered the lancers. The crowd helped by getting in the way of the support troops for long enough for them to take over the carriage and get away. I followed across the roofs and then on the ground until they got to the suburbs."

"What the hell do they want with our women?" Scott barked, he had been frantic for his wife's safety and Marty had only just got him calmed down.

"I would have thought that's obvious; they will make demands for their return," Hastings said.

"But what?" Scott cried; he was starting to get wild eyed again.

"Everyone, calm down," Marty said, "anger and fear will not help."

"Damn it, man, have you ice for blood? They have your wife as well!" Scott shouted.

Marty took him by the shoulders and stared straight into his eyes, "I am well aware of that, but I cannot rescue her if I panic and run around like a headless chicken. We have two days before they make their demands. That probably means they want to get them somewhere secure before they do."

He let the man go and turned to Adam. "Fire the recall."

Adam went out into the courtyard and, using his rifle barrel as a launch tube, fired three rockets into the air. They burst high above the temple sending large clouds of smoke drifting above the city, two red and a blue.

When the boys were gathered Marty sent Matai and Garai along the road as advanced scouts. They commandeered two of the dead lancer's horses. He returned to the house to change and re-arm, then headed out with the rest of the Shadows. They rode and had remounts.

It didn't take long for them to reach the crossroads where Matai and Garai were waiting for them.

"They turned south here," Matai said and held something out to Marty. It was a handkerchief with an embroidered CS in the corner. "It was in a bush over there. They had been travelling hard up to here, then slowed. Probably to rest the horses. There's at least a dozen of them."

They wasted no time and followed.

With remounts they could travel faster than the carriage, the tracks of which were clear in places along the increasingly wild track. Just before dark they came across the lunch site. A passable attempt had been made to conceal it, but their well-trained and experienced eyes spotted the sign.

Marty scanned the ground and spotted a small footprint he looked along the line it was taking and saw a clump of bushes. He walked towards them, keeping his eyes on the ground. There, another footprint. His nose picked up the smell as he reached the edge of the clump. Urine.

He pushed through the bushes, there was a space in the middle and from the mix of footprints the ladies had all used it. He was about to turn away when he spotted the arranged rocks. He bent and lifted the middle one. He smiled, "That's my girl." He picked up the card.

"They are about three hours ahead and there are fourteen of them including Tiger. Only three men on guard at any time. We eat in the saddle and don't stop until we catch up with them."

They had to slow down after dark. It was too dangerous to go faster than a trot on the uneven ground and at times they had to slow to a walk. It was around midnight that Adam, who was on point, stopped in the middle of the track ahead of them.

"What is it?" Marty said quietly.

"Smell," Adam replied.

Marty took a big sniff, "Food, smoke, perfume?"

"Yes, and that is Lady Caroline's if I'm not mistaken."

Marty took his word for it, He couldn't distinguish one perfume from another. They all made his nose itch. They dismounted and hobbled the horses.

They worked their way slowly down the track. The wind was in their faces and the smell of a camp got stronger as they approached. A shadow moved ahead, and they froze. Marty signalled to Antton who moved forward hunched as low to the ground as he could get. His dark clothing blending in with the night.

A faint rustle and a soft grunt. Marty moved forward again. Antton was wiping his knife when he found him, a dark shape at his feet. He ignored it and pushed ahead. The faint glow of a banked campfire. To his right, a sigh as another sentry was eliminated.

Then suddenly there was a curse and a shot. He moved fast putting a bullet into the first man he saw outlined by the fire.

Caroline was awake. She lay and listened to the faint snoring coming from the dark shape that was Flora. She had a feeling, the warm feeling she got when Marty was near. She slid her hand into the hidden slit in her dress and pulled a pistol from its garter. She felt around until she found her parasol, twisting the handle to release the hidden blade within.

"What is it?" Emma whispered.

"Be quiet, dear, help is on its way," Caroline whispered back.

Someone cursed in Hindi and a shot rang out the muzzle flash lighting up the camp momentarily. That was followed by a pistol shot and then all hell broke loose.

"We should run!" Emma cried and stood up. Caroline knocked her down with a leg sweep and followed up with a punch to the jaw.

Emma stayed quiet. Caroline found her pistol and waited. The sound of fighting was all around them. A man appeared in front of them, and another muzzle flash revealed it to be Tiger. He had a long knife in his hands and murder in his eyes.

Caroline pointed the gun at the centre of his body and shot him. He doubled up as the bullet hit him in the gut. She dropped the pistol and switched the blade to her right before trying to pull out her other pistol. It got tangled and Tiger regained his feet. She abandoned the pistol and reached up to her hair, pulling a dart disguised as a hat pin from her bonnet.

Tiger staggered forward; his knife held ahead of him. Caroline crouched in a fighter's stance and waited for him to come to her. Something moved at his feet, and he stumbled. She pressed forward and stuck the pin in his arm.

Marty fought and killed anyone that got in front of him, Zeb was to his left and Adam to his right. He was searching for the women when he heard the distinctive sound of one of Caroline's pistols. They were percussion cap models and did not make the woof noise that flintlocks made as the priming ignited.

The fighting died down as the Shadows superior close-fighting skills told. When they had control, he stirred up the fire and lit a brand to use as a torch.

"Martin! Over here!" Caroline called.

He made his way to her. She was sat next to Flora and as he got closer, he realised they were sat on a body.

"Who's that?" he said.

"Hello dear, nice to see you," Caroline said.

"Sorry, my love, it's wonderful to see you too."

He leant forward and kissed her on the cheek.

"Better," she said. "It's Tiger."

Marty swept the torch around and saw Jane nursing Emma's head in her lap.

"Is she alright?"

"I had to knock her out," Caroline said.

Marty left it at that.

In the morning they were cleaning up the mess when Garai called from watching the road, "Large dust cloud approaching."

Marty rolled his eyes. He had an idea who it was.

The women were all awake and helping Adam prepare breakfast. Emma had a bruise on her jaw and was very quiet, Flora loud and bossy and Jane stayed close to Caroline. The boys were carrying bodies out of the camp and dumping them in a dry wash. They would throw some dirt over them when they were finished. Four prisoners sat in a group. Hands tied. Tiger slept soundly. The drug that coated Caroline's pin had not worn off yet. He had a superficial wound in his stomach, the multiple layers of silk he was wearing when she shot him had almost stopped the bullet.

The dust cloud resolved into a full company of lancers with Hastings at its head. They drew up on the track by the camp when Marty stepped out in front of them.

"Where is my wife!" Hastings bellowed.

"Hello, Francis, she's right here," Marty said and Flora stepped up beside him.

Hastings was off his horse in a trice and swept his wife into his arms in a totally uncharacteristic display of emotion. Marty looked at the troopers grinning at the sight.

"Lancers! ABOUT FACE," he shouted in his quarterdeck voice.

The horsemen automatically obeyed the voice of command and wheeled their horses around.

"That was thoughtful," Caroline said from beside him.

Marty turned to face her and drew her into his arms, "I had an ulterior motive," he said and kissed her on the lips.

Chapter 11: Consequences

They arrived back in Calcutta, safely surrounded by a screen of lancers and were met at the gates of Fort William by Rocke and Scott. The welcome for their wives was more controlled but nonetheless relieved. Repercussions for the kidnapping were already underway with suspects being rounded up and establishments with suspected Maruthan sympathies raided.

Marty asked to meet with Francis Hastings.

"This purge is a blunt instrument; you know it could alienate more people than it wins over?" Marty said.

"We will not tolerate organised opposition, in any form, especially when sponsored by a hostile power. We will stamp this out and leave a message that it will not be tolerated in future."

"What will you do with Tiger?"

"He will be tried and executed on the Fort's wall by blowing from a gun."

"Messy," Marty said.

He was not surprised at the reaction but thought he should try to be the voice of moderation.

"I am not here to advise on how the Company manages its domestic policy, but I feel I should raise a note of caution if I think an action could possibly do more harm than good. I can understand you are all angry at the Maruthan actions, I am as well, but—"

"Martin, enough!" Hastings said. "As you say it's not your place to advice on domestic policy, your objection is noted."

And ignored, Marty thought.

"We need to talk about the next steps in the war," Hastings said. "The Pindaris have been raiding our territory and we know they are sponsored by Haklar and Shinde. It is my intention to eliminate this threat."

Marty knew about the Pindaris, "They are cavalry, highly mobile and evasive you will never pin them down unless you trap them."

"You have a suggestion?" Hastings said.

"Hammer and anvil, I've used the tactic against forces like these before. You need to drive them into a place of your choosing where you have cut off all avenues of escape. They come up against the securely-entrenched force that holds them while the pursuers take them from behind."

Hastings stood and looked at his map.

"Their home territory is here in the Malwa. South of the river Narmada."

Marty joined him. "That's the river the Silverthorn sailed up. What if you drive them up above that by destroying their villages? You could trap them with the river at their backs if you had an army waiting for them on the north side."

"How will we make them cross where we want?"

"I think I can help there. We should be able to get my smaller ships up the river. For the Pindaris to cross there must be fords. We can secure the ones we don't want them crossing with companies of marines supported by guns we can bring from the ships."

"Horse artillery would be ideal for that; I can arrange for you to be given several pieces," Francis said.

"Perfect! They are much easier to move than naval guns. Marty said

"This might just work. Let me discuss it with General Hislop."

"Sir, the squadron have entered the river." Adam popped his head through the door with a message slip in his hand. "There is also something about the Unicorn having a broom attached to her topmast."

"A broom?" Marty said.

"A clean sweep?" Justine said from her desk.

"That would be just what that German would do." Marty laughed. He took the slip from Adam and noted the time on it.

"They will be here around three o'clock. Let's organise a welcome." He went to see Francis Hastings.

Messages were sent and orders given. An army band was commandeered, and an honour guard detailed. It was short notice but when the commander in chief barked, his dogs howled.

Justine sent a message to Caroline in Marty's name informing her that the ships were coming home. Marty had completely forgotten to inform his wife in the excitement of organising the welcome. He was on his way to the dock when he stopped and slapped his forehead,

"I forgot to tell Caroline!" he cried.

"I sent her a message," Justine said. "She is on her way."

Marty smiled his gratitude, a look of relief on his face.

The dock was crowded, as well as the honour guard and band, most of the officials from Government House took the opportunity to stretch their legs.

"Word got around fast!" Marty said.

"It's the office telegraph," Justine said. "News travels fast."

"It is the same on a ship except we call it scuttlebutt. The men know what the captain is going to do almost as soon as he has decided."

A carriage arrived and Caroline dismounted. How she managed to look so good with hardly any notice always amazed Marty.

"Hello, darling," she said and kissed him on the cheek, "any news of James?"

"Not yet, but you will not have to wait long." He nodded at the Unicorn which was rounding the last bend before the dock.

The ships sailed smartly up and tied on to a lively tune from the band. The people cheered, Marty wasn't sure they knew why they were cheering, but he was sure the boys would appreciate it. When the gangplank dropped into place, he took Caroline by the arm and led her onboard. Wolfgang met them with a full side party.

"Permission to come aboard?" Marty said and doffed his hat to the quarterdeck.

"Permission granted," Wolfgang said with all the formality he could muster.

As Marty stepped on the deck his pennant was unfurled on the mainmast. The master had returned.

"I assume from that witch's stick on the topmast that you had a successful trip?" Marty said as he shook his hand.

"Completely successful, we eradicated the threat and captured prisoners who can tell us what was behind it."

Marty was curious but decided to wait until the welcomes were over. The Silverthorn was the fourth ship in line and moored alongside the Nymphe, the dock wall not being long enough to accommodate all the ships end to end. They stepped across to the deck.

"Commodore, Lady Caroline welcome." Angus then stepped aside so James could be greeted by his parents.

"James, you look intact," Marty said.

"Yes, Sir," he looked at Caroline, "Mother, how are you?"

"Better knowing you are safe and whole."

"We have a gift for you father," James said and signalled his men. The pirate leader and a half dozen of his men were brought forward in chains. But what intrigued Marty was the Buddhist monk who stood behind them.

"That's Izzy, he warned us about an ambush, then volunteered to come with us. He speaks Burmese and a few other languages."

Izzy came forward and bowed. "You are James's father. He looks like you."

Marty returned the bow in kind. "I am. Thank you for helping us. Can I do something for you in return?"

"It has been an adventure. That in itself is the reward."

Marty turned to the prisoners. "He is the leader?"

"One of them. They had a congress of captains which ran the fleet."

"The rest?"

"Dead, or walking and swimming home. We sank the lot," James said.

Caroline was looking around the ship when she noticed a girl stood by the rail watching James.

"Who is that?" she said.

"Who? Oh, that's Melissa, she was a captive who we freed." James blushed.

"Well, you had better introduce me."

Marty met with Wolfgang and his captains back on the Unicorn. At the start of the meeting Wolfgang had the large, brass bound chest brought in. Marty was intrigued but let Wolfgang and the captains recount the expedition in their own time. When they finished, Wolfgang went to the door and said something to the marine. A minute later James stepped inside.

"Mr Stockley, please tell the commodore what you found inside the warehouse."

James gave a concise account and then stepped over to the chest.

"Melissa told me about the chest. I picked the lock and checked for traps. When we opened it, we found this."

He opened the lid. It was full of bullion and jewellery.

Marty reached inside and lifted out a diamond and gold necklace, then he frowned, put it aside and picked up a handful of coins. He selected one, examining it, turning it over in his hands.

"Well, well, well. Gentlemen, what we have here is a smoking gun. These are damning evidence that the French consul was behind this."

"We assumed that they had attacked a French ship," Wolfgang said.

"I doubt it very much, these Louis D'Or have been marked and I have a half dozen more with the identical marks in my office. Have you questioned the pirate captain?"

"He is reluctant, we decided to leave him to you."

To keep things covert, he had the squadron move to the navy docks where he commandeered a warehouse. It was adapted by the Shadows and then, under the cover of darkness, the prisoners were transferred.

Each of them was locked in a crate that was five feet long and three feet to a side. They were kept awake for two days by someone banging and shaking the crate, made uncomfortable by having water poured through the air holes one minute and smoke the next.

Marty had the captain brought out, he stank and had fouled himself.

"Strip him and sluice him down."

The boys, all hooded, ripped his clothes off and subjected him to a thorough wash with a bucket of water and stiff brooms. They left him naked when they brought him to Marty. Izzy was on hand for translation, but Marty tried French first.

"Who gave you the gold coins?"

A flicker of his eyelids was the only reaction. Marty had Izzy ask in Burmese.

The man stayed silent.

"You must like being dirty and uncomfortable. You know, as far as anybody else is concerned you do not exist. I can keep you here forever."

That got more of a reaction.

"What will you give me for information?" he asked. If he was prepared to trade, they were making progress.

"You have courage, I will give you that. I don't need to give you anything. You will tell me eventually," Marty said.

The captain looked sly and said, "That will take time."

"I can speed up the process." Marty nodded to Billy who was stood behind him.

Billy was holding a length of heavy, tarred, two-inch cable which he struck the pirate across the kidneys with. The man collapsed to the ground crying in pain.

Marty leant forward, ignoring the gasp from Izzy, and said, "You will piss blood for a while. The next hit will be your balls. We can keep that up all day and you will not get any sleep tonight or until you tell me what I want to know."

Billy stepped forward, slapping the rope in his hand.

"A Frenchman. A Frenchman gave them to us."

"Why did he give them to you?"

"To attack British ships."

"Can you identify him?"

"Yes."

Marty signalled to Billy who dragged the man to his feet and took him out.

"I apologise that you had to see that," Marty said to Izzy.

"I thought you would have to beat him more."

"The art of interrogation is not to have to beat the truth out of the subject but to convince him that life will get infinitely worse if he doesn't talk. Sleep deprivation, isolation, stress, humiliation, the threat of more pain to come, all add up."

"You have made it a science."

Marty didn't answer, but the thought bothered him, just a little.

The ball to celebrate the governor general's birthday had been planned for months. It would be used to make a grand statement of British colonial power. There would be a parade where Hastings would be carried through the city in an open-top carriage, escorted by cavalry and serenaded by military bands. He would review the troops at Fort William. A salute would be fired and then the ball would begin.

All that was very well but it gave Marty and Frances Ridgley a security headache. That aside, Caroline was as determined as usual to make an entrance and an everlasting impression. To do that she wanted Marty in a formal tailed suit, with tight, high-waisted trousers, figured silk waistcoat over a white silk shirt and cravat. A top hat replaced his usual bicorn. His honours would be displayed on a red silk sash.

"I really don't have time," Marty protested as the tailor did yet another fitting. Caroline gave him a look and he sighed.

She was working with a talented local seamstress to create a vision in golden satin embellished with appliqued and embroidered leaves to give a natural theme. It plunged to the middle of her back which was quite daring and a shallow sweetheart neckline at the front. It was almost, but not quite off the shoulder. With the addition of her jewels, she would look stunning. All this was done with absolute secrecy. She didn't want any of the other women to have any idea what she was doing.

Come the hour of the ball Caroline wore a cloak which covered her from neck to floor as they drove up in their landau.

"Aren't you hot in that?" Marty said.

"Of course, I am," Caroline replied serenely.

Marty shook his head; he would never understand the machinations of the female mind.

They arrived at Government House and servants rushed to place the steps for them to dismount. Marty stepped down first and held out his hand for Caroline. She put her hand on his arm and stopped.

"Are you wearing your stilettoes?"

"Um, yes." Marty said.

"Why?" she asked as she stepped towards the steps to the main door.

"The pirate captain is here."

"What? Why?" Caroline said in surprise.

"To identify the French consul as the man who paid them to move to the bay."

"Are you going to cause a scene?"

"Me? No."

"Let me rephrase that, are your people going to cause a scene?"

"You know me too well. But no, there should be no scene or disruption."

"Good."

They reached the doors to the ballroom. A servant stood to take hats, cloaks, whatever the partygoers didn't want to take into the ballroom. Caroline waited until it was their turn to be announced then undid the cloak's neck clasp. Marty, who had realised what she was up to, took the cloak from her shoulders and handed it to the servant.

He had to admit his wife liked to make an entrance and had surpassed herself this time. He could almost hear the other wives grinding their teeth. Announcement made, they stepped through the crowd to the presentation line where Hastings was greeting his guests with Flora.

"Martin, Caroline. You have upstaged me again." Francis laughed. He kissed Caroline on both cheeks and shook Marty's hand.

"I am but a slave to my wife's desires where clothes are concerned."

"Wise,"

"Is the French consul here?"

"Not yet, is your man in position?"

"He should be," Marty said and looked over towards the entrance. Matai and Garai were dressed in suits and had the pirate captain firmly held between them. He was dressed in clothes similar to what he had been captured in and was getting curious looks from the other guests.

"You are sure about this?" Marty said to Hastings.

"Think of it as your birthday present to me," Hastings said.

"You have a strange idea of what a present is."

Justine appeared at the entrance, looked over at Matai and nodded.

"Here we go," Marty said.

"What's going on?" Caroline said.

Just then the French consul was announced.

"You will see," Francis said.

As soon as he saw him, the pirate wrenched himself away from his escort and threw himself at his feet begging and talking sixteen to the dozen.

"Jackpot," Hastings said.

Ize had appeared and was listening to what the man said, he translated it to Zeb who transcribed it.

The consul looked horrified and tried to back up, but Billy stood behind him, unmoving. Hastings and Marty walked over.

"Oh dear, looks like you have been undone," Hastings said, a malicious grin on his face. Marty nodded to Matai and Garai who retrieved the captain and escorted him out. He beckoned to Zeb who handed him the transcription.

"Quite damming, appears you paid him to raid our ships."

"It's just his word against mine!"

"Not quite," Marty said, "he had a chest full of these." He held up a pair of Louis D'Or.

"They could have taken that from a French ship!"

"Amazing that they all carry your personal mark. But enough of this, please present yourself to the governor general's office tomorrow at eleven in the morning." He looked at Billy, "Please escort the consul to his carriage and make sure he gets to his house safely."

Hastings had a beaming smile on his face after the consul and his wife had left, "I really don't like that man."

The ball went with a swing after that. Marty and Caroline danced with each other and others until two in the morning. He woke at nine and climbed quietly out of bed so as not to disturb her. He had his own dressing room and bathroom so shaved and dressed quietly. Adam brought him coffee and a light breakfast.

Hastings was in his office, showing no aftereffects of the party. In fact, he was, what could only be described as, chipper.

"Good morning, Martin. Lovely day."

"Francis," Marty said in greeting.

Hastings went to the window and checked his watch. It was ten minutes to eleven. A carriage pulled up in front of the steps and he watched as Jean-Claude Blanchette stepped out.

"He is here."

Hastings had arranged his office to be as confrontational as possible. He and Marty would be sat as if in judgment behind his desk with Blanchette sat in front and lower than them on a specially-modified chair.

Precisely on the stroke of eleven the door opened, and Francis's secretary showed the consul in. He looked angry and belligerent.

"I must protest at this treatment," he said as soon as he stepped inside.

"Please take a seat," Marty said.

Hastings waited until he sat and said, "Lord Stockley and his people have accumulated sufficient evidence to prove that you are working independently from your government in opposition to the British in India."

"I protest, I am the representative of the French Government."

Hastings held up his hand, "Martin, if you would be so kind."

"Where to start? Your smuggling of arms? The recruitment of French mercenaries for the Maratha Empire? The blackmailing of a British official to obtain secret information which was then sent by carrier pigeon to our enemies? The bribing of Burmese pirates to attack shipping in the Bay of Bengal? Shall I go on?"

"How?"

"That is inconsequential, the fact is we have incontrovertible evidence." Marty said. "For example, these." He handed over two of the gold coins.

"One is from your safe and the other from the pirate's chest. You will note that they have the same marks on them."

"How did you get into my safe?"

Marty just looked at him.

"You broke into my house?" his voice went up an octave.

Marty and Hastings looked at him with completely bland, cold expressions.

"That is French territory!"

"Actually, it's not. If it were an embassy, then it could be with the agreement of the host nation. As it is only a consulate, and the French government has never requested it to have French status, it is just a private residence," Hastings said.

"Semantics!"

"Facts," Marty barked.

"A report is on its way to London and from there to Paris. I am sure your government will want to have a talk with you,"

Blanchette got to his feet, "I refuse to listen to any more of this nonsense." He stormed out.

"That went well," Marty said.

"It did, didn't it." Hastings smiled.

"My bet is he will head for one of the French colonies," Marty said.

"Have you secured his house?"

"Oh yes it's being occupied by my men as we speak."

Marty took a cup of tea and sat back in his chair while he sipped it. "What is happening in the west?"

"You don't know?" Hastings laughed.

"I've been busy."

"Elphinstone is about to attack the Maratha main force. He has an army of sufficient size and is well prepared thanks to the intelligence you provided."

"We provided the false information that you asked us to, did they swallow it?" Marty said.

"It would appear so, the piece about the withdrawal of support by the French spurred Rao to dismiss most of the French advisors. By the way was that Ridgley's idea?"

"Yes, it was and even better the consul had no idea it had been sent. We will continue to send negative messages now that Blanchette has been exposed. There is no point in trying to hide his disgrace as it will be known all over Calcutta by now."

Chapter 12: The Narmada River

Caroline took an active role in the rehabilitation of the rescued slaves. Melissa in particular had caught her interest. The girl had lost everybody but was undaunted. She was intelligent and had a level of awareness and empathy for others not often found in one so young. Anabelle, Shelby's wife, had noted it in her but found the girl had no interest in medicine.

Caroline sat with her in the garden of the house they had acquired to accommodate the rescued captives.

"You were on a ship with your parents?" she said.

"Yes, the Meredith. We were sailing to Calcutta for Daddy to take a position as a clerk with the Company. The pirates swarmed the ship when we were blown towards Burma by a storm and lost contact with the convoy."

"Do you have anyone back in Britain?"

"No, my father was an only child and my grandparents died during the influenza epidemic, my mother came from France during the terror."

"You have French blood?"

"I do, but please don't hold it against me," Melissa sighed.

"I wouldn't dream of it. What education have you had?"

"I went to school where we lived in Colchester until I was fourteen. Then to a finishing school. Mama had ambitions for me to marry a man above our station."

"My mother had the same ambition; she gave me to a seventy-year-old titled man when I was sixteen."

Melissa looked astonished, "I thought you were married to Lord Stockley."

"I am, the old man died of food poisoning when I was eighteen. He never managed to get me pregnant. Then I met Martin, he was a midshipman at the time, and it was love at first sight. He fought a duel for me, and my fate was sealed."

Melissa sighed at the romance of it then looked thoughtful. "I am glad you found him. You are both so obviously happy."

"He was a catch that is for sure, but the life of a navy wife is sometimes lonely. They can be away for such long periods at a time." Caroline decided to change the subject, "What do you want to do now?"

Melisa blew out her cheeks, "I really do not know."

Caroline could sympathise, the poor girl didn't have any options.

"Can I suggest you come and stay with my family?" she said. "I am in need of a secretary." This was true, Caroline's business activities used up an inordinate amount of time and she needed help.

"Oh! Could I?" Melisa said, a spark of hope in her eyes.

"My daughter has returned to England and, when she wasn't following her father's profession, used to help me."

Melissa looked confused, "But Lord Martin is a diplomat how could she?"

"That, my dear, you will discover if you join us."

"I am intrigued! I would love to be your secretary."

"Excellent, that is settled then. Collect your belongings, we will get you installed in the house."

"I am wearing everything I own," Melissa said, looking a little abashed.

"Then we will leave now and go via the market."

James joined them for dinner. His ship would be sailing in company with the Endellion the next day. He was surprised to see Melissa there and even more so as she wore a new dress that matched her honey blond hair that was no longer a shaggy bird's nest, but glowed and was tied up in a high ponytail.

He wore a brand-new uniform as he had replaced the old ones he had grown out of. Like his father he had broad shoulders, a narrow waist, and stood erect. He was unconsciously graceful, moving with the ease of a dancer or rather a fighter.

Melissa blushed when she saw him, which was noted by his mother, and his face broke into a beaming smile when he saw her. Also noted by his mother and father. Melissa didn't join the family for dinner. She ate with the rest of the staff as she thought it would give her an opportunity to listen in on the goings on in the Stockley household. She was surprised, the staff didn't gossip much, so she asked a blunt question.

"Lady Caroline said her daughter is following in Lord Martin's footsteps, but he is a diplomat. How can that be?"

A dusky-skinned man who was married to a black woman called Tabetha laughed and said, "The boss is only a diplomat for this mission, he is in the navy."

The boss? What kind of way was that to refer to one's employer?

"Well Lady Bethany couldn't possibly follow him into the navy," she said.

Tabetha punched him in the arm, "Don't you tease her." Her voice was rich and had an exotic accent. "Lord Martin is part of Naval Intelligence."

"Naval Intelligence? What is that?"

The staff looked at each other as if wanting someone else to answer. Then a voice came from behind her.

"It's a branch of the service which gathers intelligence on our enemies and takes part in operations to disrupt those enemies."

She looked around to see a man in a smart suit helping himself to the buffet. He bowed in greeting.

"I am Adam, Lord Martin's valet and member of his team."

He sat beside her.

"So he is a?" she said.

"Spy, agent, special operative, sailor. Whatever the mission needs."

"Is his son following in his footsteps?"

Adam looked at her in a way that seemed to pierce her through, and smiled, "Only so far as he is and will be a sailor, he has no interest in the – other – part of his father's life."

"Oh," she said.

The next day the Silverthorn and Endellion slipped their moorings and headed down the river to the Bay of Bengal. Loaded with extra marines and soldiers, space was at a premium on both ships.

"What is needed here is the Hornfleur," Angus said to James as he looked across the deck. "We are not a troopship."

"What type of ship was she?" James asked.

"A wailer originally. One of the big American built ones. We fitted her out with extra davits and carried boats modelled on long boats, sharp fore and aft with rudders that could be fitted at either end."

"Easy to get on and off the beach," James said.

"And the men in and out."

They were silent as they watched the river slide by. Then Angus said, "What would be the ideal landing boat in your opinion?"

James thought about it. "Well, the men need to be able to get off quickly so something like a ramp at the bow which they could run down directly onto the beach would be useful. Shallow draft yet stable. Room for two men per oar and between ten and twenty marines plus kit."

"How many oars?" Angus said.

"Eight per side. Two men to an oar."

"A big boat!"

"It will never be built."

"No, more's the pity."

James went forward to supervise the sail handlers who were having trouble working around a mass of soldiers.

"Clear a way there!" he shouted.

A belligerent soldier who was fed up with being asked to move barked, "Let 'em work around us, there's plenty of room."

James walked up to him, "Move or I will have you moved."

"I'd like to see you try," the man challenged seeing only a fifteen-year-old boy in front of him.

James smiled at him then called, "Dennis, would you help here please."

Dennis who, as usual, was never far from James stepped up.

"Move this man please."

Before the offending soldier could say anything, Dennis picked him up and took him to where James pointed.

"Drop him there," James said, and Dennis did.

Laughter and cat calls came from the rest of the redcoats as the man landed with a thump on his arse. He was on his feet in an instant and pulled a knife. James stepped between him and Dennis.

"Don't be a fool, I could have you flogged for disobeying an order. Do you want to be hanged for attacking an officer?"

"No one lays hands on me," the man snarled.

"STAND DOWN, PRIVATE JONES!" a sergeant bellowed as he pushed his way through the men.

"Thank you, Sergeant but I can manage this," James said. He looked at Jones, seeing the rage in his eyes and knowing if he didn't settle this now then this man would do something later, probably to Dennis. "Let him try me if he thinks he can take me. We will meet as soon as we clear the estuary."

There was a collective gasp, it was unheard of for an officer to take on a ranker in the army. James, however, knew a troublemaker when he saw one and his father had always told him to tackle them head on. But, he thought, he would need all the tricks the Shadows had taught him.

"Clear a fighting circle," James said. They were in the open sea now.

The sailors grinned as they laid a rope down on the fore deck to outline the combat zone. He was stripped to the waist and the years of climbing rigging showed on his well-toned young body. Several commented on the scars he carried. He flexed his shoulders and swung his arms. His opponent, Private Jones 301, as he was known, 301 being the last three digits of his service number to distinguish him from all the other Jones in the regiment, stepped into the ring. Larger with a hint of fat around his waist. He looked odds on to flatten James in an instant.

They stepped up to the two lines on the deck and the sergeant announced the rules in a parade ground bellow.

"No gouging, or hair pulling, first man who is knocked down three times is the loser. Are you ready?" Both men nodded. He extended his arm between them.

Angus had not been keen on the idea of his mid taking on a professional soldier to prove a point, but James had been adamant that this was the only way. The men had to respect him and to do that he had to prove his worth.

James assumed a fighter's crouch, feet shoulder width apart, weight over the balls of his feet, knees bent. Balanced and ready. His opponent flexed his muscles and balled his fists.

The sergeant lifted his arm and shouted, "Fight!"

Jones roared and swung his fists only to find James wasn't there, a sharp punch to his side stung him. He turned, James had ducked his swing and gotten behind him. Another punch to the body and James stepped back out of reach. Jones roared again and started forward expecting James to keep backing up. A foot kicked him in the gut and as he doubled a knee hit him in the nose. He staggered back.

James let him recover, beating him too quickly wasn't what he wanted. He bounced on the balls of his feet while he waited. Jones shook his head, nose bleeding.

"Give up?" James asked.

"Fuck you." Jones stepped forward, fists up.

"You're learning," James smiled.

Jones feinted with his left and swung with his right. James blocked it with his left and jabbed with his right. Jones ignored the punch and bulled onwards wrapping his arms around James starting to crush him.

James's feet left the ground as the pressure came on. His breath was being crushed out of him, but Jones had made the mistake of leaving his arms free. James slapped his ears. Jones howled and his arms loosened. James's toes touched the floor, he headbutted Jones on the bridge of the nose. Jones held on, blood pouring from his nose, so he cupped his hands and slapped his ears again. This time James was released, and he whipped the off-balance soldier into a hip throw.

"First fall to Mr Stockley," the sergeant bellowed.

James was back on his line waiting for Jones to get up, but he didn't move. Fearing something was wrong, James went to him and knelt at his side. He rolled him onto his back, his eyes were wide and staring. James felt for a pulse in his neck and placed his cheek by his mouth.

"Well I'm damned! He is dead," he said, then "Get the surgeon fast!"

Angus arrived on deck and bellowed for the crowd to clear. He stood beside James who looked at the dead man with a confused look on his face.

"Nothing I did should have killed him."

"I was watching, not a single killing blow."

The surgeon came bustling up. He examined the body.

"No idea why he died. I need to perform a post-mortem examination. Let's get him down to the infirmary." He called his loblolly boys who put him on a stretcher.

From then on, James found he only had to quietly issue an order and the soldiers jumped to it. He didn't understand. One of their mates had died at his hand and no one knew why. The surgeon had been shut away in the orlop for the rest of the day and not seen on deck.

"Mr Stockley, the captain would like you to attend him in his cabin."

James handed over command to the master and went below. When he entered the room, the surgeon, and the lieutenant ostensibly in charge of the soldiers were already there along with the captain's clerk. The lieutenant was a complete drip and about as much use as doyly in a thunderstorm. He had no chin to speak of and his name was Tiffany Hindon-Beechwell Esquire. The son of a family that had been marrying its first cousins for generations in James's opinion. He spoke with a pronounced lisp.

"Ah midthipman Thtockley, tho nithe of you to join uth," he said.

He had no idea of who James was, having just arrived in the sub-continent.

Angus grinned at James and said, "Mr Simmons has come to a conclusion after performing an extensive examination."

Used poor Jones as an excuse to practise his dissection technique no doubt, James thought, but looked expectantly to the surgeon.

"Jones was a man of thirty-five years who was a heavy drinker and smoker. He had suffered several wounds during his service in the army, none of which contributed to his death. His heart and arteries around it were clogged with fat and he had a growth in his lungs. It is my belief that during the combat a lump of this fat blocked his pulmonary artery and killed him."

"He wath alwayth complaining he wath out of breath," Hindon-Beechwell said.

"That fits with a man in his condition," Simmons said.

"If I had known that I would never have fought him."

Angus squared his shoulders and said, "But you didn't and couldn't've," he then said formally,

"Let the record show that the Right Honourable James Stockley, midshipman, holds no blame in the death of Archibald Jones."

The clerk wrote it down in the record and Hindon-Beechwell looked at James in surprise at the honorific. He wisely held his tongue.

"Now, gentlemen, if you would be so kind as to join me for dinner," Angus said.

James had the watch that night when a movement on the deck alerted him someone had invaded the sanctity of the quarterdeck. He turned and saw it was Hindon-Beechwell.

"Good evening, Lieutenant what can I do for you?"

"I understand that you are the son of Viscount Stockley," he lisped.

"I am." James wondered where this was going.

"You are his heir, I wondered why you were in the navy."

"You mean in case I am killed?"

"Yes."

"My father is not one to wrap his children in cottonwool."

"My father insists that my eldest brother runs the family estate."

"A trusted friend runs our estates as manager. Father rarely interferes in either of them except to ensure the latest farming practices are adopted."

"Either of them? I know of the one in Cheshire. Do you have another?"

"We have an estate in Dorset on the Isle of Purbeck. It is where Father came from, and he bought it for his family."

"Our estate is in Norfolk."

James waited; the man would get to the point in his own time.

"I was wondering if your father might be in need of an aid de camp?"

"He doesn't, he has his own team around him."

A huge shadow approached.

"What is it, Dennis?"

"Destry say that there is a problem with the foremast stay, can you come look."

James turned to the lieutenant, "You can come with me if you like."

They walked down the deck. James easily avoiding the snags and ringbolts that trip the unwary. Hindon-Beechwell was not so experienced and tripped. James was waiting for that and caught him.

"Watch your footing, the deck is a treacherous place in the dark."

"I have to admit I cannot see a thing," Hindon-Beechwell said.

James was surprised. He could see enough by moonlight to walk around safely. They reached the sailor who had sent the message. Destry was a seasoned hand and captain of the foremast.

"What's the problem, Destry?" James said.

"This here stay is slack, Sir."

James took a hold of the stay and pulled.

"There is definitely more give than there should be. How are the others?" The stays for each mast had to be equally tensioned.

"Fore and aft be fine."

James looked up at the quarter moon then checked his watch.

"I don't think the weather will change tonight; we will tighten them in the morning. Keep an eye on them and tell the next watch when they come up to do the same."

"Aye, Aye. Sir."

He turned back to the lieutenant,

"Just how bad is your night vision?"

"In this light I can hardly see a thing."

That's not going to help when we are on the river, James thought.

"To be truthful I am looking for a staff post, I have found I am not suited to service on the line. The men know I am inexperienced and take advantage of me."

"Then how did you end up with this assignment?"

"I think the commanding officer wanted me out of the way."

That was a bombshell. They had been relying on having an experienced officer to command one of the fords.

The next morning after his usual four hours' sleep James met up with Angus and Declan O'Driscol to give them the good news.

"So, in short he can't see in the dark, has no combat experience and has been put with us to get him out of the way," James said.

"That means you will have to command one of the fords," Declan said. "S'rnt Bright will take one, Anfield another and me the third."

Angus had a slightly different view. He decided James would command the small marine detachment that would accompany the soldiers with swivel guns and have joint command with Hindon-Beechwell.

Tiff, as James decided to call him, became James's shadow after that, which Dennis thought hilarious to the point where James had to ask him to refrain from laughing out loud.

The weather got progressively worse as they sailed south. They were beating their way through a large sea with the rain slashing almost horizontally across the deck. The ship corkscrewing. Tiff was nowhere to be seen.

"Can you check on the good lieutenant?" Angus said to James.

"I was quite enjoying the respite," James grimaced.

"Nevertheless, he is our responsibility and having him die of seasickness will not go down well with his regiment."

Can you die of seasickness? James went below to the dogbox of a living space allocated to Tiff and knocked on the door frame.

"Go away."

"Tiff, it's James."

The sound of retching came from inside.

"Can I come in?"

"If you must."

James opened the door. The smell of vomit assailed his nostrils. The floor was awash. "Jesus Christ, didn't you get a bucket?"

He stepped out and grabbed two sailors,

"Get him up on deck then swab that cabin out. Tie him to a safety line so he doesn't get washed overboard."

By the time he found Tiff he was leaning on a rail, a safety line tied around his waist and secured to a convenient bollard. The rain had soaked him through and washed the worst of the puke off him.

"Your cabin is clean now, come down to the wardroom and change your clothes."

James untied him and with Dennis's help got him below. Once in the wardroom they stripped him naked and rubbed him down with cloths to both dry him and get his circulation moving. A bucket was brought in on standby, but James doubted he had anything left in him.

Tiff was exhausted and dehydrated, James had him sip lemon-flavoured water while he went to his cabin to get him some clean clothes. He rummaged through his chest and found a pair of trousers and a shirt.

"Here, get dressed, I will lend you a pair of stockings."

Tiff looked utterly miserable. He hickuped, and gulped as the ship pitched and rolled.

"Do you feel any better?"

"Not as bad, but by no means better. Does it always get like this?"

"This isn't so bad. We've seen far worse."

"Hurricane worse." Dennis laughed and clapped his hands.

"Stay in here, Dennis will look after you. I have to take the next watch."

"How is he?" Angus said as James took over the watch from him.

"Not as bad. We had to sluice out his cabin."

"I saw him on deck, he looked wretched."

"He will live." *More's the pity.*

"You have the deck. By the way, who is looking after him?"

"Dennis."

Angus left, his laughter merging with the sound of the wind making James feel it was laughing at him as well.

The storm passed as storms do and the ship settled back to an even keel. Tiff appeared on deck under his own steam. He looked up at the blue sky and enjoyed the feel of the sun on his face. He was back in uniform which had been cleaned by the wardroom steward, Perkins. He approached James.

"James, I want to thank you."

"No need, least I could do."

Tiff looked at the land on their starboard side.

"When will we reach the river?"

"In around five days if the weather holds."

Tiff looked alarmed, "It's not likely to get bad again?"

James smiled in sympathy.

"No, we are past that."

"Thank God for that." Tiff looked relieved.

James looked him over, "You don't wear a sword?"

"I keep tripping over it, so leave it off while on the ship."

"Do you fence?"

"I have had some lessons but I'm not very good."

"My watch finishes in an hour, bring your sword to the foredeck, we will take some exercise."

The fore deck was clear and relatively free of obstacles. James shed his uniform coat and removed his necktie. He was loosening up when Tiff appeared with his sword.

"What is that?" James asked, looking at the bow of something long in a scabbard.

"I got it from a dealer in Norfolk."

It was a sword with a curved blade of thirty-one inches, sharp on one side and ground to a point. The hilt was leatherbound and resembled a pistol grip. The guard was L-shaped and made of iron.

"That looks like a cavalry sabre to me," James said. He looked at the blade and noticed something engraved near the ricasso. "That looks eastern European."

He tested the balance. The balance point was a good ten inches forward of the cross guard. "This is nose heavy, fine for slashing on a horse, not so good for fencing. You can use one of mine."

He handed Tiff his old hanger. "Try that."

"Oh, that feels so light!"

"It is not much lighter than the sabre but is much better balanced," James explained. He took up his stance. "En guarde."

They practised every day and Tiff improved from terrible to average. James consoled himself with the thought that he could at least defend himself now if it came to a fight.

They entered the river, and everyone was on high alert. The plan was to get up as high as they could in the ships then use boats to take the men up to the fords.

The information they had on the Pindaris said that they fought predominantly with the spear and had very few guns. They were an ancient warrior sect and seemingly stuck in the past. All the same, as the French lancers had proven at Waterloo, the lance could still be a formidable weapon, especially against infantry caught in the open. Their planning took that into account and played on the Pindaris weaknesses. Each ford would be fortified against cavalry attack with a bank and sharpened stakes. Each fortification would have swivels and the men grenades. They had decided not to try and move the field pieces by hand.

As they sailed upstream, they saw no horsemen only a few farmers who watched them pass with studied disinterest. The main entertainment being bird spotting with prizes going to men who spotted something new.

The river gradually shallowed as they progressed, and leadsmen were in the chains continuously. When they only had a foot or so under their keel they anchored and Angus addressed the ship, "The first ford is some three miles above us and will be the responsibility of Sergeant Bright and his marines. Sergeant, please prepare to get your men loaded into the boats. Set up on the north bank and fortify your position so as to deny the Pindaris horsemen the ford.

When the boats return, we will send up the second force commanded by Sergeant Anfield, Captain O'Driscol will hold the third. Last but not least, Mr Stockley and Lieutenant Hindon-Beechwell will take their force to the fourth. You will hold until relieved."

Fifty miles to the south, the army was advancing on the Pindari villages. They drove out the inhabitants and burnt the villages to the ground. They closed down their avenues of escape and drove the Pindaris north. Any resistance was met with overwhelming force.

James and Tiff marched their men east along the north bank. It was six miles to the ford from where they were deposited on the bank. By the time they got into position it was late in the day and the men were tired.

"Before they rest, we have to throw up a berm and get the swivels mounted," James said. Tiff looked uncertain he knew his men wouldn't like that. James turned to face him, "Look every officer has to ask his men to give a bit more when they think they have had enough. The good ones inspire them the poor ones drive them. It is time you decided which you are."

Tiff blinked a couple of times then turned to his sergeant. "Get the men lined up in ranks please, Sergeant."

Tiff walked up and down, composing himself, while the sergeant bellowed orders and the men lined up in two ranks, as soon as they were settled Tiff stepped up,

"Men, we are the final brick in the wall to steer the Pindaris into the trap the general has set. We have the opportunity to end the menace of these brigands once and for all and it depends on us." He punched his fist into his hand and James noticed his lisp was almost undetectable. Tiff hadn't finished,

"We are up against cavalry. We must set our defences accordingly. We need a berm erected tonight and we need to reinforce it with stakes in the morning. Your lives and the success of the campaign is riding on your shoulders. Now you all know what needs to be done, go and do it."

The men looked at him, some in astonishment, some with surprise, none with resentment. The sergeant barked orders and they fell out, swapping their rifles for the short spades they carried strapped to their packs. The ground along the river was soft and they soon had a pile of sods stacked up. Then they piled on dirt from a trench they dug on its rear face. When a man could stand behind the wall and fire his gun while resting it on the top they stopped. Marty took care of the placement of the swivels on their spike mounts. He had three, so he set one at either end, the third in the middle. They could now enfilade any horsemen who tried the ford.

They discovered that the proximity to the river had a major disadvantage which was the mosquitoes. Marty had anointed himself liberally with citronella oil, but the most determined pests still got through. He had brought a small bottle with him and passed it out to those who were suffering the worst. Smokey fires were set to try and drive the little devils away and those men who smoked chuffed away on their pipes.

The next dawn saw the men at their breakfast. They carried enough rations for a week, but James decided to supplement them with some fresh meat as he had seen some deer on their march up. He took his three men with him. If they were lucky, Dennis would be useful for carrying a carcase back on his own and Eric and Joseph another between them.

They were lucky the wind was from the northeast, so it was easy to keep down wind of any prey and it wasn't long before they spotted a small herd.

"Half a dozen does and a buck, what do you think Eric can you take one of the does if I take another?" James said to the best shot of the three.

"I reckon so, Sir, I'll take the one on the far left, she looks to be a couple years old."

James selected another of similar age then saw she was nursing a fawn so shifted to a larger, older deer.

He took a deep breath, conscious that Eric was doing the same. He aimed for the beast's heart. "Fire," he breathed, and the guns fired as one.

The animals dropped and the rest took off. James ran forward his knife in his hand. The doe was dead. The shot was a clean kill. He noticed Eric swiftly stab his in the neck severing the main artery.

"Missed her heart," he said.

They swiftly dressed out the carcases, wrapping the livers, kidneys, and hearts in a cloth. James's kill had her legs tied together and a pole threaded through for Eric and Joseph to carry between them. Dennis simply hoisted Eric's kill onto his shoulders. They returned to the ford.

Tiff had kept the men busy and the bank had started bristling with sharpened stakes. James and the boys got a cheer as they dropped the deer by the fire so the cook could joint them up for roasting.

It was mid-afternoon and the sound of shooting drifted to them on the breeze. James climbed up on top of the berm and looked west. It was seven miles to the next ford, and he couldn't see anything.

He scanned the horizon to the south with his glass. He stopped when he saw a smudge in the sky.

"Can you see anything?" Tiff said.

"A hint of smoke or dust from below the horizon to the south. Could be a village being burnt."

"How far away do you think it is?"

"Ten or fifteen miles. Looks pretty thin as I'm not seeing it until it has risen a fair way."

They set extra sentries on the far side of the river that night with instructions to get back to the camp as fast as they could if they heard or saw anything. James and his sailors were used to night watches so took the watch from midnight to six in the morning on the south bank. They had full bellies from the roast venison and flatbreads that they had for their evening meal, and it wasn't raining. The duty no hardship at all.

False dawn came and the wind swung back to the Northeast as it seemed to every morning. James yawned; the watch would be over as soon as it was dawn proper. He checked his rifle, making sure the percussion cap was seated properly when he heard a clink. He froze then slowly stood. A horse blew. He oriented on the sound and worked around the bushes in front of him. Shapes moved in the grey light which was brightening by the second.

Four horses and riders were making their way slowly to the ford. They were passing through James's line of pickets. He put his gun down gently and pulled his knife moving up on the rider closest to him. He got ten feet behind him when he burst into a run, vaulted onto the back of the horse, and slashed his knife across the rider's throat.

Suddenly, Dennis rose up out of the shrub and punched a horse on the side of the head knocking it and its rider to the ground. The other two, alerted, spun their horses to face the perceived threat. Shots rang out and they toppled from their saddles.

"Catch the horses!" James shouted and helped by blocking the path of the two that were making to bolt. He was an experienced horseman, and noted the saddle and bridle were of a strange configuration. The horse was well schooled and seemed to obey the knee rather than the rein. That made sense when he thought about it, as the rider would have a lance taking up at least one of his hands. However, he didn't succeed in blocking both and one slipped by and galloped off.

They captured the other two and headed back across the ford. "Midshipman Stockley and pickets!" James shouted as they started the crossing.

Tiff met him as they came up onto the north bank.

"Are you hurt?"

"No, we are all fine, one of the horses got away which will warn them something's up."

"Did you take a prisoner?"

"Dennis did, he knocked out his horse then him in quick succession."

"Knocked out his horse?"

"With a right hook."

"Be damned, he is a force."

"We need to get the men ready; we can expect company soon."

Chapter 13: Skirmish at The Third Ford

Forewarned is forearmed, James thought as he organised the swivels. He had them loaded with cannister with fresh cartridge and cannister stacked close at hand. Each was manned by two marines. The loss of their rifles in the line would be more than made up for by the faster rate of fire they would achieve with the swivels. The rest of the men were lined up behind the berm in two ranks. The first rank would fire then step back allowing the second rank to take their place while they reloaded and so on. The biggest danger to the fortification was from a flanking manoeuvre. The swivels would be crucial in defending against that.

"If they have tried to force the other two fords then they might be getting desperate by the time they get to us. Hislop will be hot on their heels." Tiff said.

James smiled, Tiff was still the same chinless wonder, but he had a newfound confidence since he had addressed the men and his lisp had lessened as his confidence had grown. He wore the hanger James lent him in favour of the large cavalry sabre he had carried before.

They felt rather than heard the rumble of hooves. The ground shook and there was a discernible ripple on the surface of the river. A dust cloud was their first visible clue to the size of the force that opposed them.

"Jesus Christ! There must be thousands of the devils!" a trooper exclaimed looking at the dust cloud.

"Steady now, they can't all come at once," a sergeant said in a calm voice.

James moved from swivel to swivel, chatting to the gunners and making the odd joke. To see such a young man so relaxed settled the men and Tiff followed his lead.

"Is your powder dry, Smith 238?"

"Yes, Sir, checked it just now."

"Did you check your canteen?"

"Yes, Sir, full to the brim, Sir."

"Rum or Brandy, Smith." Tiff said, causing a chuckle from his comrades.

"Water, Sir, honest, Sir." Smith was a known boozer.

"Enemy approaching!" a lookout shouted from the south bank as he ran across the ford sending up a spray that scintillated in the sun. He was followed by the other two. James cocked his rifle, laid it on the berm and took his telescope to see what was coming.

A group of horsemen cantered along the southern riverbank towards the ford. They were dressed like their prisoner in colourful quilted coats and tight riding breeches. They wore turbans held on by looping the end of the fabric under their chins. From what he could see they were armed with sabres that had curious guards that looked more like a gauntlet and long spears. One had an old musket.

"They are the advanced party. The main force is coming up behind them," Tiff said from behind him.

"We should wait until they try the ford. Let them get their horses feet wet," James said.

"Hold fire until I give the command!" Tiff shouted.

The horsemen slowed to a walk as they got to the ford and looked across at the berm, the stakes and the rifles pointing in their direction. One spun his horse and rode back to the west along the bank.

"If they have been repelled at the other fords, they might just bypass us," Tiff said.

"They might, but the next ford is ten miles further along and it depends on how hard pressed they are."

The dust cloud resolved itself into a horde who stopped just out of musket range. A man in a golden coat, obviously in charge and giving orders.

James breathed steadily; he was excited but knew he had to keep that under control. He breathed in through his nose and out through his mouth until his heartbeat settled. Folding his telescope with a clack he exchanged it for his rifle. He was sorely tempted to take a shot at the gold-coated man as he was well within range but knew that could trigger the rest of the men to fire prematurely.

"I could knock that bugger right off his horse," he muttered then jumped when Tiff replied from behind him.

"Tempting I know, but the men are on tenterhooks as it is."

Tiff was walking the line, casually, and had been passing as James had made his utterance.

"Steady, lads," he said.

Across the river a group of around fifty horsemen split off from the main group and were trotting to a position opposite the ford. They lined up in ranks fifteen wide. The commander in front with a sword the rest with spears.

"Here they come!" James cried as they kicked forward into a walk then a trot. He was impressed by their discipline. They had been described as bandits but behaved like well-schooled troops.

They increased to a canter then a gallop obviously planning to rush the shallow waters of the ford.

"Wait for it!" bellowed the sergeant.

The horsemen got to within twenty yards of the ford when they suddenly split into two and veered away to either side. Whooping and yelling.

"Just teasing us," James said.

Discipline held and not a shot was fired.

They circled around and reformed.

They came again. This time they didn't split, and James brought his rifle to bear.

They galloped into the water. Tiff let them all get in then shouted, "FIRST RANK FIRE!"

The volley was devastatingly effective. Men and horses fell but they kept coming. The following ranks jumping any horses that lay in their path.

"SECOND RANK FIRE!" That was the cue for the swivels to open up as well. The cannister shimmered across the gap as it spread.

The § two ranks of horses fell. Their riders either dead already or thrown into the water which was turning red with blood.

James urged his gunners to reload which they should be able to do in twenty seconds. But adrenaline and nerves took their toll, and it was half a minute before the guns barked again by which time the soldiers had sent a third volley.

The surviving horsemen had reached the bank but turned and ran. Marty picked one off as he gained the far bank and quickly reloaded. This time he looked for the man in gold and carefully took aim. He allowed for bullet drop and aimed a few inches above his turban. The wind was slightly from his left, so he compensated to the right. He took a deep breath and as he exhaled, squeezed the trigger.

Something made the golden coat's horse stumble just as he fired. By the time his bullet arrived, the target's head had dropped by few inches. It passed through his turban jerking his head back.

"Bugger," James said when he saw him turn his horse and retreat into the mass of horsemen behind him.

The river took care of the dead and seriously wounded, washing them downstream. Their dead horses would take a bit of persuading to set off on their journey, but in this heat, they would bloat and float off. The living were allowed to make their way ashore. Wounded men used up resources, held the cavalry up and in any case the British didn't have the resources to care for them.

In all, James estimated they killed or wounded half the attacking horsemen. As the day was coming to an end and the sun was going down Tiff and James discussed what would happen next.

"I see they have two options, attack in force and try and press it home or move on to the next ford and into the arms of Hastings," James said.

"I don't know," Tiff said, "I just get the feeling they are up to something. I'm wondering if there is a third."

Morning dawned and the Pindaris were still opposite them. A hundred or so lined up opposite the ford in battle formation.

"Option one by the looks of things," James said. Then paused he had an itch between his shoulders.

"Wait a minute," he said and climbed on top of the berm.

"Shit! They are behind us!"

A group of around thirty horsemen had appeared on the plane behind them. The horses were steaming and looked to have been ridden hard.

"Second rank about face!" Tiff shouted. "Fix bayonets!"

The hiss of bayonets being drawn from their steel sheaths followed by the click as they were fixed to the barrels of the rifles was loud.

James got out his pistols and laid them on the berm next to his rifle.

"They must have swum the river further upstream," Tiff said.

"I will trust your hunches more in the future," James replied.

A shout from the south bank and the hundred started forward, those to the north started out a moment later.

"Now I know how the meat in a sandwich feels," Tiff said. He had gotten hold of a rifle.

"Stop the men from firing while I pick off a couple," James said.

He chose the group to the north and climbed the berm to kneel on top to give him more range. He picked the man in the middle of the line and shot for his chest having learnt his lesson from yesterday. The man took the ball in the sternum and rolled off the back of his horse.

James had practised reloading his breach loader until he could do it in less than ten seconds. He fired again and another fell. The troops cheered.

The riders kicked into a canter, he fired again. Only wounding one that time. They broke into a gallop, and he heard splashing behind him. He fired again and a fourth fell. They were only thirty yards away now and he had no time to reload. He dropped his rifle and picked up his pistols.

Tiff had fired and reloaded his Baker rifle. He waited until he gave the order for the first volley to fire a second shot.

The swivels barked and threw their loads of death across the water. Because the second rank had to defend their rear there was a twenty second gap before the second volley barked out and the Pindaris were more than halfway across. The fastest riders were almost at the north bank.

James fired his pistols, not aiming but just into the mass of men and horses. Suddenly they were surrounded with horsemen circling their position looking for gaps.

"Hold fast, keep those bayonets forward!" shouted the sergeant. In any other situation they would have been decimated in line by the cavalry, but with the berm at their backs they had a chance.

James reloaded and fired again and again. The swivels barked.

Then a few Pindaris dismounted and rushed the berm on foot. James drew his sword and met them at the top. He was joined by Dennis, Joseph and Eric all swinging swords like madmen.

They fought, men died, the line closed up and got shorter. They had to abandon one of the swivels and the gunners joined the line. The Pindaris were out to exterminate them and more and more joined. They seemed to have a never-ending supply of men, and the British were gradually running out.

James was so tired he fought automatically. He didn't think, he just fought. Suddenly there was a shout and a volley of rifles.

What the hell? James ran a screaming man through.

Another volley followed and then a third. The Pindaris turned and ran.

"Captain O'Driscol, I have never been happier to see you," James said as his position was reinforced by marines and a company of soldiers from Hislop's force that had caught up with the Pindaris on the south bank.

He staggered and sat heavily on the ground. O'Driscol was at his side in an instant.

"Are you hurt, James?"

"I don't think so, I'm just bloody knackered."

He was wrong. He had taken several wounds, most light but one on his right side from a spear was deep and bleeding.

"How come you came?"

"They bypassed the first three fords when we fired on them. Then we saw the first bodies floating down the river and knew you were having a hot time of it."

"Oh," said James, and passed out.

James woke up in the familiar surroundings of his cabin. He was bandaged around the chest and aware of a dull ache in his side. He tried to sit up, but his head spun. He fell back onto his cot with a grunt. The door burst open, and Dennis's head appeared. He grinned like his face would split.

"James awake!" he said and another head appeared. It was Tiff.

"You're back with us! The surgeon said you would be."

"Did you think I wouldn't?" James said, trying not to smile.

"Was beginning to wonder, you have been out for two days."

"Two days? What? How? Bugger!"

"You must be hungry. Shift out the way, Dennis, let them bring him his soup."

Calling the thin gruel, soup was pushing it in James's opinion, but it settled his stomach. Once he finished it, he was presented with a pint of porter. "To build up the blood," Tiff said.

After lying there for a few hours, he felt well enough to get out of bed. He pulled on shirt and trousers before stepping out barefoot after deciding finding shoes would be too much trouble. The ever-present Dennis hovering just behind him, as he walked onto the deck.

The Silverthorn was still in the river but pointing downstream. It looked like her marines and Tiff's troops were back on board. He walked slowly to the quarterdeck.

"Good afternoon, James. It's good to see you up and about," Angus said.

"It's good to be moving," he looked around, "what's happened?"

"You haven't missed much. The Pindaris ran straight into Hastings' trap and surrendered without much of a fight. Those that dispersed tried to hide in villages but apparently, they weren't so popular, and the villagers turned on them."

"All over then."

"Yes. It would appear so."

"Why aren't we heading home?" James said noting the un-readiness to sail.

"We are waiting for a dignitary to join us."

"Courier service?"

"Something like that. Now you need to rest according to the surgeon. You will join me and him for dinner tonight."

Dinner was fresh caught, deep-fried river fish followed by rare roast venison with plenty of fresh greens. The gravy was rich and the wine a heavy red.

"Eat and drink, you lost a fair amount of blood as well as exhausting yourself," Simmonds said.

"I cannot remember getting wounded," James said.

"You were probably too busy fighting to notice," Angus said. "Apparently you accounted for at least a dozen."

"I wasn't keeping count," James blushed, "it would have been different if they had guns."

"Their choice, they have an honour code around the sword and spear."

"They are doomed then; the world has moved on."

Chapter 14: A Celebration.

The next morning James rose and dressed in uniform. If a worthy was coming onto his ship, he would be dressed properly to meet him. His bandages made the coat a little tight, but he thought he should look alright. He tried to put on boots but was too stiff so settled for shoes.

He reported to the quarterdeck.

"James, you have the deck," Angus said.

"What? Oh yes, Sir, I have the deck," he said a little confused. It wasn't time for a change of watch.

Angus went below, presumably to have his breakfast.

It was quiet. The water lapping past the hull the only sound until the lookout shouted down,

"Party approaching on horseback."

Must be the person of interest, James thought.

"Boat party to the side, visitors to be picked up from the north bank," he shouted.

He beckoned over a ship's boy. "My compliments to the captain and inform him that our visitor has arrived." He looked at the shore but couldn't see who it was as he, he assumed it was a he, was stood the other side of his horse. Whoever it was, was packing a pair of chests on a pack horse.

The boat tied up at the mooring stake set into the bank and several men jumped ashore to load the baggage. Once that was done, the personage climbed down into the boat. He needed an arm to steady him. He wore a dark cloak and civilian straw hat.

"Side party, man the side," James ordered and looked around.

That's strange, he thought as there was still no sign of the captain and the ship was abnormally quiet.

The boat clunked into the side and the ship's boys ran down the battens to hold out the side ropes. James was half expecting a call for a bosun's chair when a head appeared above the side. The pipes chirped and the marines stomped, crashing the butts of their Baker rifles onto the deck.

James blinked once then twice as he recognised...

His father. He recovered himself when Marty said, "Permission to come aboard."

"Permission granted. Welcome aboard, Commodore," James said formally.

Angus chose that moment to reappear and saluted. "Commodore, welcome to the Silverthorn."

"Thank you, Angus. To tell you the truth, I have had just about as much of horses as my backside can stand."

"Mr Stockley, please show the commodore to his quarters," Angus said.

James and everyone else knew that the commodore knew very well where his quarters were, and that Angus was giving them the chance to have some privacy.

When they got into the cabin Adam was already there unpacking. He took one look at James and made a diplomatic exit.

Marty held out his arms and James stepped in and hugged him. Marty kissed him on the cheek then looked concerned when James winced.

"Are you hurt?"

"I picked up a couple of scratches at the ford."

"Where?"

"Across my side."

"Take your shirt off let me see."

"Father!" James protested.

"That's an order, Midshipman."

James stripped his shirt off and Marty carefully unwrapped the bandage.

"A scratch? That has a dozen stiches in it."

"Matches the one on the other side."

Marty looked at the puckered scar. "You have more scars than when I was fifteen."

He rebound the bandage. "Not too tight?"

"No, it's just right, thank you."

"I won't tell your mother."

"Thank you, she would have a fit."

"You had better get back to your duties," Marty said. "Did you remember it is Christmas day tomorrow?"

James hadn't.

The next evening both crews had a party on shore. This was what the men had been below preparing for. They dug two large firepits and had a steer and a boar rotating on spits. Bread was being baked in Dutch ovens and the foragers had been out to find fresh greens. Homemade bunting was strung on lines between poles.

The officers dug into their wine supplies, the men had beer and rum. Between the marines and the crew, they found enough musicians to form a band and there was the singing of hymns, carols, and shanties. Some of the more agile danced hornpipes.

After they had eaten, Marty stood.

"Gentlemen, I wish to propose a toast, to the squadron and in particular the Silverthorn and Endellion who have proved themselves yet again in combat. The Silverthorn and Endellion!"

The men roared out the toast and emptied their glasses. Once they were refilled Marty proposed the traditional Thursday toast, "To a bloody war, or a sickly season," to which the officers answered, "And so a chance of promotion!"

That made the crew laugh.

"Now I ask our youngest midshipman to propose a toast to the king. James that is you."

James stood and took a deep breath, "Gentlemen, I give you King George. King of the United Kingdom, Great Britain and Ireland! God save the king!"

"God save the king!" roared the men. Now they were free to really party.

The officers retired to the Silverthorn quarterdeck where a table had been set with port and sweet madeira, nuts, cheese and cake. They sat around the table, some partaking of a cheroot or a pipe.

Marty was asked to tell of the campaign from his position on Hasting's staff.

"We set out the day after you left with a force of some thirty thousand men and cavalry led by Hastings. Hislop moved out of Madras around the same time and moved into their territory from the south. The plan was to drive them from their villages north to where Hastings was waiting on the north side of the river."

"A bit like beating birds on a shoot!" Tiff said.

"Exactly. However, the length of the river and the number of crossing points was the weak point in the planning. We absolutely had to force them to cross the river where we wanted them to, which is where you came in. Successfully denying them the western crossing points was vital. We were chosen for the mission because a combination of marines and soldiers stood the best chance. Hastings positioned us as planned to trap them against the river and Hislop's force. The anvil to his hammer. When they saw us lined up against them with thirty thousand troops and cannon with all or their escape routes blocked, they either gave up or broke off in small parties and ran."

"We have heard that the locals are taking the opportunity to exact some revenge," O'Driscol said.

"Yes, from all reports the Pindaris have not found a welcome anywhere. Their thieving past has finally caught up with them and several have been stoned to death. Now tell me what happened at the fords."

O'Driscol cleared his throat, "We fortified the north banks of all four fords. The first two with marines and the last with Lieutenant Hindon-Beechwell's infantry and marines. James was with that team to oversee the swivels.

The three western fords were deeper than the fourth. The water being chest deep or higher on a horse. We think that was why the Pindaris only made token efforts to cross them. They moved on but we stayed in place in case it was just a feint. Then we saw bodies floating down the river and realised they were trying to cross the fourth. By the number of corpses, we knew that there was some hot action going on so set out to reinforce them."

Tiff took over, recounting what happened at the third.

"When they got behind us, I have to confess I thought we were done for. But the men fought with discipline and vigour, and we held them off. James and his marines made a huge difference as they were firing their swivels as fast as we could reload our rifles."

Tiff looked at James and grinned, "James's marksmanship took care of a good handful of them before they got in range of our volley."

James blushed and Marty beamed with pride. His son was turning out to be a thorough chip of the old block.

The party lasted into the early hours and the next morning most of the crew were hungover. There had been a couple of incidents that would need taking care of. A fight that had ended up with one man in the infirmary with a serious head injury, and a second incident that ended up with drawn knives before the marines stepped in and stopped it. Forcibly.

"When can we start for home?" Marty asked Angus.

"Tomorrow morning, I want to hold captain's court this afternoon, and the crew need a day to recover."

Marty agreed, the river was tricky and to safely navigate it they needed a crew that was sober and not hungover. At six bells in the afternoon watch, all hands were called to the main deck for captain's court. Marines lined the rail in front of the quarterdeck.

The master at arms and two of his mates brought the first offender to the fore. James had the job of announcing them and the charges.

"Able seaman Frederick Bath, foretopman. Accused of striking Terrance Arthur with an empty rum bottle causing him to bleed from both ears and his eyes. The victim is still unconscious in the infirmary and the surgeon has reported that he is not sure that he will recover as he fears his skull is broken."

Angus looked down at the man, "Fredrick Bath, until now your conduct has been exemplary. You have distinguished yourself in a number of hot actions. What have you to say for yourself?"

"Captain Sir, I honestly cannot remember what happened, the drink got a hold of me is my only excuse."

"Are there any witnesses?"

Bath was a popular man but the men looked to be unwilling to step forward. Angus tried again,

"At this time Bath is looking at fifty lashes is there anyone with information that might lend some reason to his offence?"

A sailor stepped forward.

"Yes, Cedric, what have you to say?"

"It weren't all Fred's fault, Sir, Terry Arthur was baiting him with comments about his daughter."

"Does he know your daughter?" Angus said.

"Aye, Sir, we are from the same town."

"What prompted his comments?"

"He wanted to wed her, but she weren't interested and married a farrier. I suppose he could still be holdin' a candle for her."

"Did anyone hear what caused the final conflict?"

Another man stepped forward, "Terry did call his daughter a whore, Sir."

"I see. Is that when Fred struck him?"

"Aye, Sir."

Fred was looking wretched, and Angus was considering what punishment to set when the surgeon pushed his way through to the front.

"Captain, I have to report that Terrence Arthur has just passed away."

Marty stepped up to Angus. Until then he had stayed back and let him get on with it.

"Captain, this has now to be treated as a murder and heard in front of a court martial," he said

"Yes, I agree, Commodore." He turned to the master at arms, "Take the prisoner below and put him in irons. He will stay under arrest on a charge of murder to be tried in front of a court martial." Angus was angry and when the other two offenders were brought forward, he summarily sentenced them to two dozen lashes each. Sentence was carried out immediately.

They set sail as soon as it was light the next day. They caught up with the corpses of men and horses that had become tangled in snags and tree roots. The smell was noxious, and it wasn't until they had sailed for a further day that they left them behind. Marty noticed Angus was brooding,

"Thinking about the men who came up for punishment?"

Angus sighed, "More about my behaviour, I sentenced those men in anger."

"The punishment was within bounds, they drew weapons. Look, we do not often have to flog men in the squadron, but we should not be shy of it if it is necessary. You were angry for the right reason. A man had died unnecessarily. The sentence was probably the same as you would have given if calm. The only difference was the haste it was given in," Marty said.

They called in to Bombay on the way home. Marty wanted to give the men some shore time in town, and it gave him time to go shopping for Christmas presents. He took James with him.

"You need to buy your mother and the twins Christmas presents," Marty said as they walked down the busy streets.

"What about you?" James said.

"I will be buying them presents as well."

"No, I meant what about a present for you?"

"For me? You don't need to bother about me. I have everything I need."

James didn't think that was very helpful.

They came across a shop selling silk and sarees. Marty was taken with a beautiful blue brocade that had a floral motif in silver and gold thread. He could imagine Caroline in it, so he called the shopkeeper over and asked him about it.

"Oh, Sahib, this is a saree of the finest silk from Banaris. The best in India. The zari thread is made from pure gold and silver."

"A saree? So, this is a traditional Indian dress?"

"Oh yes! Sahib, worn only by the highest-ranking ladies on special occasions."

"I would like to see it on a woman of about this height." Marty held out his hand to indicate Caroline's height.

"Is she slender?" the keeper said.

"Yes, she is rather."

Marty was offered a seat and served chai flavoured with cardamom, ginger, and black pepper. James joined him as he was intrigued to see what he was going to buy.

"I won't be able to afford much on my mid's pay," he said.

Marty slapped his forehead, "I forgot to tell you, the chest that you found has been declared prize money."

"I thought it would be declared droits of the crown."

"So did we, but the prize court declared it was found as part of an action and therefore a prize. Your share will be several thousand pounds. I will advance you what you need."

The curtains at the rear of the shop opened and an Indian woman stepped out dressed in the saree. She was stunning and showed off the outfit to its best advantage.

"Where did he find her?" James said out the side of his mouth.

Marty grinned. His boy was exhibiting exquisite taste.

Marty bought the saree along with a matched pair of silk slippers. It was expensive but he thought it was worth it on the gold content alone. James had an inspiration and headed for a jeweller he had seen earlier. He dragged Marty along, "I need to have that material nearby when I make my choice," he said.

The jeweller sold traditional Indian jewellery and a gold choker necklace caught his eye. It had three bands of woven gold laced with aquamarine beads. The strands were held apart by eight, evenly spaced, vertical bars, formed of gold flowers set with sapphires of pale blue, from which dangled tear-shaped pearls set in gold and sapphire mounts. They held it up against the saree and it was the perfect match.

"If the sahib desires I can make a set of matching earrings."

James agreed once the man guaranteed to have them ready by the morning.

That was Caroline taken care of. Now they turned their attention to the twins. At ten years old they were getting into all sorts of things. Constance was into horses. She rode well and was interested in their bloodlines and characteristics. Marty thought she would get into breeding later. Edwin was also interested in riding but had ambitions of being a soldier.

A leather shop provided James with a chance to buy Constance an ornate bridle for her favourite pony. With just his brother and Father to buy for, he parted company with Marty and set off on his own. Edwin was fond of hunting and followed the hunt run by their neighbours. A popular sport was pig sticking. Hunting wild boar with spears. James wondered about that. It was easier to shoot the damn things than spear them from horseback, but then he remembered the Pindaris lancers. Pig sticking would hone the skills of a cavalryman without doubt. Edwin would get a pair of pig spears for Christmas.

What the hell can I get Father? He wandered, but first there was one other present he wanted to get.

The ships left Bombay and made the trip back to Calcutta. They arrived too late for New Year but that didn't quell the locals' enthusiasm. The British liked a hero and Hastings had been talking up their contribution. So that when the ships arrived outside of Fort William an enthusiastic crowd cheered them home.

James was particularly happy. He was pretty much healed; the stitches were out, and the memory of the fight had faded. He did not feel like a hero. It felt like just another day, but he looked across the dock and there was his mother, brother, and sister. He looked for and found Melissa standing close to his mother.

He decided to stand back and let the worthies and senior officers get the greetings over and done with. He wanted to slip away as soon as they were given leave. But it was not to be, he and Tiff were called forward to be presented to Hastings.

"I'm told you were wounded. I trust you are recovered?" Hastings said to James.

"I am, thank you, Sir. It was nothing really."

"Just like his father. A chip off the old block, eh?" Hastings guffawed to Marty.

James smiled embarrassed.

It wasn't long before the worthies buggered off and they could go ashore. James and his followers headed straight for the house.

"Welcome home," Caroline said. "Just in time for dinner, I assume you are hungry."

"Always," James laughed. He was a growing lad after all.

After dinner came the belated giving and receiving of presents. Caroline was delighted with the saree and jewellery that Marty and James had bought for her. She resolved then and there to wear it to the ball that was being thrown at Government House that Saturday.

Edwin loved his spears and Constance the bridle. He finally turned to his father and presented him with a long box.

"What's this?" Marty said and undid the ribbon that held it shut. Inside was a Pindaris sword with its curious guard that was almost like a sleeve. Marty took it out and examined it.

"The blade is old, probably late 1600," James said, "the hilt and guard are later."

"It can still cut. The steel is surprisingly good," Marty said testing the edge with his thumb. "Did you take this at the ford?"

"I did, I thought you would like it for your collection."

"It's wonderful, thank you."

They sat and Marty said, "Did you know that after the Pindaris were defeated Hislop carried on north to Mahidpur where he found the Holkar army. They fought on 21st December and pretty much wiped them out."

"So, it is done then," James said.

"Yes, it would appear so. It's all over bar the shouting, as John used to say." Marty smiled.

James excused himself not long after that and went to the wing where the Shadows lived to find Melissa. He found her in a sitting room with Tabetha and Mary.

He knocked on the door and entered. The women glanced at each other, then at Melissa who only had eyes for James.

"Why don't you two go for a walk around the grounds," Tabetha said.

Melissa blushed when James bowed and held out his arm. She stood and curtsied before taking his arm and allowed him to lead her through the open French doors to the gardens. The grounds were patrolled so they were never really alone.

They walked without saying anything for a while then James stopped and said, "I got you a Christmas present." He reached inside his jacket and produced a narrow box tied with a blue ribbon. Her hands shook as she opened it.

"Oh! It's beautiful!" she gasped as she held up the slender gold chain with a five-petal flower pendant set with emeralds.

"Let me put it on for you," James said and was surprised that his hands were steady and not shaking when he threaded it around her neck and did up the clasp.

"I don't have a present for you," Melissa said.

"Oh, don't worry about that. Seeing you safe and here at the house is enough."

Melissa stepped forward and kissed him on the cheek.

"Thank you."

A cough from the darkness warned them they were not alone, and his father and mother walked up arm in arm.

"Have you asked Melissa to accompany you to the ball?" Caroline said.

"I was about to," James said. annoyed that his mother had pre-empted him. He turned back to Melissa.

"Would you do me the honour of accompanying me to the ball?"

"I would be honoured," Melissa said then turned to Caroline wide eyed. "I haven't got a ball gown!"

"Don't worry, you are about the same size as Beth and she left some of her gowns here. I am sure we can adapt one," Caroline said.

After that Melissa was invited to eat with the family.

"Don't you think you are pushing them a little fast?" Marty said.

"I don't know what you mean." Caroline feigned an air of innocence.

"Don't come the innocent with me, I know you too well."

"She is very suitable,"

"Have you forgotten your youth?"

"That's not fair! I'm not marrying him off to an old woman."

"But you are meddling."

Caroline had to admit she was.

"Leave them to it. If it works out, all well and good. If it doesn't, he will find a match that suits him in his own time," Marty said.

Caroline huffed, but she knew that Marty was right.

The days running up to the ball were the usual frenetic preparation for the women. The men just carried on as normal. Caroline employed the services of their Indian maids to get the saree just right as the intricate pleating was beyond her. At the same time Melissa chose one of Beth's gowns. A pale-yellow satin creation with crinoline petticoats. Caroline had a dressmaker fit it and once complete had to admit she did it justice.

Melissa had no experience of anything like this. Her family had not been of a class to attend events like this. The concentration of the dressmaker and the attention to detail that Caroline demanded was an eye opener. She had no idea that ladies put in this much effort.

"Silk stockings are a must," Caroline said and presented her with a pair of the finest along with garters. "You have good legs."

Melisa felt a bit like a prize mare, but it was made up for when she saw herself in a full-length mirror for the first time.

"Is that me?" she exclaimed.

"It's no one else," Caroline smiled.

"You em a beautiful woman," Tabetha said.

"All you need now is some jewellery," Caroline said.

"If you don't mind, I will just wear James' necklace."

"Naturally, but a few jewels in your hair will not detract from that," Caroline said and produced a box of jewelled hairpins.

Saturday evening came and a nervous James waited in the living room. Marty sat in a chair reading the paper.

"Sit down. You will wear a hole in the carpet," he said without looking up.

"Didn't you get nervous when you took Mother out for the first time?"

"Didn't get a chance. We met at a ball."

"What happened?"

"I fought a duel."

The door opened and Caroline walked in a vision in traditional Indian dress. The servants had placed a bindi mark on her forehead to signify she was married.

"Suits you. You look stunning," Marty said as he stood.

Melissa walked in at that point and for James the world stood still then proceeded at a crawl.

The dress looked like it had been made for her, her hair was arranged Venetian style and fell across her left shoulder and glinted with jewels that had been woven into it. The pendant, hung just right and sparkled in the light.

"Well?" she said.

"Well?" James said.

"How do I look?"

"Unbelievable." James seemed to have forgotten how to speak.

"Come on," Marty said, taking him by the arm, "the carriage is waiting."

The ball was two things. A celebration of the end of the Pindaris menace and a statement of British supremacy. Prominent Indians were invited and the stairs to the main entrance to the building were awash with colour. The Stockley coach pulled up and footmen rushed to place steps and clear an area for them to dismount.

Marty stepped down and held out his hand to Caroline. When she appeared, there was an audible gasp from the people nearby. Several Indian ladies bowed with their palms together in front of them, beaming smiles on their faces. The Indian men smiled and held their palms together and nodded.

Caroline reflected the greeting then took Marty's arm. Melissa and James walked behind them up the steps to the grand entrance. All the way they were greeted in the same fashion as people stood aside to give them passage.

"You've made an impact. The Indian ladies love it that you dressed like them," Marty said out the corner of his mouth.

They reached the entrance to the ballroom and the herald announced them. The reaction amongst the British fell into one of two categories. They loved it, or they thought it inappropriate. However, all had to admit she looked fantastic. Some were outraged as when she moved a sliver of slim, toned, bare midriff could sometimes be seen.

"Lord Martin, Lady Caroline," Hastings said.

"Caroline that... dress is fantastic," Flora said.

"It's a saree which Martin bought me in Bombay for Christmas, the jewels were a present from James."

"Some will think you've gone native," Hastings said.

"No, not native but an acknowledgement of the wonder of their culture. There is no denying the craftsmanship in the weaving of the cloth and the creation of the jewellery," Caroline said.

Flora took a fold of the cloth in her hand, "You are right this cloth is amazing."

They moved on so James and Melissa could be presented.

"James, how are you? Who is this beauty that you have brought with you?" Flora said.

"May I present Miss Melissa Crownbridge."

Flora took Melissa's hand. "I don't think we have met. When did you arrive?"

"I was one of those rescued from Burma, Ma'am," Melissa said, quite unsure how to address the governor's wife. "My parents were both killed by the pirates."

"Oh my! You poor girl. Where are you living now?"

"Lady Caroline has taken me under her wing."

James, seeing that Melissa was uncomfortable stepped in,

"Come, we mustn't hold the line up and the orchestra is about to begin playing."

Flora's eyes twinkled, and she said, "Yes, off you go young ones and have some fun."

James didn't get to keep her all to himself as Tiff arrived, resplendent in full dress uniform and insisted on one dance. He had proven himself in the eyes of his regiment and was a lot happier now. His lisp had proven to be a symptom of his lack of confidence and was almost indiscernible which matched his confident bearing.

Chapter 15: Endings and Beginnings

After the ball, things quietened down to a more regular existence. The squadron ran patrols in the Bay of Bengal down as far as the Strait of Malacca until Marty decided that all his ships could do with a refit. The dockyards in Calcutta were more than capable and, starting with the Unicorn, they were brought into dry dock.

The only thing that spoiled the tranquillity in Calcutta was the court martial of Frederick Bath for the murder of Terrance Arthur. A panel of four post captains chaired by Marty was assembled and the court was held in Government House.

The evidence was heard and examined then Marty summed up after the bench had discussed it.

"It is our conclusion that your action was on the spur of the moment and not pre-meditated, nor was there an intention to kill. Therefore, the charge should be manslaughter, not murder. You are found not guilty of murder but guilty of the charge of involuntary manslaughter."

Fred nearly fainted when he heard that, and they waited until he had recovered to continue.

"There are mitigating circumstances, but in the end the taking of the life of a shipmate cannot go unpunished. You are hereby sentenced to one hundred lashes in front of the fleet."

A strong man could survive a hundred lashes, for a weak man it was a death sentence. Bath was strong and Marty ordered the punishment to be given in two parts separated by time to recuperate. He had been given every chance to survive.

The sentence would be carried out on the dock. The crews of the ships in harbour would witness the punishment. They would either line up along the side of their ships or parade on the dock. The punishment was as much a warning to the men as it was a punishment for the crime.

A grating was set up and Fred marched out by marines with fixed bayonets. Shelby was in attendance. Fred was stripped to the waist and Shelby tied a leather apron around him that covered his kidneys. He stood in front of the grating and asked to lean against it in the star position. A master at arms tied his wrists and ankles to stop him moving.

Two bosun's mates stepped up. One left-handed the other right. They would give five lashes then hand over to the other until the full fifty had been given. As a further sign of mercy Marty had ordered they not be replaced with fresh men. They took the cats out of the red velvet bags. Fred had made the cats and the bags himself as was traditional.

"Let the sentence be served," Marty said

The first mate stepped up and shook out the tails.

"Lay on," the master at arms said.

Fred didn't move for the first five or the next. He uttered no sound for the first thirty-five strokes. As the thirty-sixth landed, he groaned then shook his head and took the next silently. At the end of the fifty his back was a mess. Shelby stepped forward and talked to him. Marty heard him say, "Are you sure?"

Shelby stepped forward and said, "The accused requests you finish the punishment with the next fifty."

Marty was surprised, this was unprecedented. "Is he able to take fifty more?" he said.

"The man is as strong as an ox. His heart is beating steadily albeit at an elevated rate."

"Why does he want to take all one hundred as once."

"If you want my opinion, he is suffering from acute guilt for killing Arthur and this is his way of expunging it."

"He is paying penance then."

"If you like."

Marty considered. He didn't like the idea of flogging at the best of times. He announced in a quarterdeck bellow, "The condemned has asked that we complete the sentence. What is the state of the cats?"

"Mine be fine," the first mate responded. The second piped up with, "Mine be good too."

"Let the punishment be completed."

After a full hundred they cut him down, he could barely stand, and the blood flowed freely from his back. A marine went to take his arm, but Fred shrugged him off and with a force of will stood upright and walked unaided from the dock to his ship. Shelby followed and as soon as they were aboard took him to the infirmary.

"He will go down in legend for that performance," Marty said.

"Well, he won't be performing any duties for at least a month. His back is shredded," Shelby said.

"No more than I expected," Marty said.

With the war almost over and the dominion of the East India Company assured, life settled down to pure tedium on the work front. There were skirmishes and minor confrontations but by June it was pretty much all over and done with.

Marty looked his son up and down; he was almost full grown now and filled out his uniform well.

"What day is it today?" he said.

"Why, to be honest I have completely lost track."

"I haven't. Today is June the twentieth 1818."

"My birthday?"

"Yes, your sixteenth birthday."

James had returned from an uneventful patrol and was now on shore for a month. He had developed into a competent officer and Marty would have him take his lieutenants exams as soon as he could.

"You need to get yourself fitted out with a suit of civilian clothes. Your mother is planning a party."

James groaned, if his mother was organising his birthday party, he would be the youngest there. Marty read his mind.

"Don't worry, Melissa is taking care of the guest list," he said and put his arm around his son's shoulders.

James perked up. He hadn't had a chance to see Melissa since his return. She had turned seventeen while he was away, and he had no chance to get her a present.

Marty was aware of his son's attraction to the girl and he had to be honest and say that he didn't blame him. Melissa was a catch for any man. She had blossomed in the six months or so that she had been working as Caroline's secretary and was developing her own sense of style. The East India Company had awarded her compensation for being captured on one of their ships and now she had money of her own she no longer relied on Beth's clothes.

But right at that moment Melissa was busy working with Caroline and James knew better than to disturb his mother while she was attending to business.

"Any idea what your next mission will be?" James said.

"No, I've not heard anything but the job here is done so I expect new orders any day. There has been time for the news to get back to England and for Admiral Turner and the government to find something else for us to do."

The party was not the grand affair he feared but a more intimate occasion. Melissa had invited the midshipmen James was friendly with from the squadron and a great time was had by all.

Caroline breezed into Marty's office and found her men chatting about navy things.

"You have a letter, dear, it was with my mail," she said and held out a packet.

Marty looked at James and grinned as he took it.

"Am I missing something?" Caroline said.

"We were surmising when my new orders would arrive," Marty said, then noticed that James had suddenly been distracted. Melissa had followed Caroline into the room.

"Why don't you two go for a walk," he said.

Marty slit the fouled anchor seal and removed the waxed paper wrapper. Inside was another sealed envelope and inside that a letter.

"Blah, blah, blah, aah here we go. Oh!"

"Well, what is it? Are we going home?"

"You can."

"There's a but coming," Carline frowned.

"The squadron has been ordered to Bengkoelen to support the new governor, Sir Thomas Sanford Bingley Raffles."

"Where on earth is that?"

"On the island of Sumatra. Look its here." Marty pointed to a spot on a large globe. "It's a strip down the west coast."

"Why that is halfway to Australasia!"

"Yes, and largely un-tamed. Apparently, the former governor was murdered, and the place is a mess. Raffles is going to have to put in place reforms and that will not be easy." Marty read the third page. "Apparently there is somewhere called Singapore Island where he wants to establish a free port. It will command the Malacca Strait and we are ordered to thin the pirates out and stamp our authority on the region."

For Caroline and the household, the preparations for leaving were pretty much a mirror of the ones in London. Last minute shopping for those unique items that could only be found in India, provisions for the trip home, precious stones for trade in England. It was all unnecessarily frantic in Marty's opinion.

On the other hand, there was the squadron which, under the management of Fletcher, provisioned stores, spares and fuel for the galleys. Officer's private stores came in, jars of preserves, butter, cheeses, dried meats, pulses, and rice. Livestock was housed in the mangers on the fore decks. Rolland had learned how to cook dal and bought a supply of lentils and spices. He could work wonders with them and dried meat. All this was done with the minimum of fuss and absolutely no drama.

Jeanette went to work with Frances Ridgley as she enjoyed the intrigue of intelligence. A new military attaché was on his way out from England, but his role would be more formal than Marty's and he wouldn't need a secretary of his own.

There was drama to spare at the house. Melissa was heartbroken to be leaving James and would burst into tears at the drop of a hat. The argument that he had been away more than at home during their brief courtship didn't wash and Caroline gave up and left her to it. She was surprised when Melissa turned up puffy eyed but determined in her office and asked to join her at fencing practice. The logic behind the request was quite simple. If James was going to spend his life sailing into danger, then she would learn how to fight and go with him. Caroline didn't have the heart to explain that navy wives didn't accompany their men, Melissa would have to find that out for herself.

The Pride of Purbeck, had been refitted. New copper and rigging, refurbished cabins, metal water tanks fitted. She was ready to go. The plan was she would stop off at Madras to meet up with the regular Stockley ship and the two would sail back to Britain together. This would be safer and quicker than tagging along with a Company convoy.

The day came when the squadron had to leave. Marty took his place in the Unicorn, his pennant flying proudly from the mast. The ships warped out into the channel and started down river. As they approached Fort William Marty said, "Ready the salute for the governor."

As the flagship, the Unicorn had the honour of firing the salute on behalf of the squadron and their misshapen gunner was on deck. Wolverton set the timing, not by a chant but with a watch. He was a modern man and embraced technology.

A crowd had gathered to wave goodbye to the ships and prominent were Caroline, the twins, and the household. All of whom had turned out to wave farewell to their men. The guns fired from fore to aft twenty-one times, at precisely five-second intervals. The smoke from the guns blew across the river to the south bank. Marty raised his hat to the shore as they passed, giving it a little wave to Caroline.

Melissa waited, handkerchief in hand, waiting for the Silverthorn which was fourth in line. James was at his place on the quarterdeck.

"Oh, for heaven's sake give the girl a wave," Angus said, looking at the anguished look on James' face.

"Young hearts, Sir," Yateley the helm said.

"Indeed, we were all young once." Angus smiled. He had already decided he would be keeping his young mid busy for the first week or so of the voyage to keep him from brooding.

James waved his hat vigorously at the shore answered by the fluttering handkerchief held by Melissa. Behind him waving both arms stood Dennis; a huge grin in his face.

Marty had the squadron exercise daily. His concern was that the fruitless patrols had blunted their combat readiness. He and Wolfgang worked out tactics for combatting pirates who tended to attack en masse in smaller boats.

Reports from ships that had survived attacks also led them to believe that there were several different groups of pirates from Sumatra, Java, Malay, Burma and China. The Chinese were especially concerning as they had a lot of large armed junks that could threaten even the Unicorn.

Different formations and strategies were given numbers which could be quickly signalled. Marty wanted the action on those signals to be equally fast. Rate of fire was the other important factor in a fight against massed small boats. Accordingly, gun drill burnt through an enormous amount of powder. Marty had anticipated that and had Wolverton fill each ship to capacity.

The marines were also put under pressure, Captain O'Driscol had them drill volley fire and sharpshooting. He wanted three rounds a minute from their Baker rifles in volley, which was a very hard target. Normally one would only expect that rate of fire from smooth bore muskets. The rifled barrels of the Bakers made that impossible if you loaded them traditionally. Accordingly, they adopted the method used by the 95th Rifles. Bite off the ball from the top of the cartridge, prime the pan, pour the charge into the barrel followed by the cartridge paper, spit in the ball, bang the butt on the deck three times to seat the ball. The ball was not wrapped in a wad, so this method didn't give the legendary accuracy of the rifle. It did, however, get a lot of rounds down range which was more important.

The sharpshooters, who fought from the tops, loaded their rifles traditionally for maximum accuracy. They had swivels to shoot down into any boats that came alongside, and their speed drill was to reload them as fast as possible.

"Lookout below!"

A can of cannister fell from the main top and the men below scattered as it smashed into the deck. Balls flying in all directions as it burst.

"Who dropped that?" Sergeant Bright bellowed.

"Sorry, Sarg, that were me," Marine Axel shouted down.

"Get your arse down here now!"

Marine Axel hit the deck and stood at attention in a single movement. Bright walked around him looking him up and down.

"You are an 'orrible example of a marine, your uniform is a fucking mess!"

Axel knew better than to react and stared at a point somewhere off to starboard.

"What is your excuse for dropping that canister?"

"No excuse, Sarg."

"So, you are incompetent?"

"Just trying hard, Sarg."

"Get back up there, I want to see a round every twenty seconds and do not drop another canister or you will be cleaning the heads for a week."

"Aye, aye, Sarg."

Marine Axel ran back up the ratlines to his station. Bright followed him and watched as he went through the loading procedure.

"You are five seconds too slow. Do it again."

The swivel was unloaded, not as easy as it sounds as it involved using a worm.

"Clear," Axel reported.

"Prepare to reload, start!" Bright shouted and counted.

"One and two and three and…"

Axel was calm and focussed and had just loaded the cartridge of powder when a rifle went off. Bright had fired his, "Ten and eleven."

Axel dropped the canister down the barrel followed by a wad and used a short ram to seat it.

"Done!" Axel shouted.

"Twenty-two seconds."

"Thank you, Sarg. Will try harder, Sarg."

"Keep at it. I'm watching you," Bright snarled and went back to the deck.

Marty had watched the exercises from the quarterdeck. They were approaching the Anderman Islands where they would turn south to run down the outside of them. Marty walked over to the chart table.

"We are heading for Bengkoelen, where we will meet with Raffles. After that we will patrol the straits. Unfortunately, the only two options for a base at this time are Bengkoelen, which is the wrong side of Sumatra, and George Town on Penang Island. Which is at the wrong end of the straits," he said to Arnold and Wolfgang.

"Could we establish our own base? On Singapore Island perhaps?" Wolfgang said.

"There is no British presence there yet, but I am told that Raffles is going to try and establish a trade port."

"Oh, so our presence could upset that."

"It might, we need to be wary, but Singapore would be ideal."

They arrived off Bengkoelen and Wolfgang eyed the bay. The wind was constant from the southwest.

"That is not going to be an easy harbour to get out of with this wind," Wolfgang murmured to himself.

The harbour was, fortunately, wide and would allow the ships to tack out against the wind. It would take time but it was possible as was evidenced by a merchantman flogging back and forth on short tacks to make the exit.

"Signal the squadron to anchor in line with the Unicorn," he said to the mid on signal duty.

"I want plenty of sea room for us to beat out of there. If there is decent holding ground in the middle of the bay, we will anchor there."

And that is what they did. Firing a twenty-one-gun salute as they entered.

Marty was not surprised when a carriage appeared near the dock. He had already had his barge brought alongside and the Shadows had manned it with Sam at the tiller. He dropped down into it to the serenade of the Spithead nightingales.

As they docked, a tall slender man in European dress stepped out of the coach. He waited for Marty at the end of the dock. Antton and Matai preceded Marty and took up position to either side.

Raffles looked at them curiously. When Marty joined him and they shook hands said, "Stamford Raffles, you must be Commodore Stockley. Are your men guarding you? The island is quite safe you know."

"Hello, pleased to meet you. Yes, they are, it's standard procedure when visiting a strange shore."

"We should go to the residence, it's a lot cooler and less mosquitoes," Raffles said, indicating he should join him in the coach.

They climbed into the carriage which was like a landau in design with an open top. Antton took a seat next to the driver and Matai stood on the rear step. Raffles kept up a running commentary describing the various sights as they took the ten-minute ride to the house. It was smaller than Marty expected.

When they pulled up at the front door, a servant came out to set the steps and open the carriage door to let them down. Matai, however, was faster and the sight of the well-armed stranger caused them to hesitate. When Antton joined him, it was too much, and they retreated inside.

"I say! Your men are frightening my servants. Do they need to be so... severe?"

"I could ask them to smile, I suppose," Marty said dryly. He relented once they got to Raffles' study.

"Why don't you two go and get something to drink in the kitchens," he said. Raffles looked relieved and rang a bell for tea.

"I got a letter from Hastings saying that you were finally free and could come to assist me," Raffles said.

"Interesting as I got my orders from London."

"Ah, yes. I met with Viscount Castlereagh and your Admiral Turner in London."

"What did Robert Stewart and the admiral tell you?"

"That you had a squadron perfectly suited for my needs and that you were already in Calcutta assisting Hastings. I gathered that you and your ships fall outside of the regular navy."

"We are a special unit. We take care of things the navy don't want to do or do not want to be seen doing."

"Well, you don't need to worry about that here, everything is above board. Oh, I almost forgot I have a packet for you from Turner."

He went to his desk and recovered a packet from a locked drawer. Marty took it and placed it on the table beside him without opening it. Raffles looked at it curiously, "You aren't going to open it?"

"Later, there's no hurry," Marty said. "What do you want us to do?"

"Didn't they tell you?"

"Yes, but I prefer to hear it first-hand."

"There are bands of pirates from Java, Sumatra, Burma and China roaming the straits. They hide amongst the islands and attack our ships. We need to reduce their numbers."

"And what about Singapore Island?"

"That's the key to it all." Raffles spent the next half hour telling Marty about his plans. "So, you see it's the best option, I have looked into all the alternatives including Bangka.

"To summarise then," Marty said, "setting up a trade port on the island will break the hegemony of the Dutch. Will they not object?"

"Elout, their governor, is aggressively opposed to anything British. I suspect he was behind the assassination of my predecessor."

"That is quite an accusation, do you have any proof?"

"No, none. Just a suspicion. I would be obliged if you could look into it."

"I could stay here with my team and send my ships out to patrol the straits, I suppose." He pondered the idea. "I will keep the Endellion here. The rest can leave soon."

Chapter 16: Murder Most Foul

Alone in his cabin Marty opened the packet. It contained a letter from James Turner, and copies of maps and a memorandum on the state of the area written in 1809. He read:

In 1785 the Presidency of Fort Marlborough was reduced to a Residency and made subject to the control of the Bengal Government.

In the year 1800 the Government of Bengal decided a Civil Officer with the title of Lieutenant Governor be appointed from Bengal, and who managed Civil and Military elements of the Settlement.

In 1801 the Company saw an annual loss of £87,000 by the establishment in Fort Marlborough. They decided that the residencies should be withdrawn and the permanent establishment reduced to the resident, four assistants and four writers and including the Military was not to exceed an expenditure of Dollars 61018 per Annum.

"Not profitable then," he said to himself. He read further and had confirmed that the only reason they were still here was to annoy the Dutch.

He turned to a new page and read that on his arrival, Parr reduced all the public establishments, throwing people out of employment, and reducing many to starvation. Accustomed to the strict practical forms of Bengal, and the unlimited obedience found there, Parr's approach to a people who required the opposite mode of treatment caused great offence. He changed the native courts, without the agreement of or even consulting the chiefs, and occasionally took the chair himself, which made them fear for their ancient institutions and customs. He moved too fast, without due regard to the temperament of the people and tried to force them to cultivate coffee which they loathed. He appeared to have grown discontent to a crisis... The country was in a state of revolt; but he was blind to the danger.

There was an account of the murder from Parr's wife in a letter to her brother.

My beloved husband was, on the night of the 23rd of December, torn from his bed by Malays and murdered in my sight, but do not believe that Parr's wife, and your sister, endeavoured, like a coward, to save herself by flight until she had used her weak efforts to assist the father of her children, the dear valued friend and husband of her heart. Not, my brother, until I had my hands and body stabbed did I think of my poor infant boy in the next room...

Yes, they cut off the head of my Parr to take to their chief. Blessed head! Blessed face! But his last breath was mine, He saw me struggle with the first monster who came into the room, to seize his creese that I might gain it to defend himself with — all would not do. My hands were cut to pieces, my bosom had four stabs, and I was stamped on and kicked to the other end of the room... How I should have boasted of them had my Parr's life been spared, and he would have so flattered me for my activity. Why did I not always make him keep arms? But he was displeased when I ever urged it and asserted: "I never did an injury to any man, I have nothing to fear." From a revengeful assassin he had everything to fear.

The head, it appeared, had been left in the nursery and the perpetrators had taken a watch instead.

To Marty this all seemed cut and dried. Parr had upset the natives to the point they killed him. He did note that the watch was never recovered. He also read that a contingent of marines had extracted revenge and executed suspected perpetrators. Some by being tied over the mouths of cannon. The Company paid for his wife and children to be shipped home which indicated he might have had financial woes as well. He decided to investigate to confirm whether there was Dutch involvement or not.

The squadron, less the Endellion, left port the next morning on the tide. Marty and the Shadows watched them go. They would re-join them once his investigation was concluded. Raffles had given them a house which they could use as a base and a pair of carts pulled by oxen shifted them and their gear there. Marty asked for and got the services of an interpreter.

"We will visit the scene of the crime first," Marty said.

Mount Felix had not been lived in since the murder in 1807 and had succumbed to the ravages of time. What was left was a shell which the jungle was succeeding in taking back.

Marty walked through the ruin. Stepping over roots and brushing aside vines that hung through holes in the ceiling. There was no question of going to the upper floors as the wood had been consumed by termites. The boys were stationed outside, alert for any intruders.

It was impossible to tell what room had been used for what purpose. He shrugged and was about to leave when a glint caught his eye. He bent down and picked it up. It was a broken watch chain from the T-bar to the fob, which had been removed. He put it in his pocket.

"Who were the main suspects?" he asked the interpreter whose name was Pramana.

"I was a teenager when it happened. They accused the chiefs of the village next to ours and the one beyond that. They burnt the villages and put most of the men to death."

"Indiscriminate then. I assume that the ones who were killed were not the right ones."

Pramana looked uncomfortable and didn't answer.

"I am not interested in punishing anyone," Marty said. "The whole thing is ancient history as far as I am concerned and from what I read he pretty much made his own bed. All I want to find out is whether there was any Dutch involvement."

Pramana thought for a long moment before saying, "I can take you to the son of the chief who ordered the killing."

"Is the chief dead?"

"No, but he is old and will only talk to you if his son asks him."

They were warned that it was a two-day walk to get to the village where the old chief lived. They were prepared for that and had brought packs and camping gear with them.

It was the wet season and when it wasn't raining the ground steamed. They wore oilskins and broad-brimmed hats, but it was so humid and hot that they just got soaked with sweat inside them. Keeping their cartridges dry was another problem and Marty told the boys to keep their guns unloaded until they needed them. They all went as far as to stop up their barrels with corks and coat the actions in oil.

That night they stopped in a village and were given a long house furnished with hammocks to sleep in. The villagers were friendly enough once Pramana introduced them and they were fed roast pork for their evening meal. They were happy just to get dry and slept well.

The next morning dawned misty but free of rain. They set out unencumbered by their oilskins and reached the village just after midday.

Pramana asked for the chief's son and after a short wait he appeared. The two men spent several minutes talking then they walked over to Marty.

"This is Cahya the son of the chief. He wants to know why you want to know about the killing of Parr?" Pramana said and then stood by to do a simultaneous translation,

"The new lieutenant governor Mr Raffles wants to end the slavery imposed by the Dutch and to improve the way that the islands are governed. He wishes to involve the island chiefs but there is a suspicion that the Dutch encouraged the chiefs to kill Parr. I am here to find the truth."

"Are you a chief?"

"I am what is called a viscount, a lord amongst the British and a commodore in His Majesty's Navy with six ships and over a thousand men."

"Do you know King George?"

"I do and I am a friend of his son Prince George who will be King after him."

When that was translated a murmur went around the gathered villagers. Cahya left with Pramana in tow.

Sam stepped up beside him, "You think there will be trouble?" he said, eyeing the villagers warily.

"No, they are just curious."

Marty was right. Billy and Sam were drawing admiring stares from the local women, they were probably the biggest men they had ever seen. The rest of the boys stood at ease grinning at the two big men's discomfort.

Time ticked by and Sam's stomach rumbled loudly causing the women and girls to giggle. Food was produced, there was rice and pieces of what tasted like pork served on leaves.

Cahya and Pramana returned. "My father will see you, Lord Mr Martin. Your men must stay here."

Marty handed his rifle to Adam and took off his sword belt. He gave his pistols to Sam. Cahya's eyebrows almost left his forehead as he saw the weapons. As they walked through the village Pramana said, "Follow my lead so not to do anything to offend."

The chief's hut was the biggest and most ornate in the village with a magnificently-curved roof. He climbed the steps to the porch where the old man was sat in regal splendour. Now he knew what took so long. Dressed in a costume festooned with motifs the chief chanted a series of ritualistic verses which translated into proverbs.

He learned that the people were called the Minangkabau and that each village was a separate, self-governing entity. The chiefs collectively debated and agreed overall policy. He also learned that they bowed to no one. They were prepared to cooperate with the British if it helped sell their spices. They despised the Dutch who they considered traded unfairly, squeezing the price of their pepper and restricting their trade with Malacca.

So much for a primitive people, Marty thought

Food was brought and they ate. Pramana assured Marty that he was making good progress. Marty wondered as all he had done to now was listen to the old man ramble on. *Patience,* he told himself.

While they ate the old man questioned Marty about his lands and position. Marty answered honestly and then was asked, "The chief wants to know why you are not the resident?"

"I was in India when the new resident was allocated and not available."

"The chief says you would be a good resident, you listen. Now he says you can ask him about the execution of Parr."

Marty noted the use of *execution.*

"Did the Dutch influence the decision of the chiefs to execute Parr at all?"

"The chief says, the Dutch did not need to. Parr was executed for offending the customs."

"Did he get his watch?"

The chief burst out laughing at that and produced a silver pocket watch from his waistcoat pocket and handed it to Marty. There was a remnant of watch chain hanging from it. Marty took the chain he had found from his pocket and offered it up. The parts matched. Marty handed both parts to the chief.

"You should have all of it," he said.

The chief smiled, delighted to receive a gift.

"He admitted they killed him?" Raffles said.

"Oh, the chiefs definitely ordered his execution. He had offended them mortally."

"And he had his watch,"

"Yes, I could see his family crest on the back."

"What should we do about it."

"Nothing, unless you want to start a war you don't have the resources to fight."

Raffles looked like he had sucked a lemon.

"And the Dutch had no influence?"

"No, they wouldn't listen to the Dutch as they get scrimped on the price of the pepper, they sell them."

"What do they think about slavery?"

"They don't like it especially when their people get taken," Marty said wondering where this was going.

"What do you think about it?" Raffles asked leaning forward.

"Slavery? I don't approve of it. No man should be a slave," Marty said.

"So, if I abolish it, you will support the move back in England?"

"Absolutely. But how will you grow coffee without slaves?"

Raffles sat back looking smug, "Convict labour. I have a contingent on its way here as we speak."

Marty was surprised but refrained from stating what he thought was obvious. That convict labour was just another form of slavery. Raffles listened when Marty described the democracy which the tribes lived by.

"If I honour their customs and don't force them to grow coffee they will cooperate then?"

"I would think so."

"And they trust you?

"That one chief likes me, yes." Marty got a cold feeling in his stomach.

"And he will influence the rest! You are the perfect person to be my envoy."

The gates of a very wet hell just clanged shut.

Chapter 17: The Java Sea

The ships had to short tack to get out of the bay; the wind wasn't quite a rank muzzler but not far off it. They made a long leg west out to Seberoo Island before turning south by southeast, close hauled, to head down the coast. They would maintain that heading until they reached the Sunda Strait then head northeast with the wind on their sterns to pass into the Java Sea.

It took forty-two hours to reach the turning point and as they did the lookout cried, "Big column of smoke dead ahead!"

"That would be the island of Krakatoa," Arnold Gray said. "It has a really big volcano on it that's close to a thousand feet high."

As they got closer, they could hear rumbling and banging.

"Captain, we could moor by the island. The volcano provides quite a show in the dark and we wouldn't want to try the straits in the dark." Gray said.

Wolfgang considered, Arnold was usually right, and they had made good time so far. He looked at the chart. There was a bay on the east side of the island between it and Lang Island. He looked up and saw that the smoke curved over towards where he guessed the bay was. That wouldn't do.

He looked through a magnifier and saw the ideal spot. Right between Krakatoa and Verlaten Island was a sheltered bay with deep enough water to be safe and big enough to hold the entire squadron without crowding together.

He pointed it out to Arnold, "We will overnight there."

James had the watch but as soon as the evening meal was finished the entire crew were on deck or in the rigging watching the spectacular display. The volcano did not disappoint.

"'ere, Harry you remember that there island in Sicily?" an anonymous voice from above said, and Harry answered, "Yea, what were it called?"

"Mount Edna weren't it?"

James winced at the misnaming and said, "Mount Etna."

"Aye that were it, thankee, Sir."

"Well, what about it?" Harry said.

"Weren't a patch on this."

James laughed, whoever it was, was right, this was one spectacular show. A spume of lava shot into the air glowing yellow and red followed by a whump that shook the rigging.

The show continued through his watch. He could still hear the bangs through the hull in his cabin when he was relieved. He eventually slept and dreamt of sailing on a wave of golden lava.

They made way at first light. The tide was such that there was a current running through the strait to aid them on their way. They set a course to pass to the West of Sangiang Island that sat in the middle of the Strait. James looked back at Krakatoa and, as if to say farewell, the volcano sent up a puff of smoke. He looked forward. A signal was being repeated by the Nymph.

"Preparatory, formation B," Midshipman Donaldson reported.

That warned them that Captain Ackermann was getting ready to look for their prey. Formation B placed the Silverthorn and Eagle five miles ahead and to either side of the frigates which would go into echelon a mile apart.

They passed Sangiang Island, and the signal dropped.

"Execute, make all sail, signal the acknowledge," Angus ordered.

The Silverthorn shook out her skirts and accelerated. *Now this is sailing!* James exulted silently as she picked up the wind which was on their port quarter. They passed the Nymph and he waved to Andrew Stamp. As they passed the Leonidas, he raised his hat to James Campbell. Gordon McGivern had the deck of the Unicorn, and he too warranted a salute.

Now they were heading for a point five miles ahead and to starboard of the Unicorn. James took his sextant and measured the angle to the top of the Unicorn's mainmast. A quick calculation and he had the distance. A check of the bearing and he knew if they were on track. He monitored both every ten minutes to start with and as they approached their position every five.

"On point!" he said.

"Reduce sail make ten knots," Angus said. He stepped up beside James. "Who is on lookout?"

"Gardner on the main and Hislop on the fore. Both have sharp eyes."

"Change them every hour. We need fresh eyes up there."

"Aye, aye. Sir." James went forward to select his replacements. He needed steady men with good eyes.

They were in the Java Sea and swung north toward the Belitung Islands which they wouldn't reach until after dark. The passage between the islands was a scant nine miles wide and Wolfgang was not keen on passing through at night because their charts didn't show the depth or the bottom. They had several options, sail slower, heave to at dusk, or try a different route.

"We could circle them to the east," Arnold said.

"The added distance would take roughly the same time as stopping and going through at daylight."

Wolfgang frowned, "There is a full moon tonight. We will close up the squadron and go through at night. Slowly and with care."

On the Silverthorn, Angus was about to hand over the watch to the master for the night when the lookout called out, "Deck there, Unicorn has fired a gun and signalled."

"James, nip up and see what it is."

James grabbed a glass and shinnied up to the main top. He adjusted the glass to his mark and swept the horizon. He found the Unicorn and read the signal, "It's the recall," he shouted down. Before he landed on the deck the acknowledge had gone up and Angus was shouting orders.

"What do you think the captain will do?" James asked.

"Knowing him we are in for a long night. I wager he will navigate through the passage tonight."

Angus was correct. They formed up in line astern, a cable apart and, as the sun set, approached the gap between the two islands. It looked to be around nine miles across, but they knew that there would be shoals and sandbars as well as swirling currents. They slowed to five knots.

On the Unicorn, two men were in the chains with deep-water leads sounding the bottom. The Island of Banca to port and the Island of Bilhtoo to starboard. Across the passage were three small islands with a scattering of small islets between the second and third. Their course took them between the first, Lepar Island, and the second, Lait Island.

James and Angus stayed on duty as they followed the Nymph with the Eagle behind them. Angus had it in mind that if Wolfgang got it wrong and the ships ahead of them ended up aground, he would be ready to pull them off. Consequently, he had a full extra watch. James was in the bow, he had good night vision and Angus wanted him to relay any changes in course or speed to him.

They had just entered the gap when the lookout called, "Sir, there be a bloody big cloud bank coming up from the southwest."

James swung around and looked. The cloud bank had snuck up on them when all eyes were forward. The forward edge of it lit up as lightning coursed across it.

"Get ready to reduce sail!" Angus shouted through a speaking trumpet.

It couldn't have come at a worse time.

It was a monsoon. The clouds covered the moon. They were plunged into complete darkness. The rain came down. It was like standing under a waterfall and water poured out of the scuppers. The wind was finicky and shifted without warning, gusting, and veering.

James had to peer ahead to catch glimpses of the Nymphe's stern lights. The rain and the loss of the moonlight made that almost impossible, and he was peering forward to try and pick it up when the Nymphe's stern suddenly appeared out of the gloom a mere fifty feet ahead.

"Hard to starboard!" James yelled.

The helmsman swung the wheel immediately and the bow swung around. The Nymphe came closer and the Silverthorn's bowsprit was dangerously close to her transom windows.

James held his breath as they turned, just missing the other ship to pass up her starboard side. Andrew Stamp was at the rail and shouted down to James.

"I'd rather you come for dinner when I invite you!"

James shook his head, that was close.

They reduced sail to storm sails and managed to get back behind the Nymphe but their trials weren't over.

"Waterspout!" the lookout cried.

The waves became confused and increased in size. The bow pitched and the Silverthorn shook her head. The waterspout crashed into them two thirds along the port side. James was thrown to the deck and grabbed a coil of rope as it pitched over. Rigging snapped with a series of bangs like rifle shots, and he felt a rope snap past his head.

Suddenly as they started to right there was a creek and the sound of wood breaking. He tried to get to his feet when something hit him on the head.

He came around. He tried to sit but his stomach spasmed and he threw up. He had no idea how long he had been unconscious, and he had a lump on his head. It was still dark and raining. The ship felt strange. He sat up.

A large shape lay on the deck nearby. He crawled to it and saw it was Dennis. For a moment he thought he was dead then he felt a heartbeat and he was breathing. He struggled to his feet. The ship was a mess. The fore mast was gone, the mainmast was hanging over the side. He heard Angus shouting orders and made his way towards his voice. Men were chopping away at the rigging holding the mainmast to the ship. It was dragging them around and would sink them if they didn't succeed.

He found Angus. He had his left arm tied across his chest.

"James! I thought you lost."

"Knocked out, Dennis is still down at the bow unconscious. What happened to your arm?"

"Got hit by a spar. Broken it."

"What can I do?"

"Get below, find the carpenter and check the hull. See how much water is in the bilges. Then report back to me."

James went below, hanging on for grim death as the ship pitched violently. He went down passing through the orlop where the surgeon was treating the injured. He was below the waterline, and it became steadier. He heard voices and followed them to a pool of light. It was the carpenter with one of his mates.

"Hello, Mitch, how is she faring?"

"Hull's still tight apart a couple of sprung seams." Mitch showed Marty the seepage and they dipped the bilge.

"Better than up top. We only have the mizzen left. Let's go and talk to the captain."

The fought their way up to the main deck and found that the crew had successfully cut away the main mast.

"Hull's good and there's only a couple of feet of water in the bilge," James reported.

"Good. Ah you brought Mitch. We need to jury rig a foresail."

"We'll get on to it." James led the carpenter to the bow.

They found Dennis propped up against the rail; a bandage around his head. James knelt by his side,

"How are you?"

"Dennis head hurt, and stomach not happy. Ship is wobbly."

"He has concussion," Sergeant Anfield said as he knelt the other side of him. "Here drink this," he said as he held a mug up to the big man's lips.

"What is it?" James said.

"Rum cut ten to one with water and a dash of lemon. Works wonders."

"Give me some, I need it as well," James said and gulped some down.

When Dennis had drunk and he was sure he was safe he said, "Stay there until you feel better."

He found Mitch who was preparing a spare spar to fish onto the stump of the fore mast.

"We will bind it with rope, and once it's up you can attach stays," Mitch said.

They had no idea where they were as they had lost touch with the rest of the squadron. It was pitch black and the rain continued to hammer down. Angus put men on the pump for an hour to keep the level of the water in the bilge under control.

James was preparing to raise a foresail when he heard something. He stopped working and called for silence.

"Oh my god, that's surf! Get that sail up now!"

He ran to the quarterdeck.

"ANGUS!"

"What's the matter?" Angus said turning to him.

"Surf dead ahead!"

"The fore sail?"

"Another ten minutes."

"We can't turn her on the mizzen alone. Get back forward and keep a lookout and get that sail up!"

James chivvied the men to work as fast as they could. They knew the danger, but the soaking wet canvas and ropes didn't want to cooperate. He went to the bow. The sound was much louder. He peered ahead and caught a glimpse of white.

It was only twenty yards ahead.

"BRACE, EVERYBODY BRACE FOR COLLISSION."

The Silverthorn rode a wave which lifted her stern then, as it rolled under, lifted her bow. It carried her forward onto the reef which she rode onto with a shuddering crash. Anyone not braced was thrown forward. The overstressed mizzen snapped and went over the side.

James moved around the deck, getting help for the injured. Ironically the storm was lessening, moving on as fast as it had arrived. The wind was dropping, and it was getting light. An inspection of the hull revealed they were holed. It would only get worse as the waves worked the hull until she broke apart. They needed to get ashore.

As the light increased, they could see they were actually aground on a coral reef that was two miles or so off a shoreline.

"We still have one boat. If we throw hatch covers over, the boat can tow them to the shore. We can get everyone ashore in three or more trips," Angus said.

James took charge of getting the men ready to abandon ship. They had no idea what they would find, so they would need to take what they could. Discipline would be key to saving both the men and the wherewithal to survive.

Angus organised the boat and got the hatch covers over the side and tied on. It wasn't long before the first trip across to the shore was on its way. The sea, however, hadn't finished with them and a seventh wave tipped the hatch covers throwing men into the water. Only around one in four sailors could swim and none of these could. Their mates threw ropes and one brave soul jumped in to attempt a rescue.

"We lost three men on that trip," Angus said.

"We need at least five trips to get everyone off," James said.

"I know, I want you to go on the next one to organise the men ashore."

"But—"

Angus stopped him. "I have to be last man off, injured or not. You need to be there to keep the men together and organised. Now go."

James made sure his men were with him when he lowered himself into the boat. They got to shore with no losses and James sent the boat straight back with a fresh set of rowers. He rounded up the men and took an inventory of what they had. They had some food that wasn't spoiled by salt water, a few hand axes, and tomahawks. The marines had their guns but whether their powder had survived was another question.

"Search for dry wood we need a fire." He delegated the task to half a dozen men. He ordered the rest, "You men get some long timber to build shelters."

A groan of tortured timbers reached them from across the water. The wind was blowing directly onshore now aiding the third load of men.

"We lost another couple and the captain said to tell you there are fifteen dead onboard."

They had lost men overboard when the masts went. James had already done a headcount of the injured.

"Tell him that if we get everyone alive ashore, we will have seventy fit men and twenty-three invalided." Out of a crew of one hundred and twenty that was disastrous.

By the time the last group was brought ashore, that had worsened as the Silverthorn was breaking up, injuring more men. Angus had to be lifted out of the boat. His arm was in agony and needed to be set. Fortunately, the surgeon was one of the survivors and with Dennis's help set the arm and splinted it.

It was fully light now and James could see there were tree-covered hills behind them. He sent men to find fresh water. They returned with the news that there were several streams running down into the sea.

Water was no problem, but they were very short of food. They also had thirty injured men laid out under crude shelters. James went to Angus. He found him sat against a rock. His face pale from the pain of his arm.

"I don't need to ask how you feel, I can see it," James said.

"I'm not sure which hurt more, breaking it in the first place or Simmonds and that ox of yours setting it."

"I am going to take a party and see if we can find some food. Joseph rescued my rifle and cartridges. I will try and bag a pig or a deer."

"Take Alf Rowel and Stan Foyle, they were poachers."

"I can take Alf. Stan is one of the injured."

"Damn, he would have been useful." Angus winced as a stab of pain hit him.

"Do you have any idea where we are?"

"My guess is Lepar island. It has a boundary reef on the north side."

James selected a foraging team of five men and set off heading west along the coast looking for a stream to follow inland. Now it was fully light, they could see that the beach turned two miles ahead and they quickly reached, the corner of the island. From the apex of the curve, he could see there was a village a mile along the coast with fishing boats pulled up on the shore.

"Do you think they'm friendly?" Alf said.

"I don't know," James said, "I suppose there is only one way to find out."

They started down the beach and got to within two hundred yards when dogs started barking at them. A child came out from the huts and stared at them for a long moment before running, shouting, back into the village.

"We will wait here," James said as they got to a hundred yards from the first house.

James left his rifle slung over his shoulder by its strap and made sure the others didn't have weapons in their hands. A group of men approached dressed in loose-fitting shirts and sarongs, their heads wrapped in a bandana or light turbans and carrying a variety of spears and harpoons.

They stopped ten feet away and James held his hands out to his side, palms forward and stepped ahead. A small older man, they were all short but he was shorter, stepped forward to meet him. James remembered how the Indians greeted each other and bowed with his hands together in front of him. The man smiled and reflected the gesture.

"James," James said and pointed to himself. Then he pointed at the old man. "You are?"

The old man pointed to himself and said, "Pratam."

"Do you speak English?"

The man looked confused and turned to his men who shook their heads. He turned back to James and shrugged. James pantomimed sailing, pointing to the sea, then a storm and then crashing into the rocks, making all the noises. He pointed to where they had been wrecked held up his hands with fingers spread and open and closed his hands seven times. He finished and pointed to his stomach, made a sad face and pointed to his mouth.

The fishermen put their heads together and discussed what they had seen. James stood patiently. The old man came back and made a sweeping gesture that encompassed the village, then he pointed to the boats and finally to where they were shipwrecked. Then he made a shooing motion.

"I think he wants us to go back to the others," James said. "I think he is saying they will come with the boats."

James bowed, hands together again.

"Come on we will go back."

They reached the corner where there was a stream. James made an instant decision. "You men follow the stream and see if there is any game. I will catch you up after I have told the captain about the village." He traversed the two miles to the camp at a dog trot and went straight to see Angus. He looked better. His face was still pinched with pain, but he had some colour back.

"Do you think they will bring food?"

"From his gestures, I think so," James said, noticing men coming from the forest with fruits and other foraged greens.

"They remember what they learnt on the river and are searching the forest for foodstuff, but it's not enough to feed everyone." Angus looked thoughtful. "If there is a village on the coast, do you think there are more inland?"

"Probably, it looks to be a pretty large island."

"Will they be friendly or hostile?"

"I don't know, fishermen tend to be more likely to help another sailor, but the inland tribes will probably be hunters."

"We are not far from Borneo, and I have read stories of head-hunters. I think we should be vigilant."

"I will post sentries."

James found Sergeant Anfield and gave him instructions then he found Dennis.

"How are you?"

"Dennis good."

"Excellent you can come with me."

They set off to catch up with the hunting team and were soon following the stream inland. The tracks of the men were easy to follow. James kept up a good pace and they were negotiating a swampy area when there was a shot from not too far ahead. They left the stream and followed the tracks through the trees.

They entered a clearing to find the men stood around the carcase of a small deer.

"Is that full grown? It's not much bigger than my dog," James said.

"Looking at its teeth it looks like an adult," Alf said.

James looked around the clearing. The forest floor was covered in ferns and the canopy shut out a lot of the direct sunlight. He couldn't actually see very far in any direction.

"I don't think we are going to see much wandering around in here," he said.

"I saw tracks where something with split hooves had been drinking by the stream," Alf said.

"Bigger than those?"

"Yes, I reckon we could set up a hide and wait for it to come back."

James didn't have a better idea, so they returned to the stream and set about building a hide on the opposite bank to the tracks. Thin vines were used to tie branches to make a frame and ferns used to create a concealing screen. Alf added a few ferns as a roof to keep off the rain.

It was getting late, and the light was fading when James and all but two of the men returned to the camp. Alf and his mate stayed to see if something came down at night. The need for food was acute. The smell of fish cooking on a fire greeted them.

"The fishermen came," Angus told him. "We traded a couple of knives for a dozen big fish."

James could see the fish which were of a good size and silver in colour. The men had filleted them and cut the fillets into steaks. Those were cooking over the fires. There was enough that every man would get a portion which solved the immediate problem. He hoped the fishermen would return tomorrow.

That first night it rained. The men crowded together under the shelters they had made. James and Angus shared one with Simmonds the surgeon, and Philips the master. In the morning the men started building more shelters and thickening the roofs of the existing ones.

Alf and his mate returned around midday with what at first glance looked like a cow. It was certainly a bovine and about the size of a cow. It had a dark grey coat and stubby horns. Slow roasted over the cook fire it smelt like beef and tasted something like it as well.

The fishermen came back in the evening and more goods were traded. The old man, who they thought was the leader, pointed to his boat then out to sea then to James.

"I think he wants to take you out," Angus said.

James thought it couldn't hurt so nodded and followed the man into the boat. He was impressed at the old man's skill as they negotiated the reef past what was left of the Silverthorn. James enjoyed the feeling of the wind in his hair and the water spay that landed on his skin. The boat sped along with the wind on its quarter. They continued for an hour then the old man smiled and pointed ahead. James stood, holding onto the mast and shaded his eyes against the setting sun.

It was the Leonidas.

The fishing boat went alongside, and James thanked the old man before going up the side.

"Where have you been and why are you in a fishing boat?" James Campbell asked as soon as he hit the deck.

"Sir, I have to report the Silverthorn is lost." James said.

"What? Good grief! How?"

"A waterspout hit us and we lost the fore and main. Before we could get her under control we were driven onto a reef. She broke up but we got everybody who was alive off. "

"Captain Fraser?"

"He has a broken arm and was the last man off."

"Can the fisherman guide us to the survivors?"

James went to the side. The old man was still there. It was getting dark rapidly, so he called for a lantern and took it down. He signed to him that they should return to the island. The man shook his head and pointed to the west. James looked and saw storm clouds approaching.

The next morning Angus was wondering where the hell his number two had gotten to when a shout went up. The Leonidas was approaching. She was following the fishing boat and once they reached the reef, anchored a safe distance off and lowered boats.

James came ashore with the fisherman.

"I have no idea how he did it but he took me directly to the Leonidas. We had to sit out the storm over night before he would guide us back in," James said to Angus who had joined him on the beach to wait for the boats to land.

"These people are amazing. They seem to just know where to go and how to get back with no compasses or instruments at all," Angus said then stepped forward as Captain Campbell stepped out of his boat and said, "Angus, sorry you lost your ship. How many men have you?"

"Sixty-three able and twenty-eight wounded. Two more died last night."

Campbell blew out his cheeks, "Thirty lost. That is hard. We will get you onto the Leonidas and re-join the squadron. We were looking for you while the rest of the squadron carried on the patrol."

"Sir, I would like to give a gift to the chief," James said.

"Yes, that would be appropriate he has been invaluable." Campbell said, "What did you have in mind?"

"Axes and adze. Maybe five of each?"

"We should have those aboard I will send them ashore. Now let's get your men off. The wounded first."

James asked the chief, as he now thought of him, to stay. He found a rock to sit on and watch the navy work. The hurt men were gently carried to boats and taken out to the big warship. Then the men were loaded up and rowed out. He was impressed with the discipline and noticed the young man, who the men obviously deferred to despite his lack of years, and the older man with the broken arm would be the last to leave.

James and Angus approached followed by two men carrying canvas-wrapped bundles. James bowed his hands together in front of him. He touched his heart and pointed to the chief, *I think that means thank you,* he thought. The two men were beckoned forward, and James took one of the bundles. James laid it at his feet and opened it. Six shiny new axes with four-pound heads and ash handles lay inside. The second package held six adzes. He knew good quality tools when he saw them.

"For me?" he said.

James guessed what he meant, nodded and smiled. Tools like these were invaluable for making boats.

James bowed again and the men left. The old man carried his gifts to his boat. His wife would be happy with their new wealth, and he would remember the young man who commanded for as long as he lived.

Chapter 18: Confrontation

The crowded Leonidas rendezvoused with the rest of the squadron and Angus had to go aboard the Unicorn and report. James was reinstated as senior midshipman on the Leonidas and the fit crew were distributed around the ships as needed. He didn't see Angus again as he stayed on the Unicorn as a guest of Wolfgang where Shelby could oversee his recovery. Shelby's wife Anabelle came aboard the Leonidas to help with the sick and wounded.

James visited the infirmary where the worst hurt men were being treated. The others had been moved to the Unicorn or discharged as walking wounded.

"Hello, James," Anabelle said. She had a lock of hair hanging across her face from where it had escaped the bun she had pulled her hair back into. She was quite beautiful, even in her white apron and surrounded by the sick and wounded.

"Hello, Doctor."

"You must call me Anabelle."

He bowed, "Why thank you," he grinned looking just like his father. "How are my men doing?"

"Most will recover but there are two that will never sail again."

James asked to see them. One was from his guns division.

"Peter, how do you feel?" he asked the first.

"My foot hurts sommat proper," Peter said.

James looked at Anabelle in question.

"His leg was amputated above the knee. We call it phantom pain."

James placed his hand on his shoulder, "You will recover, and the pain will get less. It's a life ashore for you now."

"I don't want to go ashore. Please, Mister Stockley can you get them to take me on as a cook's mate or something?"

"I will ask the captain."

"Thankee, Sir, I am much obliged."

They moved on to the second man who was strapped to his bed, eyes wide and staring.

"He is not physically hurt now but his mind has gone. We will have to ship him home to Haslar for treatment," Anabelle said.

Haslar was the naval hospital at Gosport where they had founded an asylum for sailors with mental problems.

"As far as I can tell his mind is locked in the moment the ship sank, he repeats the same cries over and over."

James looked at the man sadly. "I knew him, he was a fine hand at drawing and entertained the crew with caricatures. He did one of me that was really funny."

The man started to struggle and cried unintelligibly in terror. Then screamed, "She's goin', she's goin. Oh God, Jimmie!"

"Oh, that's it. Jimmie was his brother. He didn't get off," James said.

"He must have seen him die," Anabelle said.

"Maybe, they were in the same watch. Poor sod."

They patrolled the straits. Escorting ships through. Only catching sight of potential enemies at a distance. One captain said they had never known the straits to be so quiet. Even Dutch ships joined the convoys. James was enjoying dinner with the other mids in the cockpit.

"Do you think we have frightened them off?" Gabriel, the youngest of the mids, asked.

"Who? The pirates? No, they are up to something, and we can expect them at some time," James said.

"And you know that because?" Felix Rathbone the senior mid until James' return said. He was royally miffed at being replaced. "Did the captain tell you because your father..." He stopped as James stood.

"Would you care to accompany me to the cable tier," James said and walked out without looking back.

By the time Felix reached the cable tier James had lit a lamp to illuminate it. He stood in the middle of the open space that was left after the massive anchor cable had been coiled in.

"Felix, ever since I got back you have been firing shots at me. That has got to stop, so I am giving you one chance to get whatever is bothering out of your system. No one can hear us here or witness what we do. So go ahead, get it off your chest."

No one would ever know what was said or done in the fifteen minutes they were in the tier but after they came out. Felix had gotten over his gripe and James was secure in his seniority. It didn't come a moment too soon.

"Sails ho! A point off the starboard bow," the lookout cried.

"Unicorn signalling. Enemy in sight," Felix reported as signals officer.

"Deck there, the horizon ahead is full of them!" the main mast lookout cried.

"Full of what, man? Be precise!" Campbell barked back.

"Sails, all across the horizon ahead of us."

"Dammit. Mr Stockley get up there with a glass and give me a proper report and replace that man with someone else," Campbell barked.

James grabbed the largest glass and slung it over his shoulder by its strap. He flew up the ratlines to the futtock shrouds, went around the outside of them without slowing and was up in the tops in short order.

"I have the lookout go below," he said, "send up the next in line for watch duty."

He settled and looked ahead. His eyebrows raised in surprise. He pulled the glass around and opened it to his focus mark.

"Junks. Chinese and Javanese by the looks of them." He counted the ones in the front row. "There are twenty big square-rigged ones in the first rank, more behind." He scanned the line again. "At least another twenty. Mixture of Junks and Javanese ships."

He waited above until the replacement lookout arrived and with a caution to tell what he saw precisely and without exaggeration he took a stay to the deck. He arrived just in time to hear, "Unicorn signal, F 4."

"Wolfgang's going to take them on," Campbell said. "Helm, get us out a cable off the Unicorn's starboard quarter. Simon get us to quarters please."

James made his way forward to his station at the forward half of the main battery as soon as the first lieutenant gave the order. His gun crews were already there and hauling the guns back to load. Wolfgang had deployed his ships in an arrowhead with the Eagle as the shaft and the Unicorn at the tip. The Leonidas was on the starboard side and the Nymph on the left. The formation was approaching the pirate fleet at a closing speed of twenty knots. James knew from briefings that Wolfgang would only clew up his mains at the last minute to blast their way through the superior numbers and prevent them from being mobbed.

"Load double shot. Carronades, smashers."

James passed on the order.

"Run out!"

The main battery rumbled forward on both sides.

The big fore deck carronades were loaded with massive sixty-four-pound balls. Two men being required to lift them into the barrels.

Simon arrived and said, "Go to cannister over shot after the first broadsides. Aimed fire. We want to damage and disable as many of them as possible on the first pass. Load the carronades with small ball."

"Aye, aye, Sir." James grinned.

"And try and stay safe."

The two sets of ships approached each other at speed. James could see that the junks were sprouting guns down both sides. He couldn't tell what size they were but if they were nine pounders or higher, they could hurt them badly.

At around two cables' distance the captain ordered the mains clewed up and their speed dropped to around eight knots. James focussed; it was time. The forward carronades barked, and he could see the huge balls fly straight and true at the two ships they would pass between.

The port side ship was hit just off centre of their square bow the ball careened down the inside of the ship and several of the guns on that side disappeared from their ports. The ball exited the ship up through her deck, presumably after taking a deflection, scattering sailors in all directions.

They were in the gap.

"Fire as you bear!"

That same junk came in for a pounding as gun after gun fired as she passed. The guns on both sides fired in sequence.

James was yelling for the men to reload as fast as possible and hardly noticed the balls that whistled over his head from the return fire. The Chinese were going for their rigging. A block fell into the nets above him. He glanced up then ignored it.

There was a rending crash from forward. He ran forward to see what had happened. He looked down to see a Javanese junk under their bow the men scrambling up to try and get aboard.

"Dennis with me, the rest of you keep firing."

James drew a pistol and shot at a man hanging from the bowsprit lines. He missed. There was a thunderous roar from beside him. Dennis had fired a swivel gun he held like a shotgun. He looked back and the man had disappeared. He looked down in time to see the junk disappear beneath the sea.

More men had managed to get a hold of lines, or chains and a head appeared above the side. This time he was too close to miss and shot him in the face. The guns behind him were keeping up a steady rhythm. Dennis grabbed another boarder by the head lifting him up before giving it a viscous twist and breaking his neck.

James looked around. They were through the second rank and approaching the third and final one. Several pirate ships were burning or crippled behind them, and it didn't look like the squadron had suffered any serious casualties at all.

As soon as they were between the second and third ranks Wolfgang ordered them to wear to port to run between them. The other ships turned to take up positions in line astern. James could see that the first rank was trying to turn to engage them, but the junks were nowhere near as agile as their French-made frigates and a certain amount of chaos ensued as they got in each other's way.

The guns were jumping when they fired. Their barrels getting hotter and hotter. They were doing their job. Junks of both types were being hit and either sunk or damaged. Then a large Chinese ship ran across their bow.

"Get down!" James cried and threw himself to the deck as the ship's side lit up with cannon fire. A clang came from above and behind him and he turned his head to see the port carronade slewing around on its pivot.

"Is it damaged?" he asked the gunners when they stood.

"No, it was a glancing blow, Sir, see?" the gun captain said pointing to a scuff on the breach.

"Good get it firing again."

The junk was approaching, and he could see the crew franticly try to get her turned to avoid being rammed. However, the last thing Campbell wanted was a collision. Mobility was their main asset, so he ordered the helm to port, and they slipped past her stern. James's guns came to bear and charge after charge of cannister over ball ripped her from stern to stem leaving a shattered hulk that bled.

James realised that the Chinese ships were made of a combination of soft and hard wood. They were doing far more damage than they would against a European ship and although they were taking hits not a lot of damage or casualties was being caused.

The Javanese ships were a different matter. Though smaller they were made of multiple layers of teak and considerably tougher than their Chinese counterparts. A couple had turned and were closing in to attempt to board. Men stood by swinging grapples ready to hook onto the Leonidas's side.

The marines in the tops were picking off the grapplers.

"Load with grape, fire down onto their decks," James ordered. The gunners had nets of grape prepared. Bigger than cannister but smaller than small ball, it was devastating.

The first gun fired but the angle was too shallow. It shredded any men stood above the gunnel but didn't go deep into the boat. The second and third had a better shot the fourth the best. The boat drifted to a halt. There was nobody left to steer or sail her. The second boat managed to get under the guns with men left, but there were not enough to pose more than an annoyance to the marines.

On the Eagle, Trevor Archer was having a harder time. More on a par for size with the Chinese Junks they were exchanging fire at close range. His well-trained gun crews and their rate of fire made the difference. The guns were so hot they jumped and bucked when they fired.

"We're nearly out of small ball," Midshipman Gerald Sykes reported to him.

"Langridge and chain. That will be just as effective against their thin hulls," Trevor ordered.

A scream from behind them made them spin around. A sword-wielding pirate had snuck over the stern and stabbed the helmsman in the back. Trevor drew his sword and rushed to take him on. It was no time for subtlety, he swung his sword down at the man's head. He blocked with his sword. Trevor kicked him in the stomach and hacked down on his neck.

Another appeared over the stern followed by several more.

"Captain! Down!" Gerald shouted

Trevor didn't hesitate and dropped to the deck. Shot howled over his head as Gerald fired a swivel then led a party to finish off the survivors. Trevor got to his feet and joined them.

"Grenades!" he called.

A pair of marines arrived with a crate and started lighting and dropping the lethal steel balls into the boat below.

"Gerald, get back to the guns," Trevor said, "I can manage this now."

It was hot work. They were constantly fending off attacks and sinking any ship that got close.

James was also busy. His guns were doing a tremendous amount of damage to the pirate ships, but the continuous incoming fire was taking its toll. He was wondering whether they had bitten off more than they could chew when cheers started from the stern spreading forward to the bow.

"Good grief, Company liners!" he said as he saw the cause.

Three big well-armed East Indiamen had joined in the fight. These 3rd rate sized ships with fifty guns had the firepower of a frigate and solidly-built hulls. They were sailing in behind the pirates and serving them broadsides. The effect was instantaneous. The pirates broke off and started to run.

The eighteen-pound guns on the Leonidas switched to ball and fired at the retreating ships until they were out of range.

James was exhausted and as he looked around his division, he saw he wasn't the only one. He checked on the injured, there were no dead thank God. Simon Fitzwarren, the first lieutenant, arrived. His uniform was splattered in blood.

"Are you hurt?" he asked James.

"No just knackered, what about you?"

"This isn't mine. We had some unwanted visitors. What is the butchers bill in your division?"

"Four injured, one is bad with a splinter in his gut, the rest are walking. No dead."

"It's amazing we have gotten away with three dead and a dozen wounded," Simon said and went to report to the captain.

"What ammunition do we have left?" James asked one of his gun captains.

"No grape, a half dozen cannister and some chain. Plenty of ball."

The gunner had appeared from his isolation in the magazine and walked up to the bow. James joined him.

"They really are running," Evan said.

"Yes, the appearance of the Indiamen was too much for them."

"Just as well."

"Why?"

"We only have two broadsides of cartridge left."

"Oh my god.," James said.

Chapter 19: Trial by Combat

Marty and the Shadows were sent back into the rain forest to meet with the council of chiefs. His mission, to get them to agree to work with Raffles in the administration of the territory. It was alternately wet then humid to the point where it made no difference. They sweated and developed sores where they gear rubbed. Pramana was their guide again.

"Where do they meet?" Marty said.

"They rotate the meetings around the villages. This time it is one in the hills."

"Is it cooler up there?"

"Yes, but the villagers are more warlike."

"Warlike?"

"They used to be head-hunters."

Marty dropped back to where Antton was walking behind them, "Did you hear that?"

"Yes, the villagers used to be head-hunters. When did they stop?"
Marty called to Pramana.

"Just three years ago, the council decided to stop the villages fighting each other to concentrate in resisting the invaders."

Antton looked at Marty and raised his eyebrows. Marty pursed his lips and focussed on walking.

The ground gradually rose then got steeper. The up side was the forest got thinner and the ground firmer. His calves started to burn. He just wasn't used to all this walking.

"Boss, we are being shadowed," Matai said.

Marty was surprised he hadn't spotted anyone.

"Where?"

"Out to our left."

He casually scanned the forest to both sides. Whoever was out there was good. He couldn't see anyone.

"How far to the village, Pramana?" he said.

"Another hour's walk."

Marty checked his watch. It was three in the afternoon.

"Let's take a break," he said.

The men closed up and Pramana joined them.

"I need a pee." Marty stepped off the trail.

As soon as he was in the undergrowth, he slipped further out into the forest and circled around looking for the person following them. He moved silently from tree to tree, using all his senses. He detected a faint smell. He stopped and checked the direction the very slight air movement was coming from. He crouched and moved through the bracken slowly to not alert whoever was ahead. He stopped when he caught a glimpse of colour.

It was a girl. A local by the looks of the dress. She was watching the boys sitting around resting. He waited to see what she would do next. She just watched for a while then sat with her back to the tree.

Marty didn't like being spied on so decided to act. He stood and walked towards her. She looked up as he got within five feet of her, shot to her feet in alarm and made a break for it. Marty snaked out an arm and caught her around the waist and in one movement hoisted her up and over his shoulder.

She squealed and kicked and pummelled his back with her fists, but her held her tight and walked back into camp. He put her back on her feet in front of Pramana. She tried to strike him, but he caught her hands. "Tell her I won't hurt her."

Pramana spoke to her sternly and she stopped struggling. Marty let her go.

"She is from the village. She heard we were coming to the congress and wanted to see what the white men looked like." She struck a proud pose and babbled something else. Pramana's eyes widened.

"What did she say?" Marty said.

"She said she wanted to see your faces before her father took your heads."

"Oh, and who is her father?"

"The chief of the village, he is not in favour of working with the British or any white men."

The girl looked back and forth from Pramana to Marty. She was about the same age as Beth.

"Bring her along, she might as well accompany us into the village. I will make her father a present of her," Marty said.

They entered the village to see a lot of men gathered. Pramana pointed out that the different symbology on their clothes indicated which village they came from. Many men looked at them with interest and several grinned when they saw the girl being escorted along between Sam and Billy who towered over her.

Pramana guided them through the crowd to a huge house with the typical boat roof of the region. Marty noticed that Chin stayed in the centre of the group and kept his head covered. He focussed back on what was in front of him as they started up the steps to the floor where the council was being held.

There was a small commotion as the girl was spotted. A man stood; he was in his late middle years but still muscular and agile. He barked something at the girl who walked forward with her head bowed.

"He is asking her why she is captive. I cannot hear what she said."

The man looked at Marty and snarled something.

"He asks why you laid hands on his daughter."

"She was spying on us. I just brought her back where she belongs."

"He says his daughter is no spy and that you are a liar."

"Ah well this is the part where he challenges me to trial by combat so he can take my head I suppose."

Pramana translated that verbatim. Several of the council members looked alarmed and others kept carefully neutral looks on their faces. Others grinned, whether at the prospect of Marty losing his head or his jest he didn't know.

"The chief says he does challenge you. You are not worthy to touch his daughter or to sit at the council. He is quite entitled to challenge you and it is up to you whether you accept the challenge or not. If you accept it shows courage and he may make a magnanimous gesture and not actually fight you."

"I doubt he will do that; he wants my head on a plate. Tell him I accept."

There were gasps from many of the men. Chin appeared beside him.

"You will have to fight using a pair of their swords. It will be like fighting with the sticks we have practised."

"You know about these people?"

"Some of them made submissions to the emperor. They made demonstrations of their prowess with the swords."

"Pramana, ask the chiefs if it would be in order for me and my men to demonstrate our skill with weapons before the combat," Marty said as he suddenly got an idea.

There was a general discussion and it seemed that the majority thought it a good idea.

Billy and Sam took centre stage and gave a demonstration of grappling. Their height and muscular bulk not lost on the watchers, especially the younger women.

Then Antton and Garai faced off and astounded the audience with a flashing display of knife fighting. Their moves were so fast that most couldn't follow them. Chin and Matai faced off with staves and soon the air rang with the clack as they attacked and parried. The staves blurred as they spun, and the combat continued until Chin froze in place his stave tip touching Matai's sternum.

Marty noted that the appearance of Chin caused a few worried looks. Marty stepped forward bare chested. His untanned torso in stark contrast to his tanned arms and face. He held a pair of the local swords and swung them experimentally.

"Not a bad balance," he said. "Are you ready?" he said to the challenger.

"You have to go to the combat ring," Pramana said.

"Lead on MacDuff." Marty said.

He looked happy and in fact he was. His adrenalin was pumping, and he was focussed, the adrenalin a ball in his stomach. His awareness was intensified. He could hear the people chatter. The squawk of a bird, the bleat of a goat. He stepped into the circle.

His opponent stood across the circle flexing his muscles. Marty relaxed his and held his swords by his side. He stepped forward as Pramana had told him too. The other man mirrored him twirling his swords before he brought them up in a ready position.

Marty didn't move. He looked calmly into the man's eyes. He waited, the eyes flicked to his shoulder and the swords moved. Marty parried, his blades flashing. He was getting the feel of the swords and his opponent. The man had a unique style, it felt almost formalised as if he had rehearsed the moves. Marty took care not to fall into the trap of falling into his opponent's rhythm and varied his attack speed to see how he reacted.

The chief pushed forward with an attack trying to force Marty up against the edge of the circle. Marty circled backwards and let him come on. He felt good, wrists supple, arms not tired.

Suddenly the chief broke of his attack and stepped back. He was blowing and sweat ran down his face. Marty circled back to the centre of the ring.

"You cannot defeat me," he said.

The chief growled something and took up his stance again.

Marty shrugged and stepped forward and took his guard. The chief attacked. Marty parried; knocking both his swords aside then stepped inside his swing.

The chief froze. There was a blade laid across his throat and another at the back of his neck. The crowd were silent. The chief's eyes were wide.

"Do I have to kill him to win?" Marty called.

"He can withdraw his challenge, otherwise yes," Pramana said.

"Ask him."

"He says you are worthy."

"Does he withdraw the challenge?"

"He does not."

Marty looked him in the eyes, "I would spare your life."

There was a scream of rage and a warrior in the crowd rushed forward with a sword raised. There was a shot, and he was smashed backwards to the ground. Marty looked around and saw Billy with a smoking pistol in his hand.

The chief's head hit the ground followed by his body

Pramana joined them and spoke to the rest of the assembled chief.

"They say there is no shame being defeated by a warrior like you. They are sorry that man behaved badly. That he died is just."

The council reconvened and discussions progressed. There was a lively debate between the older chiefs who wanted to go back to the way things were before and the ones who thought that there could be an advantage in working with the British.

Marty spoke eloquently about how Raffles understood the mistakes his predecessor made and was resolved not to do the same again. He assured, even guaranteed, that the chiefs would be a part of the government of the province and have a full say. He also told them they would not be forced to grow coffee unless they wanted to but if they did, they would see a fair share of the profits. The news that slavery was being abolished was particularly well received.

The vote when it was held wasn't a foregone conclusion, but Marty needn't have worried. It was carried in his favour by a two thirds majority. The end of the council was celebrated with a feast which went on for two days. Along with the food there was dancing and singing. The dead men were not forgotten; the one who was shot dressed and honoured as a guest. When he got a little ripe, he was interred with some ceremony. Marty found out that the hill tribes venerated the dead and the corpse would be taken out regularly and dressed to spend time with his family.

The body of the chief had disappeared, and Marty wondered what had happened to it. He found out what had happened to the head when they were about to leave.

The trip back to the residence was completed in company with the chiefs and their retinues that lived en route. It was consequently slower as they had to stop at each village and attend a feast after the chief announced the decision of the council. It was a full week later when he walked back into Raffles' office. Sam followed him in carrying a wicker basket with a lid.

"Lord Martin, welcome back. How did it go?"

"I'm very well Raffles, thank you" Marty said.

"Oh, my apologies, I have to confess to being on tenterhooks awaiting your return," Raffles said embarrassed by his lapse.

"Our proposal was accepted by the council."

"In full?"

"In full. You had better live up to it because they have a high expectation."

"I have every intention to." He looked Marty over. "Will you join me for dinner after you have bathed and refreshed yourself?"

"As long as it's simple fair, I have been feasted for a fortnight. Those people know how to celebrate."

"Oh, by the way I had to fight one of the chiefs."

"You did, good God, man, what happened?"

"I killed him when he wouldn't withdraw the challenge. There is a condition to them sitting on the council because of it."

"What is it?"

"That his head has a seat. It's in that basket, they preserved it to remind them of me."

Raffles looked at the basket and swallowed hard.

At dinner, Raffles told him he was negotiating with Jahor for the right to establish a trading port on Singapore Island. He had been corresponding with the sultan and he needed to visit to finalise the agreement.

"How are you going to do that? The area and the sultanate are controlled by the Dutch," Marty said.

"Tengku Rahman is, but Tenkhu Abdul Rahman and his officials are actually loyal to his older brother, Tenkhu Long, who is in exile."

"The Dutch won't let him back in."

"No, but if we can get him onto Singapore there is an enclave of around one hundred Temenggong there who will accommodate him and give him a foothold to take back power."

"In return for granting you permission."

"Exactly. That and an annual payment of five thousand pounds to him and three thousand to the Temenggong."

Chapter 20: Foundation

Marty and Raffles boarded the Endellion. The Shadows joined the crew as several crewmen had succumbed to fever while in port. The shortage of men enabled them to build Raffles a cabin of his own.

They retraced the steps of the squadron but instead of heading to the Straits of Malacca they headed north to the Riau Peninsula and Penyengat Island. There the sultan was being held by a coalition of Malay and Dutch captors. Marty and the Shadows had work to do.

Penyengat Island was a small island in the shadow of the much larger Toapaya Island. It was overlooked by the port city of Tanjung Pinang which was under Dutch control. From the correspondence that Raffles had with the sultan they knew he was effectively under house arrest in a palace complex situated on Kursi Hill which also had a garrison housed in a block house.

"The hill is in the middle of the island. First problem is getting onto the island," Marty said to the assembled team. Raffles sat the side and observed.

Zeb produced a chart he had created from what they knew. The island was shaped somewhat like a left foot with only a big toe. The palace was situated slightly to the north of centre on the ball of the foot.

"Along the instep is a fishing village and the main landing, which we can expect to be patrolled," Marty continued.

"What's the coast like the other side of the island?" Antton asked.

"We don't know but my guess is there will be a beach somewhere along it."

"What I'd give to be seagull for a day to fly over these jobs before we grope our way in," laughed Zeb.

"Would make life easier, but we have what we have. We will look for a landing on the north shore. Then make our way inland to the palace. Chin and Sam will take point. The rest of us will follow twenty minutes later. Chin will carry out a reconnaissance of the blockhouse and Sam the perimeter. We will rendezvous directly to the north of the Palace. Once we know what we are up against we will infiltrate the palace and extract the sultan."

"May I come with you?" Raffles asked. "The sultan will be expecting me."

"You can if you give me your word you will do exactly what we tell you."

Raffles looked around the faces of the Shadows and saw cold determination and a certain ruthlessness in eyes that had seen too much and shuddered.

"Absolutely and without question," he said.

"Billy, he is your responsibility. He is not to be captured." Marty didn't add alive, but Billy knew it was what he meant. So did Raffles who paled.

The Endellion made good time and in two days were passing through the gap where the Silverthorn met its demise. The wreck was too far to the west for them to see. The Shadows and Marty embarked on an extensive exercise routine, and after watching them for an hour or so Raffles joined in. He didn't have their athleticism or brute strength, but he was willing and worked on his fitness.

Marty visited him in his cabin.

"I brought you these," he said and dropped a bundle of black cloth on his cot.

"What is it?" Raffles asked.

"Coveralls, shoes and a hood."

Raffles unfolded the bundle and held up the coveralls.

"Made of silk?"

"Yes, it doesn't rustle."

"Shoes?"

"Silk slippers with chamois leather soles."

"Make no noise?"

"Exactly."

"Will you all be wearing hoods?"

"No, we apply burnt cork to our exposed skin."

"Why can't I?"

"Because we don't want to frighten the sultan."

They sailed north by northwest into the peninsula past Lingen Island. They flew French colours. The few ships they saw were either Malay or Dutch and generally ignored them. They were largely the remnants of the Dutch East India fleet that had been disbanded in 1799 when the Company went bust. Now they were owned by private operators supported by the Dutch Navy.

The master set their speed so they came up on the island at dusk. Marty was in the tops with Antton looking it over with a telescope.

"Beaches everywhere except the harbour and a town opposite it the other side of the island."

"Looks too easy."

Marty scanned the island slowly.

"There are patrols, look."

Antton took the glass and emulated Marty's scan.

"Two-man patrols. By the look of it they are patrolling fixed sectors. They look alert. Do you think they suspect we would try something?"

"No, there's no reason they should. My guess is their hold on the region is tenuous and they aren't taking chances."

"We go tonight?"

"No time like the present."

The boat slid up onto the beach with a gentle hiss. Chin and Sam went over the bow and disappeared into the dark. Marty and the rest of the Shadows followed and set up a perimeter. Billy and Raffles were last and moved up behind Marty. Two of the sailors brought up the rear and swept the beach of footprints before pushing the boat out. They would lay offshore until they got a signal to come in and pick up the team.

They waited in the brush behind the beach until Chin and Sam returned.

"Just like you wanted we are between two patrols. They don't come down as far as here but patrol back and forward one hundred yards inland," Sam whispered. "There is a company of Malay infantry and a platoon of Dutch in the fort. They have patrols running all the time."

"The palace is one hundred yards the other side of the fort to here. All the entrances have sentries. We can get between the patrols but would have to take out the sentries. At most we would have five minutes before they were discovered." Chin said.

"Other entry points?" Marty asked.

"We will have to go up the side to the top of the turrets and then in through a window."

Marty turned to Raffles. "That counts you out, you will not be able to climb fast enough. Do you have something I can show the sultan that will convince him to come with us?"

Raffles removed the gloves they had made him wear and took off his signet ring. "He will know this."

Marty took it and slipped it on his finger. It was a good fit.

"Billy will get you as close as he can. We will be back soon."

The team slipped silently into the dark. Not guns but blackjacks were the order of the day. As they flitted from shadow to shadow, they stopped and listened. The tread of a boot on gravel warned them and they all froze. The sentry passed within four feet of Chin and never saw him. He rounded the corner and they moved. The wall was too smooth for even Chin to climb so a padded grapnel was tossed up and on the second throw bit. Chin was up in a trice followed by Marty and Antton. The rest faded into the shadows.

The palace wasn't large, and they soon discovered that the upper floor was just two rooms. The question was which one was the sultan in? Marty moved across to the window and looked in. It was a sitting room. Marty slipped the catch with his slim-jim.

Inside it was absolutely luxurious. Gold leaf covered everything, and the coverings were silk in extraordinary colours. Marty ignored it and moved to the door. He listened, there was the murmur of voices followed by a single set of footsteps that sounded like they were walking downstairs.

He signalled to Antton, miming blowing through a pipe. Antton extracted two tubes from his belt and fitted them together. He looked at Marty and drew his finger across his throat. Marty nodded and Antton selected a dart.

Marty cracked the door and squinted through the smallest of gaps. There was a guard outside of the doors to the other room. He quietly moved to one side so Antton could see and ease the blowpipe through.

The guard was dead by the time they reached the door. Chin hung back to keep a watch on the stairs while Antton and Marty moved the body. The doors were not locked and opened outwards which made their entrance quite dramatic.

The sultan was sat up in bed reading a scroll when they entered. A nubile female lay asleep beside him. He looked at them quite calmly.

"Tenkhu Long?" Marty said.

He looked surprised at the English accent and nodded.

Marty held out the ring for him to look at.

"Raffles?" he said.

"He is waiting for you, we have come to take you to Singapore Island."

"Who are you?"

"That will be clear later. Now we have to get you away from here."

The sultan looked at the girl and sighed. "You will have to kill her?"

"Is she likely to scream?"

He nodded. Marty took a cloth and a small vial of liquid from a pouch. He carefully tipped the contents of the vial onto the cloth then clamped it over her nose and mouth. She struggled for a moment or two then went limp. Marty held the cloth in place a moment longer then pinched her earlobe hard. No reaction.

"She will sleep until we are away," he said and put the rag under the pillow.

As the sultan dressed, it was clear he wouldn't be going out the way they came in. He was overweight and they would need Billy and Sam to lower him down by rope. Marty went out the window and signalled that they would go out the main door.

Chin went down the stairs. There was a second guard snoring on a cot in a side room who would wake up with a headache. The guard at the door was harder. Chin waited until the patrol had passed then opened the door and hit him with a Japanese Yawara as he turned. He dragged the unconscious body into the palace then whistled softly.

Marty and Antton escorted the sultan down the stairs and followed Chin out into the night. The rest of the Shadows formed up around them in a perimeter. They practically carried the sultan along as fast as they could. To give him his due he didn't complain.

There was a shout from the palace and a whistle started blowing.

"Times up. Sorry, Your Majesty. Sam, carry him."

Sam stepped up and indicated the sultan should ride piggyback. Marty got them into a dog trot. They soon reached the place where Billy and Raffles waited. Sam put him down. Raffles had his hood off and greeted the sultan deferentially.

Marty moved ahead and lit a shuttered lantern which he used to signal the boat. The rest caught him up.

"Soldiers moving up on us about a hundred yards behind," Matai said.

"Rear guard action. I will send up a flare as soon as we are in the boat."

Marty and Raffles escorted the somewhat breathless sultan to the beach and the boys faded back up the hill. The boat was far enough out to need several minutes to get in. There was a shot from inland.

"Your boys?" Raffles said.

"No, they will kill silently."

A soft splash announced the arrival of the boat, and they hurried the sultan forward, bodily lifting him over the side. Marty took a small rocket and lit it with a striker. It whooshed skyward and a minute later the Shadows started to arrive. Chin was last and he was halfway across the beach when a soldier appeared in the moonlight and brought his rifle to his shoulder.

"Chin down!" Marty shouted. His arm swung forward as he shouted, and a tomahawk flew through the air. The soldier got the shot off and it smacked into the hull of the boat. The tomahawk appeared in his forehead, and he gently rolled forward onto the sand. Chin vaulted into the boat after pushing it off.

"A singularly unique experience," the sultan said after they had joined the ship and settled him in the main cabin. Marty had introduced himself on the way back and now scrubbed the black off his face and hands.

"You are really a viscount?"

"Yes, Your Majesty, I have the honour of holding that title."

"Yet you work for Naval Intelligence."

"Since I was a young man."

"Extraordinary."

"I suppose you will deny you had any part in this at all," Raffles said.

"Of course, wouldn't do to have that bandied around," Marty said.

"How do we explain my miraculous escape?" the sultan said

"If you must, then give Raffles and allies amongst the Temenggong's credit."

The Endellion sailed into Singapore and docked at a wooden wharf. The word was sent out that the sultan was aboard and soon a delegation of Malays arrived to escort him ashore. A palanquin was brought up and he was taken to his new home in procession. Marty and Raffles in attendance.

Marty wasn't sure how it happened, but the sultan was soon resplendent in new robes and turban with jewels and adornments. Raffles made sure Marty was present when the agreement was signed and that February sixth 1819, the free port of Singapore was founded.

It was time Marty re-joined the squadron.

Epilogue

The Endellion pulled up alongside the Unicorn for Marty to transfer aboard. He had noticed immediately that the Silverthorn was missing, and his heart was in his mouth as he stepped across.

"Commodore, welcome aboard," Wolfgang said

"Wolfgang. Where is the Silverthorn?"

Wolfgang leaned in as they shook hands and said quietly, "James is fine. He is on the Leonidas."

Marty recovered himself and managed to do the rest of the ceremony. In his cabin afterwards Wolfgang told him the full story.

"There will have to be a court of enquiry," Wolfgang said.

"Of course, in this we will have to follow navy protocol," Marty said. "Our task here is complete. The Company Marine will take over now and we can return to Calcutta."

Marty interviewed Trevor Archer, who still had his arm in a sling, and read his report. James had also submitted a report and Marty was pleased to see he had kept it factual and without embellishment. With the facts in his hands, he felt more comfortable that the enquiry could do nothing but exonerate the Silverthorn's officers. He held off from visiting James for fear of being seen to favour him. In reality the crews wouldn't have cared and would have been happy to see their commander and his son together.

The squadron left the Malacca Strait and headed back towards Calcutta. Halfway across the Bay of Bengal they spotted a Company Marine Frigate.

"She is signalling our number and dispatches aboard," Midshipman Stirling reported.

"Signal the squadron to heave to," Wolfgang said.

The ships came to halt, rising and falling on the gentle swell while a boat was sent across. Mail bags were hoisted aboard and the midshipman in command of it told them they were tasked with patrolling the straits. Marty had some personal mail and a couple of dispatches from the admiralty.

He read the personal ones first. They were from Caroline and Beth with an insert in Caroline's from the twins. Then he opened the ones from the admiralty. He sat back in stunned disbelief.

"Call Wolfgang in please."

Wolfgang arrived and sat at Marty's invitation.

"I have had a dispatch from the admiralty, they are disbanding the squadron."

"What? Why?" Wolfgang said.

"Apparently, they have decided that with the world at peace it is no longer required. The ships will be absorbed back into the regular navy."

"What about you?"

"I will stay part of Naval Intelligence, maintain my rank but with no ship. That is all it says."

"Anything from Admiral Turner?"

"No nothing. It's very odd. We are ordered to replenish at Madras and return to Portsmouth."

"Also odd as the Medway is our home base."

Later that day there was a knock at the door and Fletcher the purser stepped in. He held a letter in his hand.

"Martin, this was in my personal mail. I believe its intended for you."

Marty took the offered papers and immediately recognised they were written in code. He also noted the initial T at the bottom. It had to be from James Turner. The question was, why did he feel the need to use an indirect method to contact him? He thanked Fletcher and sat down to decode it.

Fifteen minutes later he had the decoded version in front of him.

Dear Martin

By now you will probably have seen the directive from the admiralty that the squadron is to be disbanded. The politicians are the reason as they are looking for a peace premium but our opponents in the navy itself have been actively saying the squadron is just your personal playground. They have short memories or do not want to understand what we do. I doubt the loyalties of some as they are far too close to the Russians who I judge will be our next great test.

I am trying to keep the Unicorn for you. Be careful when you get back there are many who are jealous of your freedom and relationship with Prince George. When you return come directly to my house not the admiralty.

On the subject of royalty. I do not expect the king will survive another year. Prince George is not popular amongst the people but he is already regent so they will have to put up with him. I am also worried about his health. He has gotten very fat.

There was more but this was all that really mattered. The squadron was the victim of budget cuts and apart from funding it himself he couldn't see a way out of that. Turner had obviously felt that their opponents were strong enough he had to avoid the risk that his warnings were intercepted.

They anchored at Madras and replenished their stores, fuel and water for the voyage home. The officers enjoyed a day or two looking around the city, buying presents for their loved ones. Marty had not told them yet. He was hoping for a crisis to come up in India or at home so that they would have a stay of execution. More importantly there were no navy ships in port only Company Marine so a court of enquiry could not be held into the loss of the Silverthorn.

They set sail with a fair wind and sailed south. The world was at peace, and they were a strong force. They wouldn't be hindered on their passage home and with the ships in good condition and more than enough crew it wouldn't take more than three months. He wondered what the future would bring.

Historic Notes

Naval Measurements

Cable – Two hundred yards plus eight inches

Knot – One point one five land miles an hour

Fathom – Six feet

Pistol shot – Fifty feet

A grey goose at a mile – Dawn

The Third Maruthan War

This was the final conflict that gave the Honourable East India Company control of most of India. The final conflicts were as I have written with the exception that I have written in my main characters. The Pindaris still exist but no longer raid or steal. Their final meeting with Hastings put paid to all of that.

Java Sea and Islands

I have used the names that were used in the period so please don't write to tell me they are wrong because you looked on google maps. I used a map from 1826 which was the closest I could find online.

Singapore

The foundation of Singapore was done by Raffles in the time of this book and he even brought the sultan back from exile. I just spiced the story up a bit with Marty and the Shadow's involvement.

Excerpt from Treasure of the Serpent God

Chapter 1: Lord Kingsborough

Charlemagne Griffon, Charlie to his friends, was just finishing breakfast in his Whitechapel house when the front doorbell rang. Etherton, his valet, housekeeper, engineer, and armourer, went to find out who it was and returned after a minute.

"It's Seamus and some lord, I've put them in the drawing room."

"What do they want?"

"No idea, but they want to talk to you."

Seamus was the gang leader of the Whitechapel area of London. He ran the docks, prostitution, pubs, and protection. Charlie was stepping out with his daughter Samantha who had her sights firmly set on him as her husband. It was a nervous relationship as he did the occasional job for Seamus and knew he was quite capable of dealing out beatings or even worse to people that displeased him. What he was doing rubbing shoulders with the aristocracy he had no idea.

Intrigued Charley mopped up the last of his eggs, stood and pulled on his smoking jacket. The drawing room was at the front of the house which caught the morning sun.

"Charlie me boy, top of the morning to ya," Seamus said and shook his hand. "Allow me to introduce an acquaintance of mine Edward King, Lord Kingsborough of Cork."

King stood and shook hands; Charlie's eyes were drawn to a large volume he had placed on the side table.

"Pleased to meet you Mr Griffon, Seamus tells me you are an explorer and adventurer."

"I am. I have been on a number of expeditions including Egypt and Nepal."

"Excellent, excellent," King said and sat back down.

Charlie exchanged a questioning look with Seamus and sat down in the chair next to King, Seamus took the third chair and Etherton arrived with a tray of tea. Once they all had a cup Charlie asked, "What is it you are looking for me to do?"

"Oh! Yes" King said, pulled out of thinking deeply about something. He turned the book around so Charlie could see it and opened the cover. The first page caused his eyebrows to rise.

ANTIQUITIES OF MEXICO:

COMPRISING

FAC-SIMILES

OF

ANCIENT MEXICAN PAINTINGS AND HIEROGLYPHICS,

PRESERVED

IN THE ROYAL LIBRARIES OF PARIS, BERLIN, AND DRESDEN;
IN THE IMPERIAL LIBRARY OF VIENNA;
IN THE VATICAN LIBRARY;
IN THE BORGIAN MUSEUM AT ROME;
IN THE LIBRARY OF THE INSTITUTE AT BOLOGNA;
AND IN THE BODLEIAN LIBRARY AT OXFORD.

TOGETHER WITH

THE MONUMENTS OF NEW SPAIN,

By M. DUPAIX:

WITH THEIR RESPECTIVE
SCALES OF MEASUREMENT AND ACCOMPANYING DESCRIPTIONS.

THE WHOLE ILLUSTRATED BY MANY VALUABLE

Inedited Manuscripts,

By LORD KINGSBOROUGH.

THE DRAWINGS, ON STONE, BY A. AGLIO.

IN SEVEN VOLUMES.
VOL. I.

LONDON:
PRINTED BY JAMES MOYES, CASTLE STREET, LEICESTER SQUARE.
PUBLISHED BY ROBERT HAVELL, 77, OXFORD STREET;
AND
COLNAGHI, SON, AND CO. PALL MALL EAST.
MDCCCXXXI.

"This is a work I put together to collect a number of different Mayan documents in one place. As you can see from the list, I have copied documents held in museums and libraries from Berlin to Vienna. This is volume one of nine that I have published, but it is volume ten that holds the key."

He stopped talking and looked at Charlie expectantly.

"That looks like the work of a lifetime, what do you want me to do with it?" Charlie said still none the wiser.

Seamus stepped in.

"Lord Kingsborough, has managed to decipher a document which tells us that, at the time the Mayan empire collapsed they hid a large number of golden artifacts in a lake in Yucatan."

That explains Seamus's involvement, Charlie thought but Seamus wasn't finished.

"His Lordship believes the artifacts will prove his theory that the Mayans were descended from a lost tribe of Israelites."

King became animated and launched into an extended explanation of his thesis, which, as far as Charlie was concerned, boiled down to that the Mayans were a lost tribe that made its way from the Middle East to Mexico after the Israelites fled Egypt at the time of Moses.

When he ran out of steam Seamus said,

"I have agreed to fund an expedition to recover the artifacts and I want you to lead it."

"Mexico?" Etherton said later, "Never been there. America, isn't it?"

"Sort of. The bit we are interested in is here." Charlie turned a large globe he had in his study and pointed to the Yucatan peninsula. "There's a place in the middle somewhere called Hormiguero and near that is the lake."

"All that from a volume of his book that he hasn't published yet." Etherton said, not convinced.

"Which is why he hasn't published it and may never do so. He thinks the content is so important that it may turn history as we know it on its head. He went so far as to fake his own death in debtors' prison in '37 so he could continue work on it in secret."

"How did he get linked up with Seamus? That's as unlikely alliance as I've ever seen."

"Apparently their families have been 'doing business' for years and when he wanted to disappear, he asked Seamus to help him."

Etherton barked a laugh, "I bet he found a convenient cadaver to substitute for King."

"Actually, he did, a homeless man who bore a passing resemblance to King who died of typhus."

Etherton chewed that over then said, "Alright, what do we do next?"

"I need to talk to Felix," Charlie said.

Books by Christopher C Tubbs

The Dorset Boy Series.
A Talent for Trouble
The Special Operations Flotilla
Agent Provocateur
In Dangerous Company
The Tempest
Vendetta
The Trojan Horse
La Licorne
Raider
Silverthorn
Exile
Dynasty
Empire

The Scarlet Fox Series
Scarlett
A Kind of Freedom
Legacy

The Charlamagne Griffon Chronicles
Buddha's Fist
The Pharoah's Mask
Treasure of the Serpent God

See them all at:

Website: www.thedorsetboy.com
Twitter: @ChristoherCTu3
Facebook: https://www.facebook.com/thedorsetboy/
YouTube: https://youtu.be/KCBR4ITqDi4

Published in E-Book, Paperback and Audio formats on Amazon, Audible and iTunes

Printed in Great Britain
by Amazon